Praise for

Slipsliding by the Bay

"With a sharp eye for detail and a complement of perfectly peculiar characters, Barbara Mcdonald has devised a wonderful satire of the academic world. Her portrait of a small liberal arts college—its lecheries and larcenies—exactly conjures the atmosphere of that unique modern institution where absurdity and logic are married so closely: the campus."

—Louis B. Jones, author of *California's Over, Particles and Luck,* and *Radiance*

"Intriguing. You got me hooked with the moving plot and interesting characters. I was curious to see what mischief Gudewill and Stein would cook up. Magdalena and Lucy continued to surprise." —Louis Owens, author of *Sharpest Sight* and *Bone Game*

"Barbara McDonald's *Slipsliding by the Bay* is an absorbing novel. A comedy both dark and light, it recounts an often wild search for survival of an embattled small college in 1970s San Francisco. The battle is within: a new president recruited to save the college, diverse students, faculty and alums, and most engagingly, a famed artist, Sister Magdalena, whose sculptures embody a fierce war against corporate America, notably the college's chairman of the board. McDonald's gift for lively dialogue carries the college from one crisis to another, the denouement in suspense until the very end. An intriguing read from start to finish."

—John Boettiger, author of *A Love in the Shadows*

"I am always cautious when approaching a novel written by a published r--t b-t B-rb--- M-D----ld m-d- r--d--- *Slipsliding by the Bay* e   ead it with

Slipsliding by the Bay

Slipsliding by the Bay

A Spoof of San Francisco in the Seventies

BARBARA McDONALD

SHE WRITES PRESS

Published 2017
Printed in the United States of America
ISBN: 978-1-63152-225-3 pbk
ISBN: 978-1-63152-224-6 ebk
Library of Congress Control Number: 2017934120

Book design by Stacey Aaronson

For information, address:
She Writes Press
1563 Solano Ave #546
Berkeley, CA 94707

She Writes Press is a division of SparkPoint Studio, LLC.

This book is a work of fiction. Any references to historical events, real people, or real locales are used fictitiously.

To Deirdre, Mike, and Brian

CAST OF CHARACTERS

Noah Adams: student

Sister Agnes: faculty

Richard Babcock (Frieda): trustee

Bill Bennett (Nancy): faculty

Eliot Blanc: faculty

Dominic Cavallo: union representative

Inspector Chin: SFPD

Bert Connor: property developer

Miles Dooley: gardener

Luz Gabriella Fumando-Seer: guru of the Way

John Gudewill: Lakeside president

Jack Harrison: student

Eunice Howard: Whitman Foundation director

Marian Jackson (Will): academic dean

Pete Johnson: maintenance

Keiani Jones: student

Lily Lee: administrative assistant

Bernie Levin: front man for the Way

CAST OF CHARACTERS

Sister Magdalena: faculty

Jim Miller: property developer

Carmen O'Doyle: faculty

Charlie O'Leary: security

Dorothy Owens: student

Margaret Phelan (Barry): alumni

Larry Preston: extra security

Gary Rubin: faculty

Rick: cafeteria

Terry Shea: alumni

Sister Stack: president of board

Harry Stein: assistant to president

Lucy Stuart: librarian

Sarajane O'Connor Thomas: alumni

Carlos Torres: student

Justine Tuliver: dean of students

Katherine Wright (Gladys, hound dog): student

Susan Wood: outside mediator

one | MEET THE PRESIDENT

ister Magdalena? You're where? In jail? I'll be there as soon as I can. Nice meeting you too." John Gudewill leaned forward to replace the receiver on his desk phone.

"Trouble in paradise?" Harry Stein raised his left eyebrow.

"Nothing that can't be handled. It seems that Lakeside's illustrious sculptor has gotten herself locked up in the tank for protesting with Cesar Chavez."

A smile edged its way across Stein's face. "Lakeside is full of surprises. May I join you in your rescue of the fair damsel?"

The two left the office and drove downtown. Lakeside College overlooked San Francisco's Lake Merced. Gudewill picked up the 280 at John Daly Drive and followed the freeway to its intersection with 101. Gudewill had recently been hired as the new president to rescue Lakeside College from its financial crisis. The board of trustees decided that the situation demanded a businessman at the helm, a captain of industry, rather than the usual academic. Gudewill had started a bank after a stint in World War II and the completion of his BA at Stanford. As a man of many interests, he served on innumerable civic boards, acted as a consultant to the bureaucrats in Washington, and was the man behind the scenes in local politics. His introduction to

the college community had been more akin to that of the inves-
titure of a mayor, quite a switch from the prescribed tea and
sherry parties to which the academic community was accus-
tomed. The mayor, city officials from the chief of police to the
park and recreation director, the Montgomery Street CEOs—all
were in attendance, plus the presidents of Cal, Stanford, San
Francisco State, USF, UCSF, and representatives of the Bay
Area Consortium of Colleges and Universities.

The day after the party, the campus buzzed like bees on a
Sierra summer afternoon. Gudewill made an impression. Hard
liquor, catered hors d'oeuvres instead of the food service's usual
Ritz crackers and cheddar cheese. With a Dixieland band, no less.
If these were signs of things to come, maybe there was hope for
the old school. Yes, Gudewill exploded on campus as brilliant as
the Fourth of July fireworks at Crissy Field, just as he had intended.

Gudewill had a plan. "Give them what they want. That's the
secret. That's what the Wizard of Oz did. But we're going to do
one better and get Dorothy back to Kansas without the aid of the
magic slippers. Bring in some of the Army buddies." Stein and
Gudewill had met in boot camp, and the two had been linked ever
since. "As I see it, this place, whether it knows it or not, is on the
cutting edge of what is happening in California, and what is happening in California will soon be happening in the rest of world.
What Lakeside needs is something to give it legitimacy! The sixties
counterculture movements are fast becoming mainstream. Maybe
if I brought in some of the Army gang, set up a board, maybe even
an institute, I could bring it off. The school would have veracity."

"I think you're expecting a tremendous gift of faith if you
think the Army buddies can substitute for red shoes."

The two seldom agreed on anything except their mutual taste
for Dewar's Scotch. Stein was a sharp contrast to Gudewill,
whose massive frame and leonine head were maned by waves of

white hair. Thick glasses veiled his piercing blue eyes. Stein was slight, impeccably dressed and of a pessimistic nature, certain to point out the darker side of any situation.

"Not just the Army buddies. Their connections. Hell, BJ is on all those boards. He could get the right people involved. Between us all, we could put together a board that would dazzle the outside world. And if we convince the outside world that Lakeside is the place to be, then our financial problems will be well on the way to being solved."

"Knowing your convoluted mind, you think the money will start coming in to rescue this sinking ivory tower."

"Right. But I have another twist you haven't foreseen."

"Yes?"

"A board will help community relations and the outside perception of Lakeside. Intrinsically, the place is a can of worms, and since change can come only from within, I'm beginning by putting you in charge of maintenance and security as the director of institutional services as well as my assistant."

"You're nuts!"

"Not so quick. If you're overseeing the boys in the trenches, then I can focus on the faculty, where the real problem lies. They're planning to unionize, and it wouldn't surprise me if your boys were thinking along the same lines. With you in command, at least I'd be aware of what's happening."

"It's a cockamamy plan."

"Think about it. If you gain the confidence of the troops, you can find out what they really want. Then the wizard can give them their heart or brain or whatever they think is missing. I won't have to worry about them, and you'll find you have access to all sorts of inside information. It's been my experience that the guys behind the scenes really know what's going on. Remember Max, the doorman at my apartment in DC?"

And so Stein became both the director of institutional services and Gudewill's assistant.

Gudewill turned off Highway 101 at the downtown exit and found a parking spot on Bryant Street across from the new Hall of Justice. Stark in its rectangularity, it looked exactly like what it was, a jail. Gudewill arranged for Sister Magdalena's release. The officer in charge shook his head as Gudewill paid the bail. "So you're rescuing one of Chavez's people. They're all alike, them bleeding hearts. Don't get the picture that they're gonna get thrown in the can every time they try one of these demonstrations."

Gudewill nodded. He turned to find a tall, dignified woman next to him.

"John Gudewill?" She eyed him curiously.

"Sister Magdalena." He extended his hand. "A pleasure, Sister. I've admired your art and am delighted we'll be working together, although I didn't expect our first meeting to be in jail." Gudewill chuckled. "I'd like you to meet my assistant, Stein."

Peering down at Stein, the sister firmly clasped his hand. "How do you do, Mr. Stein?"

"Just Stein, Sister, just Stein."

"In that case, just call me Magdalena."

The two sized each other up, and, apparently approving of what they saw, both turned to Gudewill, who led the way to the long, gray Lincoln sedan. Magdalena held court in the passenger seat like a member of the royal family. Although she was as massive as Gudewill, she had a certain delicateness about her, and she exuded a definite sense of her own femininity. She was unlike any nun either man had ever met.

Gudewill chose a different route to deliver the esteemed artist back to Lakeside, one that meandered through the city and Golden Gate Park. Steering the Lincoln down Fell Street and the Panhandle, he drove into the park. They passed the Conservatory in its Victorian splendor and the Rhododendron Dell with its wealth of Himalayan beauties, guarded by a life-size statue of John McLaren, the park's creator. Continuing down John F. Kennedy Drive, they passed the Rainbow Falls and Portals of the Past, Lloyd Lake's marbled columns.

"How was jail, Magdalena? You don't mind if I call you that also, do you?"

"Of course not, John. Jail was jail. What more can I say? Sometimes it's necessary to make sacrifices for the cause. I consider it all part of the job."

"Job?"

"'Job' in the sense of Christian responsibility. I'm a member of a religious order and am only following Christ's directives. Spending a night in jail really isn't much when you consider what Cesar is doing for democracy."

"Of course not. Are you giving up your art for the cause?"

"No. My current piece has to do with the cause. Incorporating my politics into my art. I hope it provokes outrage, because that's how I feel."

Beyond Spreckels Lake and its miniature yachts tacking in the breeze, the buffaloes grazed in their paddock, oblivious of the gawking tourists.

"What about teaching?"

"I have one class of undergraduates and several students I work with individually. I spend most of my time on my own work and the cause. There are other things to do than teach. I've done that already. It's time to move on to more urgent matters."

"I have noticed that there are very few sisters left at the college. That's one of the reasons I was hired. To replace Sister Clark. It's a changing world. I'm giving up the financial world to return to academia, and you're leaving academia to battle, indirectly, the financial world."

"I'm not abandoning academia, John. I still have a loyalty to Lakeside. Don't misunderstand me. I will continue to teach; it's just that, at this point, I see the importance of other things."

Gudewill turned left onto the Great Highway and headed south toward Lakeside. The Pacific breakers gleamed offshore.

"I'm relieved to hear that, Magdalena. You're key to Lakeside for many reasons. From what the students tell me, you're a real asset, one of the most liked faculty members and a fine teacher. You also give Lakeside visibility because of your national reputation. I'll be happy to do all I can to ensure that you'll stay with us."

"You needn't worry. I'm happy to do what I can to help the college."

"Delighted, Magdalena. I was wondering if you'd listen to an idea I had for a faculty retreat."

"What a splendid idea. It could serve as a forum."

Gudewill grinned across the plush gray seat. "My thoughts exactly. It's good to know we think along the same lines, Magdalena."

Magdalena smiled coyly back at him. "Where do you plan to hold it? At the college?"

"No, I think it would be most effective if it were off campus. Some place more pastoral in setting. Sonoma. I know just the right spot."

"That sounds perfect, John. Do you have a facilitator?"

"As a matter of fact, I do. Someone from my days at Stanford."

Stein reclined in the backseat, listening, occasionally nodding his head. So Gudewill had done it again. Magdalena was on the team.

two | MISSING TAPESTRIES

quinting one eye, Stein peered at the cards in front of him, pursed his lips, and drew one from the stack. Glancing at the card, he laid it face up on the table and methodically followed it with those in his hand. "Gin," he said. Only the slightly upturned corner of his mouth revealed any emotion.

He was in the boiler room with Pete Johnson, the maintenance foreman. The boiler room was also the tool room, and it was as orderly as a hospital operating room. Stein was impressed. So was Pete, by Stein's prowess at gin and even more by the way he treated him as an equal. Stein hadn't arrived on the scene like some know-it-all big shot. Pete and Charlie O'Leary, the security chief, had expected changes with the new president, had even anticipated getting laid off, and had devised a plan that if they were replaced they would sue the college. But that wasn't necessary. Instead, Gudewill had reorganized in such a manner that the two now worked under Stein in a department called institutional services. Nothing else had changed.

The boiler room door swung open.

"Checking to see if I forgot to make my rounds, Charlie?" Stein called out.

"No, Stein. There's been a burglary in the library. I thought you'd want to come along."

Charlie led Stein and Pete, who was as lean as Charlie was round, out of the boiler room, through the basement, and out the main building across the quad to the library. Once inside, the trio marched to the office next to the main desk. A slim blond with black-rimmed glasses, a gray tailored suit, and a white blouse stood looking at a large book.

"It took you long enough to get here," she remarked icily, removing her glasses.

"I wanted to bring the new boss. He wants to get a handle on the situation."

"Really."

"I'm Stein, the new director. I don't believe I've had the pleasure." Stepping forward, Stein extended his hand.

"Lucy Stuart. I certainly hope you're more competent than your staff."

"We try to do our best, madam. What seems to be the problem?"

"As I told your person, three of the tapestries are missing from the reading room. When I came in this morning, they were gone. Only the rods were left."

"When did the library close yesterday, and who was the last person in here? Do you know?"

"Of course I know. Do you think I'm a ninny? It closes at ten o'clock and Mary Holland is the night librarian. She always locks up at ten and checks all the windows and doors. I could set my clock by her punctuality."

"Where is she now?"

"At home, I imagine. She doesn't come on until two."

Stein turned to Charlie. "What's the usual procedure? Don't you call in the cops?"

"Right! I'll do it now." Charlie grabbed the phone on the desk and dialed.

Stein's eyes darted around the room. "Do you think the thieves were in here?"

"The only things I know missing are the tapestries. When I went to shelve a reference book, I saw that the walls were bare. Since the library doesn't open until ten, the theft wouldn't have been noticed until then."

"The police are on their way," Charlie interrupted. "Inspector Chin of Burglary. I talked to him. He said don't touch anything."

"Of course," Stein nodded. "Why don't we revisit the scene of the crime? Ms. Stuart, you lead the way."

Lucy Stuart intrigued Stein. He always had been attracted to tall blonds, and if they were unapproachable, even better. He would have to make the library part of his daily rounds. It promised more than books and missing tapestries.

To the left of the circulation desk, a large room overlooked Lake Merced. Heavy oak tables were flanked by tall leather chairs. Brass lamps with parchment shades studded the tables in military file. The beams of the high-ceilinged room were decorated with gold leaf. Leaded glass doors covered the bookcases that lined the walls and paralleled the tables. Stein felt as if he had been transported back to a fourteenth-century monastery library.

"You have quite a place here."

"It is impressive. You can see where the tapestries hung. They were even more impressive. Tapestries hang throughout the college, a reminder of the days when it was an all-women's school."

"If the missing ones are anything like those that are still here, they must be something." Stein referred to the five that still hung between the small paned windows. "Do you have pictures to show the police?"

"Heavens, no! We don't even have a catalog of the recent acquisition of rare books from the Delaney family. We can barely keep up with the day-to-day circulation and new books, let alone burrow into all the special books."

Lucy's complaints were halted by the appearance of two security guards, three gardeners, and the electrician, followed by a slight Asian man in a sport coat, slacks, a blue shirt, and a tie. He looked at the group gathered under the vacant wall and asked, "Charles O'Leary?"

"That's me, I'm Charlie. Inspector Chin?" Charlie turned to Stein. "This is my boss, Stein."

three | NOAH

A wall of fog rose from the ground, erasing the circular driveway in front of Lakeside's administration building. With his tall frame slouched over, Gudewill peered out the office window and shuddered. "What happened to Indian summer?" He turned to Stein and continued. "I just talked to the auditors. There seems to be a slight discrepancy. Apparently the business manager was a creative bookkeeper. It wouldn't surprise me if Babcock was aware of it when he came to me about this job. It wouldn't surprise me in the least." Gudewill folded himself into his chair and looked across the desk. He wore a well-tailored suit, one of many hanging in his wardrobe. The large man had a distinct presence, so distinct that one was seldom aware of what he was wearing, usually a gray or dark suit, white shirt, and nondescript tie. No one really noticed. It was his presence that commanded attention. "What do you want to see me about, Stein?"

Stein sat down. "Money's not the only thing missing." Stein, with an Italian tailor and impeccable taste, was a dapper dresser and paid great attention to his clothes. Today he sported tan slacks, a blue Brooks Brothers shirt, and a navy blazer with shiny brass buttons. His cordovan loafers would pass military inspection.

"Some of the tapestries have disappeared. And there's no catalog of the recent rare book acquisitions. A shoestring operation."

"What's your read on the tapestries?"

"An inside job. How else would they get in? Chin's getting back to me. That's what he'll say."

"Stealing tapestries, embezzling money. No wonder Babcock was eager for me to take over. Now I know why the business manager left. No one said much when I asked; all they said was that it was for health reasons. Health, my foot! He's probably off in the Bahamas, toasting his newly recovered health and laughing at the mess he left behind. That's the way it is with these religious outfits. When there's a hint of scandal, they send the culprit packing and cover it up to avoid publicity. So the business manager suddenly develops poor health and disappears. Very handy, and the public isn't any wiser. What an MO!"

"No longer, I hope."

"Don't worry." Gudewill peered over the top of his horn-rimmed glasses. "No catalog, you say. That's tricky. Anyone who knows that could walk away, book by book, and no one would be the wiser. Why haven't the books been inventoried? The new acquisition is priceless."

"No funds."

"There are now. Tell the librarian that a catalog is the number one priority. She needs to put someone on it immediately."

"With pleasure."

"Hmm . . . I think Stein has found himself another damsel in distress. I can tell by the tone of the voice and raised eyebrow. Let me guess. She's tall, blond, and unapproachable."

"How did you guess?" Stein grinned.

"How can I not? Do what is necessary to get those books inventoried. Also, look into the library security. The more precautions the better."

A knock on the door interrupted Gudewill. "That must be the work-study student. I told Lily to expect him. Come in."

A big-boned twenty-something entered. All arms and legs, he resembled a young redwood that hadn't quite filled out. In dungarees and a faded flannel shirt, he wore his hair pulled back in a ponytail, a tattered backpack on his left shoulder. With his long face and mournful eyes, he resembled a hound dog. He extended his hand across the desk.

"Morning, Mr. Gudewill. I'm Noah Adams. Financial aid said I should start today."

"Right you are, Noah. Why don't you call me John? This is Stein, director of institutional services. Have a seat."

Noah settled in the chair next to Stein, who eyed him suspiciously.

"What brought you to Lakeside, Noah?"

"A scholarship and the independent study program. I like being able to create my own program and do what I want. There's none of that bullshit about mandatory classes. I had enough of that in high school and the community colleges I went to. In fact, I never did graduate from high school. Took the GED and traveled to Alaska. Then came back and went to City College. High school was a bore, man, a bore. Anyway, my home life was the pits. My old lady never cared. Too busy with her husbands and the bottle, and my old man, he took a walk when I was a kid and never came back. It was better to just get out."

"How long have you been here?"

"My second year. Worked in the library last year. Lucy gave me a good recommendation, so the financial aid office sent me here."

"Yes, I read it. I want someone responsible and discreet. Everything you see and hear stays within these walls. You'll be working mostly for Lily, but on occasion you'll do the odd job for me. Act as runner, deliver things."

"Sounds good. I always wondered what a college president's office was like."

"It's no different from the president's office in any business or corporation. I'm glad you're aboard, Noah." Gudewill stretched across the desk and shook the young man's hand. "Why don't you see if Lily has anything for you to do?"

Noah nodded and left.

"What do you think, Stein?"

"I don't like him." His mouth quickened into a tight corkscrew.

"I do. He reminds me of myself at that age."

"Maybe that's why I don't like him. You have a lot in common." The corkscrew uncurled into a grin. "You're both full of yourselves."

"Is that so? I think you don't like him because he is on a first-name basis with the librarian. A little competition, my friend?"

"Get off it, Gudewill. My gut tells me not to trust him."

"I had forgotten. Stein and his intuitive gut. We shall see."

four | TEA AT ELIOT'S

arian Jackson, Lakeside's dean of academics, sat poised at the edge of a Louis XIV chair, balancing a bone cup and saucer on her lap. The large sitting room overlooked the San Francisco Bay, where a regatta was in progress. Gilt-framed eighteenth-century etchings lined the wall. A cherry credenza displayed a collection of foot sculptures. Mozart's Piano Concerto no. 21 discreetly sounded in the background.

"What a lovely piece of Imari, Eliot," Marian nodded toward the large bowl on the hand-carved mantelpiece.

"I didn't know you're a connoisseur of porcelain." Eliot Blanc was the English chair.

"There are many things you don't know about me, Eliot." Marian set the cup and saucer on the butler's table. And don't underestimate me, she thought. You've invited me to your flat for only one reason. Like the spider asking the fly to tea. Whatever your motive, it doesn't bode well for Lakeside. "How's the revolution class going, Eliot?" Marian referred to a new interdisciplinary class taught by Eliot, Magdalena, and Sister Agnes from the religious studies program.

"I have my reservations."

"I understand student enthusiasm is quite high. Magdalena's

pleased. And Agnes and I have a meeting about it scheduled later in the week."

"You'll find Agnes's and my definition of a class on revolution quite different from that of Magdalena." Eliot was dressed in a white lightweight suit and white buck shoes. A pink shirt accentuated his white skin and hairless face.

"That's a plus for the students. The more exposure to different viewpoints, the better."

"Would you care for another sweet?" Eliot picked up the silver tray of Italian pastries and English biscuits.

"No, thanks."

"Wouldn't you say the class on revolution is somewhat prophetic?" He returned the tray to the butler's table.

"What do you mean?"

"Just that it's less than twenty-five years until the millennium, and you know what Yeats said." He sipped his tea.

"Refresh my memory."

"The center's not holding. I feel this is especially true of our situation at Lakeside." Eliot dabbed at the corner of his mouth with a small linen napkin.

"What else did Yeats have to say?"

"It's all in his poetry. You're welcome to borrow one of my copies of his works."

"We have our own at home."

"Of course! Your husband, the lawyer-poet."

The hairs on Marian's neck rose. Why did she find Eliot so offensive? The tone of his voice made her feel that he was snickering at her. Was it her blackness? Her femaleness? The fact that her degree was in social sciences, not the humanities? He was a vain little frog in a very small pond. She must remember this and try not to let his condescension bother her. She watched Eliot across the elegantly upholstered sofa. He even looked like a frog, an albino frog, with his pop-eyes, flat broad face with barely a nose, large tubular lips, and receding chin and hairline.

"Will enjoys his poetry. It's a good release from the DA's office. What have we here?" Marian looked down at the sleek Siamese rubbing against her legs.

"Maud Gonne. Maudie, Maudie, come here, come to Daddy." The blue-eyed cat segued along the rose damask sofa to her master.

"What a lovely cat, Eliot."

"Maud is more than a cat. Maud has a soul. I'm sure in another life she was Cleopatra." He picked up Maud and held her to his chest, slowly stroking her.

Marian raised an eyebrow, but Eliot was engrossed with the cat and didn't notice. "She's beautifully marked. Have you had her long?"

"Seven years."

"That's about when I came to Lakeside. Getting back to Yeats and revolution, what did you mean? Is something about to happen?"

"I really couldn't say, my dear, but I think you should watch the center. That's all I'm at liberty to say for the present."

"I must go, Eliot. I'm meeting Will at five. I'll consider your reference to Yeats. Perhaps next time you'll be more explicit. Thank you for the tea." Stiffly, Marian rose from the chair and straightened her gray skirt. The message was loud and clear. The faculty was about to unionize.

five | ENTER KATHERINE

*L*ike one of the lions at Fleishhacker Zoo, a mile from Lakeside, Gudewill paced back and forth in his office. A fog bank hovered over the campus. The sun had yet to break through, and right now he could use a shot of sunshine. Last night's board meeting had been a zinger. The trustees had come clean about the missing funds. They expected him to get rid of the mess left by the departed business manager. He noticed a police car pulling into the driveway. What now? Another crisis?

Lily's high-pitched voice shot through the open door. "I'm sorry. You can't bring it into the president's office. It's definitely against school regulations. Please, take it outside."

"What a ridiculous rule! Gladys goes everywhere with me. Everywhere! You tell President Gudewill that Katherine Wright is here."

"I'm sorry, Miss Wright, but you can't bring it in."

"'It' happens to be Gladys. I won't have you refer to her as 'it'!"

Gudewill popped his head around the door. "Lily, may I be of assistance? What seems to be the problem?" He looked down to see an oversize basset hound. The hound gazed up at him. Gudewill stooped and patted the long-slung animal on the head.

"Hello, fella."

"She is not a fellow. She's a bitch!"

"My mistake. I'm John Gudewill." He stood up. "I don't believe I've had the pleasure."

"Katherine Wright. It's imperative that I talk to you. I am a Lakeside student! This woman won't let me bring Gladys into your office. She says it's against the rules."

"I'm sure we can bend the rules for Gladys. Come in, Katherine." He motioned to the door.

Katherine led the way into the office taking long, sweeping steps as if she were marking off property boundaries. A tall, spindly woman, she had pulled her mousy hair back in a severe bun. She was swaddled in a massive green cape, which she loosened as she settled into one of the orange chairs, revealing a madras plaid skirt and a baggy chartreuse turtleneck. On her feet were white bobby socks and clunky suede heels.

"I'm here on important business, Mr. President." Katherine locked his eyes in a viselike grip. "It's the Elvis play. I've written a musical based on Elvis's life and I want Lakeshore to produce it."

"An Elvis musical. An interesting idea."

"Of course, the music is Elvis's. I wouldn't think of writing anything for him. There's no one greater than Elvis."

"He is the king."

"Exactly. I knew you'd understand."

"Your idea is most unusual, but it's not up to me to say. There are channels."

They were interrupted by a knock.

"Excuse me, Katherine. Come in."

Stein poked his head around the corner.

"I see you're busy."

"It's all right. Come in. There's someone I want you to meet. This is Katherine Wright. Katherine, Stein."

Stein cocked an eyebrow, first at Katherine, then at Gudewill.

He arched his shoulders and gave his head a quick shake. In turn, Gladys let out a low rumble and bared her teeth. Katherine narrowed her eyes.

"Who are you?"

"Gudewill's assistant. And you?"

"I'm a Lakeside student and I'm discussing a proposal with President Gudewill."

"That she is. Sit down, Stein. Katherine wants to produce a biographical musical of Elvis that she's written. Using his songs, of course."

Stein raised an eyebrow.

Gladys rumbled and revealed her molars.

"And who is Katherine's friend?"

"Gladys," Katherine answered. "Gladys is a pedigreed basset hound and very intuitive. She doesn't trust you, Mr. Stein."

"The feeling is mutual."

"Getting back to the Elvis musical, Katherine," Gudewill said, "a proposal such as yours has to go through the music department. You say you're a student?"

"Yes, part-time. I sing with the Glee Club and act in some of the plays."

"As interesting as your idea is, you do have to go through channels. It's not up to the president to make departmental decisions."

"I thought you were in charge."

"Unfortunately, that's not the way it works. I'm more like the captain of a ship, but it's the engineer who really runs the ship, and that's what Kevin Grady is to the music department. You'll have to see him about it." Gudewill rose out of the chair and walked over to her. "I'm sure you can work something out with the music department. Thank you for taking the trouble to come see me."

Katherine stood up. Gladys rose, too, sniffed at Stein, and growled. Stein glowered back. Gudewill walked Katherine to the door and closed it behind her.

"Well, *mein kapitän*, I'd say you're the captain of the loony bin. That one's a real nutcase! You'd better watch out for her, JG."

"She's harmless, Stein, harmless. She'll get the runaround from Kevin and then from the drama department, and it will never get off the ground. They know how to play the game."

"That's not what I'm referring to. She's trouble."

"As usual, Stein, you're making a mountain out of a molehill. Some part-time students audit art and music classes. She must be one of them. Now what did you want to see me about?"

"Another tapestry's missing from the library."

Gudewill spun around. "I thought you'd beefed up security."

"The extra guard begins tonight."

The tall man sighed, his shoulders dropping slightly. "I wonder what else is missing."

*L*ucy, Lucy in the sky with diamonds," Noah sang as he straddled Lucy. They were on the multipillowed bed in her Divisadero Street flat. An oriental rug covered much of the blond oak floor, and a highboy dresser held a cloisonné vase with a single red rose. Across from the bed was a vanity with a crewel-covered stool patterned in red roses. The mirror above the vanity reflected the occupied couple in the bed. Beyond the window the bay sparkled and white sails bobbed up and down like the feathers in Lucy's blue eiderdown quilt. The four-poster bed was its own ship of pleasure in the high-ceilinged room.

"I wonder how many people would believe that the ice queen is doing the dirty deed with her former work-study student?" Lifting Lucy's hair off her neck, Noah grinned down at Lucy and burrowed his head into the ivory column.

"Stop it, Noah," she demanded. "I have to go. The damn CORE meeting starts at seven. Why the Governance group decided to form the Committee to Order and Revitalize Education is beyond me. I'm not sure it's working."

"Or that she's a neck freak and has erogenous zones that take her over the edge," he muttered as he kept burrowing.

"Noah! I mean it. I've got to get dressed."

"Yeah, what if the proper librarian shows up late, looking like she just had a roll in the hay? That would give the committee something to talk about besides program changes."

Noah rolled over and propped himself against the embroidered white pillowcases. "By the way, my uncle has a buyer for the tapestries. The guy from Hillsborough wants more of the same. How's the Wednesday after the retreat sound?"

"The night the board meets?"

"I forgot about that."

"Perfect!" Lucy sat up and kissed Noah.

"What was that for?" He grinned.

"For being such a clever boy. You do have talents other than your obvious one." She licked her lips, grinned, and hopped out of bed. "I like the idea of stealing with the trustees in the building." She laughed and tossed her blond hair off her face. "By the way, how was your meeting with Gudewill?" She opened a drawer of the highboy.

"Fine. I'm going to be a gofer and do odd jobs. He made a big deal about keeping the confidentiality of the office. I told him not to worry. It'd go no further than this bedroom." Stretching, Noah crossed the room. "I'm going to scrounge something to eat. A growing boy needs to keep up his strength." He squeezed her bottom.

"The cupboard is pretty bare." She removed a pair of black watch plaid slacks and a black turtleneck from the closet and pulled them over her black lace panties and bra.

Noah reappeared with an apple and a hunk of French bread. "What do you live on? Yogurt and apples?" He settled back on the pillows and watched Lucy brush her hair up into a bun.

"How come you never wear your hair down, Lucy?"

"People think librarians are straightlaced. I wouldn't want to disappoint them." She winked and played her tongue over her lips.

"If they only knew." Noah laughed and bit into the apple.

"All the better to fool them, my dear." Giving her hair a final twist, she turned to Noah. "I'll see you tomorrow in the library. Make the arrangements for Wednesday. And turn on the porch light when you leave."

*T*he president had an open-door policy at certain times during the week to encourage dialogue. With his office door ajar, Gudewill pondered the latest business-office figures. More money was needed for financial aid. Lakeside's endowment was minimal. He glanced up to see a cloud of purple smiling down at him.

"Hello, John Gudewill," purred a heavily made-up woman somewhat over fifty. Swathed in shades of purple ranging from the faintest hint of lavender to deep merlot, the woman wore gold bracelets and bangles up to her elbows, and through the veil of scarves around her neck glittered chains of gold. "I'm Sarajane O'Connor Thomas. I was so disappointed to miss your reception, but I was in the South of France."

Rising from his chair, Gudewill moved quickly around the desk and grasped her hand in his.

"A pleasure, Sarajane. You don't mind if I call you Sarajane, do you? I've heard about you and your plans. You've caught me when I have a few minutes. Why don't you fill me in?"

"That would be lovely. May I call you . . . John?" Sarajane drawled Gudewill's first name as a separate question and, dropping her head to one side, peeked out from thick eyelashes that could have come only from Elizabeth Arden.

"Of course." Good God, he thought. I'd better watch out. She has more on her mind than the alumni.

"Thank you, John." Her voice assumed a proprietary tone. "What a lovely view of the lake. I see you've some of Magdalena's paintings. And one of the angel sculptures. The early series." Sarajane's green eyes narrowed as they roamed the office like a security camera on surveillance. "What an interesting color scheme. I'd have picked something a bit more restful." She drew a long, purple nail along the border of the orange-striped chair as she turned to sit down.

"I'm colorblind." Gudewill laughed. "Lily salvaged some furniture from the storeroom. It's fine. Tell me about your idea to endow a chair of religious studies. The search committee mentioned it at our meeting." He sat in the chair next to her.

"Yes, it's what Lakeside needs. Something to bring in new students . . . the right kind. So many of us are disillusioned by the changes." Shuddering, Sarajane released a strong scent of Tabu. "You don't mind if I smoke, do you?" She reached into a tapestry bag the size of a valise and groped around until she extracted a gold cigarette case and matching lighter. "Would you be dear and light this for me?" She touched Gudewill's wrist and handed him the lighter.

"That's quite a case."

"Thank you. A gift from my late husband. I'm a widow." Sarajane sighed, closed her eyes, and slowly inhaled the smoke.

"I'm sorry. Has it been long?"

"Several years, but one never gets over the loss. But you know. I understand you're also widowed." Sarajane looked at John for a long moment, then dropped her eyes.

"About six months. In fact, Julie's death was one of the reasons I took this job. I needed a change."

"Lakeside's certainly that. Some of the alumni and I were

hoping you could do something to make it, shall I say, a little less different, more like it was when I was a student here. My dear friend Sister Agnes and I have many ideas. She's marvelous, believes in the old ways. Of course, she teaches all the new theology, but if I were to endow a chair, it would have certain provisos." She raised a carefully plucked eyebrow.

"Oh?"

"That's only one of my ideas for Lakeside. Advertising, or the lack of, is another problem. I worked at Barnaby and Thomas before my marriage." Sarajane paused and inhaled deeply on her Benson & Hedges.

"Really."

"Of course, I gave up my career to marry Edward." She lowered her eyes.

"I would like to hear more about your plans. Perhaps we can set up an appointment for later in the week. Meanwhile, I hear some students in the outer office." Gudewill unfurled his large frame. Sarajane also rose. She was shorter than he expected, even in her three-inch heels. The armor of scarves, bracelets, and necklaces gave her the appearance of a much larger woman.

"I'd like that." She crumpled the cigarette in the large enamel ashtray on the desk and shuddered, releasing Tabu. "This ashtray is rather tacky for the president."

"It's fine. Check with Lily about an appointment. It's been a pleasure to meet you." He shook her hand. Sarajane's fingers lingered on his.

She looked at him directly and said, "I look forward to it."

tein, Inspector Chin, and Lucy stood in the back of the reading room. The library was devoid of students. It didn't open until noon on Thursdays. Outside, the fog swirled against the leaded windows like cats swishing their tails. Inside, the mood was anything but playful. Another tapestry was missing. The three stared at the wall. Only the beveled rod remained, like the scar from an old incision.

"I agree, Chin, it's an inside job. Whoever did this knew there was a board meeting and that security would be occupied. I'll post security in the library for all the hours it's closed. The librarians can handle it when it's open. Is that agreeable with you, Ms. Stuart?" Stein shifted his weight, his polished Italian loafers catching the light from the wall sconce, and turned to Lucy.

"Fine, Mr. Stein. I've hired some students to catalog the rare books. I appreciate that the president sees the urgency, especially with this. We can't be too cautious."

"Any other suggestions, Inspector?"

"A list of everyone who has a library key."

Lucy laughed. "Then you'd better get all the student rosters for the past ten years. Everyone who took a class during that time had access to a key. Security is nonexistent."

"Is that so?" The inspector turned to Stein.

"You'll have to take Ms. Stuart's word for it. I'm new to the organization. I guess the next move is to rekey. It's probably the only way to secure the place."

"By all means. And put in a system where only you and the president have the master key. I think that wraps it up for now. If anything new turns up, call me. You have my number." The slight man left.

Stein looked at Lucy. "Madame Stuart, if you don't mind, I'd like to ask you a few questions about the library. May we adjourn to your office?"

Lucy nodded and led Stein into a small room to the side of the main reading room. Outside, the east garden was barely visible, the rose bushes shivering under the blanket of fog. She pointed to a straight-backed chair in front of the desk. Stein scanned the clutter.

"It looks like you're a busy woman."

"You don't know the half of it." Lucy sighed and leaned back in the chair behind the desk, swiveling it so that it was at an angle, and crossed her legs. Her black wool skirt stopped a few inches above her knee. She swung her top leg back and forth so that her sling-back shoe played at the tip of her foot. The definition of her legs was accented; a hint of black lace peeked from under her skirt. Stein watched. A grin flickered at the corners of his mouth.

He asked, "So how does the library work and how do you see its role in the college?"

Lucy met Stein's gaze. "You're posing a complex question, Mr. Stein. It can't be answered in the few minutes I have."

"That's all right. You don't have to answer it all today. And by the way, call me Stein. Everyone does."

"To answer the first part of your question, Stein, the library doesn't work well. You can see that yourself. It's a case of the college cutting off its nose to spite its face. And 'cut' is the operative word. The board's made such drastic cuts in our budget that I'm barely able to meet the students' needs. It's a joke. As anyone in academia knows, the key to a college or university is its library, something the board seems to have forgotten." Lucy recrossed her legs. Her skirt edged up an inch.

Stein watched her swing the other foot and smiled. "So the financial crisis has hit the library in the solar plexus."

"Definitely! I have barely any staff. Consequently, the library's open only a few hours a day. It closes at ten at night rather than midnight, and some days, like today, it doesn't open until noon."

"As I recall, the adage of burning the midnight oil is particularly applicable to students."

"Lakeside in particular," Lucy nodded. "Many have off-campus jobs, so they need late hours to fit in with their schedules."

"A dilemma, Ms. Stuart."

"I hope you and President Gudewill can do something to alleviate the problem." Lucy swiveled the chair back to the center of the desk and leaned forward. Her silk blouse gapped just enough to cause Stein to breath deeply.

"We'll do our best. Gudewill's reputation is built on his ability to troubleshoot. Thanks for the information. I'll pass it on." Stein rose and left. Humming, he headed down the hall.

nine | INTERIOR DESIGN

*G*udewill strolled out of the cafeteria and nodded absent-mindedly to the students he passed. Another tapestry gone! And, to add insult to injury, during the board meeting! He shook his head. Stationing an extra man in the library should help. It had to be an inside job. On the upside, the meeting with Babcock and the bankers had gone well. He was holding them at bay, at least temporarily. Cash flow was the real problem.

Outside in the quad, he could see Katherine arguing with Kevin from the drama department. He chuckled. Kevin could handle it. Mounting the stairs to his office corridor, he sighed. There were several proposals from the faculty he had to review before meeting with Marian. He checked out the wall hangings along the corridor. Were they inventoried?

When Lily saw Gudewill, she bounced up to greet him. "President Gudewill, I didn't . . . she just stormed in and took over. There wasn't anything I could do." Wringing her hands and dancing on the tips of her does, Lily looked as if she were about to flood the office with tears.

"Take a deep breath, Lily, and tell me what you're talking about."

"It's that woman, Mrs. Thomas. She marched in and told me

to keep typing. I know she's important to the college with all her money. I didn't know what to do, and you were out to lunch with Mr. Babcock and . . ." The tiny woman quivered like a monarch butterfly in a strong October breeze.

"Whatever she did, it's not your fault." He patted her arm. "What did she do?"

"Replaced all the furniture in your office." Lily's eyes widened.

"The furniture?"

"The furniture."

Good God, I should have known. That woman! So Sarajane's taken it upon herself to decorate my office. I remember now. She didn't like the color scheme. Said something was tacky. I'd better check the damage. Gudewill entered his office. An elaborately carved library table had replaced the simple desk. Gone was his swivel-backed chair, replaced by a forest green plaid wingback that was matched by two similar chairs opposite the oak table. Eight barrel chairs flanked a leather-covered conference table. On one wall was an armoire and on the other a credenza.

I bet it's a bar, Gudewill thought. He opened the door. Sure enough. Jack Daniels, Johnny Walker Red, Tanqueray gin, Russian vodka, B & B, top California wines, and the mandatory mixes and soda. The lady knew her booze. He shut the door and walked to the armoire. Inside were filing cabinets, with his current papers neatly ordered. She hadn't missed a thing, even adding early photos of the college and some angels from Magdelena's later series, ones with which the public was familiar. The woman had taste, but she was as subtle as a baseball bat.

On the desk was a lavender envelope addressed in florid purple handwriting. The note read:

Dear John,
I know you will approve of your office's new look.
I'll be in touch.
Sarajane

Gudewill crumpled the note and tossed it in the wastebasket. "I bet you will."

ten | VALHALLA

Gudewill peered from under his Yankees cap like a giant sea turtle rising out of the ocean to survey the shore. The Lakeside community squinted back at him. Overhead, the October sun sparkled in the blue sky. In the front row, radiating her own brilliance, Magdalena smiled at him from beneath a ribbon-festooned Panama hat. Next to her sat Lily, incognito behind oversize dark glasses and a 49ers cap. Others in the audience sported yachting caps, straw hats, floppy hats, football helmets, berets, visors, and every type of headgear imaginable. One student even wore what appeared to be an upside-down flowerpot. Gudewill tipped back the brim of his cap while the audience shifted in white wooden chairs.

"Good morning, everyone! I'm delighted to see so many of you this early on a Saturday morning. And in your chapeaux of choice!" He grinned and adjusted his glasses. "As you know, we've convened at this beautiful Sonoma retreat center for the purpose of dialogue. It's crucial that we sit down and discuss common goals. We're also here to energize Lakeside. That's why everybody needs to be involved: secretaries, custodians, students, the faculty and administration. By reaching out to one another, we'll renew and re-create Lakeside. Like the mythical phoenix.

"But you didn't drive all that distance to hear me talk. Before we break into groups, I'd like to introduce a longtime friend of mine, a woman who's going to join our community, and she's just what the doctor ordered. A woman with impeccable credentials, on the faculty of Stanford, who has worked with many corporations to bring accord. A woman of honesty, charm, and clear-mindedness, who listens better than anyone I know. I'm delighted to present my friend and Lakeside's new facilitator, Susan Wood."

Gudewill stepped aside to make room for the pink-faced woman standing next to him on the podium. Dressed in a blue denim Indian-style dress, Susan wore a feather-trimmed vaquero hat that topped her long, gray-streaked braid. Her apple-like cheeks rounded even more as she beamed down on the crowd.

"It's a pleasure to be here with you and have the opportunity to become part of the Lakeside family. Lakeside has such an outstanding reputation. It's recognized by the government, the foundation and business worlds, and other academic institutions as being on the forefront of educational innovation. I know that, working together, we'll reach consensus, restore harmony to the college, and achieve peace.

"But I won't keep you any longer. The point of the day is to communicate with each other on a personal level, not to hear me pontificate. When we reconvene this afternoon, I'll be facilitating the meeting. Now it's time to move on to your focus groups. Thank you."

As the group scattered, Susan turned to Gudewill. "They seemed receptive enough, although it's really too early to tell. I'll be in the main house reviewing the information you gave me. I'll join you in the gazebo for lunch."

"Good. It's important that you meet my focus group before the afternoon meeting. They're the key players. I'll see you then." Gudewill turned and crossed the manicured lawn to the gazebo on the hill above. Valhalla nestled in the middle of the lush

Sonoma wine country. An old estate, it had been converted into a retreat center. The main house was a sprawling colonial mansion surrounded by guest cottages, meeting centers, and a pool and health center, all sheltered by large oaks and madrones. The various focus groups were scattered around the grounds under the spreading trees or on the verandas.

As he climbed up to the gazebo, Gudewill could see Marian, the academic dean, and Eliot, the English prof, already in the semicircle of folding chairs fronting the newsprint-covered easel. Jack Harrison cut across the manicured grass and caught up with him. "It looks like we're in the same group, John." Gudewill stopped and shook the hand of the gangly man in a tattered T-shirt and jeans with a red bandanna sweatband over his forehead.

"Good to see you, Jack." The two passed a border of yellow and orange chrysanthemums. "As one of the editors of *Foggy Bottom*, you're the man with his hand on the pulse of the college. I'm glad we're in the same group. I'll get a sense of what's going on with the students." At the gazebo, Gudewill greeted Marian. Carmen O'Doyle, a language teacher, and Eliot huddled at one side of the round table. They both nodded a greeting.

"Susan's done a fine job of scheduling the day, don't you agree?" Gudewill said to the group. "By the way, I've taken the liberty of inviting her to join us for lunch. Afterward we'll reconvene for the general meeting. The latter part of the day will be spent relaxing and shooting the bull."

"I didn't come here to 'shoot the bull,' as you phrase it," Eliot sniffed, distending his flat nostrils. A broad-brimmed plantation hat covered his head. He wore white linen slacks, a Mexican wedding shirt, white socks, and huaraches.

"I agree," Carmen said. "I didn't drive two hours to waste the day. There are a million things I should be doing, but since my language hours have been cut in half, I need to be part of the process or I might not have a job at all. Don't misunderstand me." She adjusted her black straw hat. "I do feel it's important to be part of the process. Don't you agree, Eliot?" Without waiting for an answer, she rattled on. "I should be preparing for my acting classes. That's what the academic commission decided I should teach instead of French. What the college is doing dropping languages, I don't know. But they have, and only Spanish remains and only as a support. My colleagues are just out the door. Can you believe it? It's absolutely appalling."

"I'm familiar with your situation, Carmen," Gudewill said, "and I understand how you must feel. That's why we're here today, to discuss your concerns and priorities. Don't worry, Eliot, something of substance will be accomplished today. I see the other members of our group are here. Hello, Charlie, Dooley." The chief of security, Charlie, had on an Irish wool cap, and the gardener, Miles Dooley, wore his Red Sox cap. Keiani Jones and Carlos Torres, student council officers, followed them into the wisteria-covered structure. Carlos pulled his hand from under his serape, tipped his sombrero, and laughed. Keiani, in a Dodgers cap, nodded and sat next to Jack.

Gudewill looked at the group. "Now that we're all here, why don't we decide on a facilitator, chairperson, and recorder. You're all familiar with the procedure." He settled back in the folding chair. The games were about to begin.

eleven | LUNCH

*T*he noon sun blazed down on the gazebo where Gude-will's focus group was eating. An assortment of pastel-colored box lunches was spread across the table. Pushed aside were the easel and its stack of newsprint covered with red, green, blue, and black notes. Bright marking pens were scattered among the cardboard boxes, each of which had contained a turkey sandwich, a plastic cup of a variety of salads, chips, an apple, a brownie, and a soft drink.

"What do you think of the Lakeside community so far, Susan?" Jack Harrison asked as he stretched his long body, tipping his chair so that it was at a forty-five-degree angle to the ground and grinning his jack-o'-lantern smile. "We're quite a group, aren't we?"

Susan set her Tab next to her brownie and smiled. "I'm delighted at the diversity of opinions. It's very healthy."

"Lakeside's a place that cares, but it's got a lot of problems, a whole lot of problems." He pushed his chair upright.

"That's why we're here." She removed the plastic wrap from her brownie.

"Everyone agrees that communication's the main problem. That's why it's cool that you'll be working with us, Susan," Keiani said. "I hope you'll be involved a lot with student government. As

student council president, I'd like some sort of ongoing dialogue."
She popped her apple into a pocket of her Dodgers jacket.

"It's not like we're Berkeley, with forty thousand students."
Carlos took a bite of coleslaw. "One of the reasons I came to
Lakeside was because it's small and I could work with the profes-
sors. Faculty and administration are more accessible."

"Theoretically," Jack said.

Carmen bristled, her back suddenly ramrod straight. "Our
professors are accessible, Jack." In the oak trees behind the gazebo, the stellar jays squawked and hopped from branch to
branch, their black crests bobbing like tiny weather vanes.

"I'm not talking about you, Carmen. Don't get your hair up.
I mean the administrators. Like you, Marian."

"Just make an appointment, Jack." She opened her bag of
chips.

"It's easier to get an appointment with President Ford."

"This is an area we can work on," Susan interrupted. "Marian freeing up some of her time for students."

"And faculty," Eliot grumbled.

"And faculty, Eliot. Getting back to our primary concern,
we're in agreement. It's communication. Correct?" Susan looked
around the group. "You've been quiet, Charlie. Is there anything
you'd like to add?"

"Now that you're asking, I have to say that student services
doesn't always let us know what's happening, and then we don't
have enough men to cover events."

"Like the poetry reading last week," Carlos said.

"Actually that was scheduled through academics and Eliot,"
Marian said.

"Have you considered a master calendar?" Susan asked. "It
could solve a number of problems."

"That might handle it." Marian removed a chip from the bag.

"Another problem that no one's addressed but that's on everyone's mind is faculty cuts." Keiani's face grew serious.

"Keiani's right. That's what people aren't talking about." Carlos nodded.

"What do you mean, Carlos?"

"In the reorganization last spring, some departments were cut."

"Languages!" Carmen waved her apple in the air. "I should be home preparing my drama classes, but I felt I needed to be here today to make sure nothing else happens."

"The paper's doing a story on it in the next issue. The students are pretty upset. We didn't have any say. That stinks." Jack crumpled his chip bag and shot it into the garbage can.

"But that was the accreditation committee's recommendation and the budget committee's proposal. And it was the faculty who made the recommendations to the board of trustees." Marian threw up her arms in frustration. The din of the jays increased.

"The students weren't involved."

"It wasn't up to the students, Jack." Marian shook her head.

Susan had pulled a yellow legal tablet from her bag and was making notes. "So you're saying that you didn't touch on the real issues?"

"Definitely!" Eliot sat back stiffly in his chair, arms folded across his white shirt.

"Could you expand, Eliot?" Susan looked up from her notepad.

"Lakeside is not Valhalla. Some of the faculty are unhappy with the outcome of the cuts. And they're concerned enough to want to protect themselves." He stared intently at Marian.

"That's true, Susan," Carmen interrupted, "and I'm one. I can't tell you how upsetting it is to have to reorganize your whole life. At least I have drama to fall back on. My poor colleagues!

You don't know how awful it's been for them. One's taken to her bed. Eliot's right. Lakeside is anything but Valhalla."

"Is that what you want to bring back as your number one priority to the general meeting? Faculty and student dissatisfaction with the cuts? Or is it still communication?" Susan frowned as she looked around the semicircle.

Gudewill leaned over, resting his elbows on his knees. "I haven't said much because I'm new, but what I've been hearing tells me that communication is still the number one problem. The fact that no one has addressed the discontent over cuts is really a lack of communication. If we can solve the communication problem, tackling all the others will be easier. If no one addresses the real issues, our meeting is a sham. I say communication, then cuts."

"I'm with you, John," Keiani said.

"Me, too." Jack leaned back and helped himself to a brownie. Eliot flattened his lips and whispered something to Carmen. In the redwood trees, the jays continued screeching, their cacophony rising above the valley.

twelve | THE POOL

he October sun had traveled to the mountains west of Valhalla, and the feathered redwoods to the north cast long purple shadows on the lush valley. In the Olympic-size pool behind the colonial mansion, students splashed water and dodged one another, drenching the students and faculty lounging in the recliners along the side. Stein leaned against the bamboo bar at the far end of the pool and sighed.

"Kids," he remarked to no one in particular. "Where do they get the energy?" He took a matchbook from the glass jar on top of the bar, then pulled a pack of True Blues from his khakis pocket, extracted one, and lit it. He drew deeply on the cigarette and slowly exhaled.

"Goodness! Don't tell me you still have that nasty habit! How can you stand those awful things and what they do to you? I gave them up years ago. I couldn't stand the way everything smelled of tobacco, such a dreadful odor. Aren't you the new maintenance man?" A woman in a black straw hat, blue gauze skirt, and white blouse stood next to Stein, her brown eyes darting accusingly back and forth from him to the cigarette.

"I'm director of institutional services, if that's what you mean. Why do you ask?" Inhaling, Stein swiveled the rattan stool to look at the slender redhead.

"There have been problems getting setups for my productions. The system, or should I say nonsystem, doesn't work." She asked the bartender for a tall gin and tonic. "I thought you might help me out. You look like a man who gets things done." Her brown eyes traveled up and down Stein's compact body, taking stock from his curly gray hair to his brown topsiders, which he was wearing without socks.

"And to whom, may I ask, am I speaking?" Stein flicked the cigarette ash in the tray.

"I'm Carmen O'Doyle, formerly professor of French and Spanish, now of Spanish and drama. You've heard of the cuts? I'm one of them."

"You look all right to me."

Carmen frowned and then flickered a smile. "I'm reduced to teaching acting classes, and I want to make sure that when I have a production, the room will be set up just as I've requested, with the exact number of tables and chairs. There have been problems before. That Pete Johnson ignored my requests, and my students had to set everything up at the last minute." The bartender set a gin and tonic in front of her.

"I'll see what I can do, madam." Stein drained his glass.

"Do call me Carmen. Lakeside's quite informal."

"I've noticed. Would you like another drink?"

"I haven't touched this one yet."

"Another Dewar's," he said to the bartender as he motioned to the empty glass. Then he turned back to Carmen. "I'm Stein."

"Really? No first name?"

"Just Stein."

"Fine, Stein. I'm counting on you. Don't let me down. Do you know Sister Agnes? She's the religious studies survivor. There she is, and I need to talk to her, so I'll leave you. Don't forget the chairs." Nodding, Carmen turned from the bar and walked to the other end of the pool. Her pale blue skirt swished around her bare legs, and her red hair bobbed up and down under the black hat. Carmen O'Doyle, Stein thought. That's one I won't forget. She doesn't come up for air. He lit another cigarette and watched her sit down. So she's in cahoots with Sister Agnes and Eliot, conspiring as I watch. He took the fresh drink and thought, I wonder where Gudewill is.

thirteen | THE GAZEBO

till at the gazebo, Gudewill leaned on the edge of his chair, his baseball cap tilted back, his arms on his knees, and his hands in a prayer position under his chin. Jack sprawled across from him, propped up between two wooden chairs. The others had wandered off to the pool or to one of the yew-hedged gardens that pocketed the center. A family of quail scurried across the lawn in front of them, the father leading, followed by the mother and chirping chicks. Beyond the boxwood border was a bed of lavender, sage, baby's breath, Shasta daisies, and blue and white salvia. On the hill, a deer grazed, eyeing the two men.

"The students are gonna make the difference, John," Jack said. He dropped his feet to the grass and rubbed his stubbly chin. "As co-editor of the paper, I interact with most of the students. Until last year we wouldn't have anything to do with the college. You don't know the change that's taken place. All summer a bunch of us worked our tails off. We yelled and screamed a lot, but we came together for the first time in three years. We helped with the grounds, weeding and planting. You know what that means?"

"I have a pretty good idea. I could sense it in our focus group. Now's the time for everyone to become part of the team, and the students are vital."

"You'd better believe it. If it weren't for the students, there'd be no team. You're damn right we're important." He grinned at Gudewill.

"I never underestimate the value of students, Jack. Why don't we get a beer? I have even more reason to celebrate. The Yankees are looking good—they might make it to the playoffs!"

"Let's go!" The two headed across the lawn. The deer continued grazing.

fourteen | UNION OR NOT

Carmen rejoined Agnes and Eliot at the end of the pool. Setting down her gin and tonic, she gathered her skirt and settled into one of the turquoise-and-white-striped chaise lounges that clustered around the pool. Beyond, terraced flowerbeds of perennials unfolded like a Chinese fan spreading out to the vineyards. A red-tailed hawk circled overhead.

"What a relief the meetings are over." Carmen pulled her dark glasses out of her straw bag. "These days are such a strain. Talk, talk, talk, that's all anyone does. It hardly gives one a moment to think. Don't you agree? And of course no one was addressing the real issue, the cutbacks. I still can't believe they've gone ahead with them. I am teaching freshman acting techniques!"

"Rest assured, my dear," Eliot said. "That's what happens when someone not versed in the humanities is running the college, someone whose discipline is social sciences." Eliot fanned himself with his hat. "The dean should have the proper credentials."

"I don't know if I agree with you, Eliot. Marian knows what she's doing, even with her background in social sciences. I'm concerned about the elimination of languages and history." Carmen paused to take a sip of her drink and peered over her dark glasses to examine her forearm. "I hope I'm not too red. My doctor has me using a sunscreen, but I still seem to burn."

"That's why it's important to protect ourselves, against the administration, that is," Agnes said. "Have you talked to the union people any more, Eliot?" She was sitting under the expansive white umbrella, cupping a glass of white wine in her hands. Her pale skin was even paler against her beige-and-tan culottes outfit. She wore white hose, brown sandals, and a large coolie hat.

"We met yesterday. I also talked to the people from USF. They offered excellent advice. After all, they were the first private university faculty to unionize." Eliot massaged the few remaining clusters of white hair on his balding head.

"Who offered advice, Eliot?" Gary Rubin, head of the psychology department, pulled up one of the striped chairs and sat down next to Agnes. A tall man in his late thirties, he wore gray cotton trousers, a black turtleneck, and Birkenstocks. Blond curls haloed his baby face, and his blue eyes were perpetually widened as if they had just witnessed an eight-point earthquake. An Australian outback hat hung down his back.

"The University of San Francisco union people. They've been through it already."

"Good idea! Better than reinventing the wheel." Gary nodded and blinked thoughtfully.

Agnes placed her empty glass on the table. "I do have reservations. It goes against the grain of the university tradition."

"Because of the blue-collar nature of organized labor?" Gary asked. He took a handful of chips from the bowl on the table and lined them up in front of him like checkers on a board next to his Coke.

"Yes, we're not teamsters."

Eliot stopped massaging his head. "That's why we're looking at the Association of American University Professors, the AAUP, instead of the AFT, or the NEA," he said impatiently. "The American Federation of Teachers and National Education Association are not quite the image we want to project for Lakeside. After all, the AAUP was founded by John Dewey."

He looked at Gary. "What did you think of Susan Wood's little closing game?" Following the afternoon session, Susan had gathered the group in a giant circle around a campfire at the edge of the assembly. Each person had written what he or she disliked most about Lakeside on a white piece of paper and what he or she liked most on a green one. Each person then chucked the white paper in the fire and passed the green paper to the person to the right.

"The students liked the symbolism. I thought it rather effective, using the bonfire as a sign of rebirth to carry out Gudewill's theme of the phoenix."

"A bit of hocus-pocus for the students. A panacea to make them think all's well. Mumbo jumbo." Eliot sniffed and took a sip of his Bloody Mary.

"You're such a cynic, Eliot," Agnes giggled. "Have you no faith in the new facilitator?"

"Time will tell, Agnes, time will tell."

fifteen | GARY'S DIP

*T*he red-tailed hawk soared over the herbal knot garden, one of several gardens that bordered the lawn. In
the center, gray dwarf sage enclosed English lavender
and another purple-flowered variety. Overlapping circles of sage,
yarrow, thyme, more lavender, and golden sage edged out to the
bricks. Under the oaks, squirrels hurried to bury acorns for the
winter. At the pool's edge, miniature rainbows sparkled on the
spilled drops of suntan lotion. Gary popped the last of the line of
chips into his mouth and sauntered off to the bar to get refills for
Agnes and himself.

As he passed by a group of students sunning themselves on
large beach towels, a basset hound cut in front of him, ears flap-
ping up and down and short legs furiously pumping her low-slung
body. She was followed by a band of screaming towheads aged
three to thirteen years, all dressed in brown shorts, orange-striped
T-shirts, and PF Flyers. "Get the dog, get the dog," they chanted.

Gary stepped aside to avoid the unholy herd, and one of the
smaller ones veered toward him dripping an orange Popsicle.
Jumping back, he fell into the pool. "Christ," he sputtered as he
rose to the surface, his outback hat floating behind him. "Look
what you've done." But the marauders had disappeared without a
backward glance.

The students in the pool began to splash him, yelling, "Gary, Gary, Marco Polo, Marco Polo! Want to play?"

He grinned sheepishly, his turtleneck bagging around him like an oversize piece of black kelp. "Another time," he called as he climbed the three-rung ladder out of the pool.

The students burst into the Bee Gees' "You Should Be Dancing," substituting "swimming" for "dancing." Gary laughed and shook his head, droplets of water cascading from his ring of curls.

Carmen rushed over with a towel. "You poor dear! Look at you, dripping wet! What are you going to do? And those awful children. Bill Bennett should have left them at home where they belong. They're incorrigible."

"Thanks, Carmen. Nothing to worry about. I've a change of clothes in my car. I'm staying overnight." Gary sloshed over to the group at the table. "You'll have to wait on the wine, Agnes." He puddled off to the parking lot, trailed by a trickle of water.

"I don't think it looks right if I go over to the bar," Agnes said. "The students might get the wrong idea."

"Really, Agnes, we all know nuns are no different from the rest of us. But if it makes you more comfortable, Gary will be back soon," Carmen said. "Where are the brats now?"

"Up the hill." Agnes pointed to the slope climbing to the redwood grove. The children seemed to be gaining on the hound.

Gary returned a few minutes later in an identical black turtleneck and slacks with a fresh Coke and a glass of wine for Agnes. He eased himself into a chair. The pool was emptying and people were changing for the barbecue and talent show that would end the retreat.

"Black refracts the heat," Gary said. He sipped his Coke.

"I find that hard to believe. When we wore habits, I remember sweltering in all that black."

"It was all the layers, Agnes. It had nothing to do with black.

I wore black when I was in Baja last spring and was quite comfortable," Gary said.

"I know I prefer white or light colors, regardless of the season." Eliot stroked the sleeve of his embroidered shirt. "But back to Gudewill. We were discussing the new president, the company man. He and his henchman, Stein, are really Rosencrantz and Guildenstern and will go to any length to please the king, in this case, the board. They're men of secret intentions." He leaned forward and stared at Gary, his frog eyes popping out.

"How can you make such a snap judgment, Eliot? He's only been here a short time." Carmen put her sunglasses in her purse.

"I don't need time. He's a banker, my dear, out for his pound of flesh, only in this case it's ours. And look how Marian, our dean, welcomes him with open arms, like Gertrude with Rosencrantz and Guildenstern."

"But as an administrator, doesn't she have to work with him?" Agnes tipped her glass until it was empty.

"Exactly! It's 'them against us.' This entire day is an example of their deviousness. A plot to lull us. And if you noticed, he really didn't say anything. He's all smoke and mirrors." Eliot sipped his Bloody Mary.

"Do you think Susan Wood is part of his scheme?"

"Definitely. You heard him say they were pals from Stanford."

"Just because they attended the same university doesn't make them conspirators." Gary tasseled his yellow ringlets in an attempt to dry them. "You're reading too much into it."

"Wait and see." Eliot nodded knowingly. "My real concern is the union. The more faculty members we enlist on our side, the better off we'll be."

"I agree." Agnes set her empty glass on the table. "What about the library staff? They're auxiliary, but their numbers would give us more power."

"Agnes is right. Have you talked to Lucy at all?" Carmen crossed her legs and straightened her skirt.

"Indeed." Eliot's thick lips parted in a smile. "We had tea Thursday."

"Speak of the devil, here she comes." All eyes followed Gary's to see Lucy waving to them from across the pool. She skirted the diving board and approached their table.

"Do join us, Lucy." Eliot patted the chair next to him. "We've been discussing the meeting. What did you think?"

Lucy draped her blue cardigan over the turquoise chair and sat down. She was wearing a navy blue sundress and white sandals; her hair was pulled back in a French knot. "The game at the end was a bit much."

Eliot's smile broadened, revealing pink gums. "My sentiments exactly. Too California. But it appealed to the masses." He chuckled. "I was just telling my colleagues that we had tea the other day."

"I didn't realize we had so much in common." Lucy looked at the group. "Anyone care for a drink? It's been a long day."

"A glass of white wine, please." Agnes raised her glass.

"A Bloody Mary." Eliot raised his.

sixteen | STEIN AND THE ICE QUEEN

Lucy nodded and walked down to the bar. Only a few students remained in the pool. Several stood at the bar talking to Stein. He turned from them when he saw her. "If it isn't Madame Stuart. What a pleasure. I didn't know you were here."

"My focus group met again after the healing ritual."

"How dedicated."

"Or foolhardy. There wasn't much I could do. Everyone was insistent. What a waste of time. Some of them even want to continue meeting after the retreat. I don't have the time and told them."

"Time's a precious commodity."

"The most, according to some." Lucy motioned to the bartender.

Stein watched her, noting approvingly the way her snug sundress clung to her curves. No bra either. She sat down on the stool next to him. Her straight skirt stopped above her knees. Her tanned legs were even better without stockings, smooth with a slight definition. She crossed one leg over the other. Her skirt edged up higher. She smiled as his eyes shifted to her face.

"You don't sound convinced," he said, unaware that she had been watching him.

"Right now I'd like a tall drink. Bartender, a tall Scotch and soda, a white wine, and a Bloody Mary."

"You are thirsty."

"Two are for my friends." She pointed to the group at the end of pool.

"The queen of Babel and cohorts."

"The queen of Babel? Oh, Carmen." Lucy laughed.

"Madame Stuart can actually laugh. Another surprise. I thought you were made of ice."

"Am I the ice queen?" She laughed again.

"Are you the ice queen?" One corner of Stein's mouth turned up in a grin.

"You'll have to find out, won't you?" Smiling, Lucy slid off the stool. Her dress rose even higher. She pulled it down, smoothing it carefully and further defining her body, and then picked up the drinks and walked back to the table. Stein analyzed every move.

The sun was behind the hills on its path across the Pacific and a fall chill was in the air, the shortening days and cooler mornings reminders of impending winter. Lucy handed Eliot and Agnes their drinks and settled down in the chair with her Scotch.

"Did you hear what happened to Gary?" Carmen wrapped an Aztec blue rebozo around herself. "Bill Bennett's pack of children pushed him in the pool."

"So that's why your hair's wet," Lucy said. "I thought you'd been swimming."

"Never swim. The Bennett rug rats were chasing a basset hound."

"Katherine's, probably. I've had all kinds of problems with her in the library. Because of that dog, the college council passed a no-dogs-on-campus rule. But no one enforces it," Lucy said dryly and sipped her drink.

"You mean Katherine from the drama department?" Eliot sucked the lime from his Bloody Mary.

"She's really not in the drama department, Eliot." Carmen hugged the rebozo around her. "She's an occasional extra in musicals. She's not a regular student. I won't allow her in my classes!"

"That woman's a good example of what happened when the college reached out to the community, opening some of the art and music classes to the general public They brought in the dregs, and now they're stuck with them." He dropped the lime in the ashtray. "She accosted me in the hall last week with a hairbrained idea for an Elvis musical."

"Do you think the president has more plans for community outreach?" Lucy asked.

"Let's hope not. We were just talking about Gudewill and his banking background, Lucy. It reminds me of something Addison said: 'A money lender. He serves you in the present tense; he lends you in the conditional mood; keeps you in the subjunctive; and ruins you in the future.'"

"That's very harsh, Eliot, and certainly not Christian," Agnes giggled.

"The terms 'money lender' and 'Christian' are antithetical, Agnes. If our plans work out, we won't have to worry about Gudewill or his gang. The union will take care of us."

"Is there any progress since Thursday?" Lucy stirred her drink with her finger.

"Bennett from Biology is not interested. An idealist. He says unionizing will force up tuition prices. He thinks unions are opportunistic and political, and he's not comfortable having us linked with plumbers and auto workers."

"What about the others?" Alan lined the empty glasses up in a row.

"It takes time," Eliot snapped, "but soon we'll have a majority of the faculty, and then the banker won't hold all the cards." He drained his drink.

Seventeen | THE RIDE HOME

lack Point Cutoff was dark as Gudewill guided the gray Lincoln along Highway 37. He passed Port Sonoma Marina, at the junction of the Petaluma River and San Pablo Bay. Striped bass, sturgeon, and flounder hid in the murky water below the high bridge. The waters were famous for a granddaddy of a sturgeon that hung out around the pilings of the nearby railroad drawbridge. Gudewill chuckled as he recalled his own battle with the crafty old sturgeon. Stein rode shotgun. They were on their way back to the city after the retreat. The moon hid behind high cumulus clouds, and the only light was the occasional beam from an oncoming car.

Stein leaned against the plush upholstery. "Stage one complete, JG. What's next?"

"Have Susan set up a series of meetings with the different constituencies. What happened in your session?"

"Not much. Bill Bennett, the biologist, that nun, Agnes, the editor of the newspaper, Dorothy, your friend, Noah, but he left early, and some other students were there. Bennett's in an ivory tower. He rambled on about the invasive corporate mentality and the necessity of returning to the purity of higher education. I guess that's academia for you. The high point of the day was when Bennett's gang of hoodlums knocked the school psychologist into the pool. You should have seen his expression." Stein threw back his head and laughed.

"I built some bridges, especially with the editors of the paper, Jack and Dorothy. Those two are all right. We had a few beers with Magdalena and Susan after our meeting. They're doing a feature on Susan and another on the faculty cuts. They renamed the paper *Foggy Bottom* after the neighborhood in DC and because of the perennial fog."

"They got that one right. Do you think anyone at Lakeside is aware there's a national election going on?"

"They're too wrapped up in their own personal battles."

"Do they expect you to restore the cut positions?"

"I hope not. We're going ahead, not backward. And the cuts happened before I was hired."

"Don't get cocky. You never know what's going to happen, especially around Lakeside. By the way, it was that cockamamy basset hound that knocked the psychologist into the pool."

"Gladys the hound dog?"

"None other."

"The routine that she and Katherine staged should be recorded for posterity."

"I'm sure they'd do a command performance."

"No, thanks." Gudewill laughed as he steered the car past the fields on both sides of the highway. "I couldn't believe my eyes when Katherine appeared onstage as Elvis in his thin period with Gladys accompanying her to 'You Ain't Nothin' But a Hound Dog.'"

"The beast is certainly trained."

"She sings better than Katherine."

"You ought to have her perform for the Army buddies."

"That's not the image Lakeside needs to project."

"I wonder why." Stein pulled out a cigarette and lit it, tossing the match in the ashtray. "Incidentally, the faculty was conspiring at the end of the pool. The queen of Babel and her cohorts."

"Who?" Gudewill looked across the seat.

"The queen of Babel."

"Let me guess. Carmen, the former French teacher, now Spanish-slash-drama teacher."

"Right! Babel, the ice queen, the shrink, the religious chair nun, and the frogman, with occasional drop-ins."

"The librarian, eh? That's unexpected. The faculty's been quite clear about drawing the lines between the staff and themselves."

"Recruiting her to the ranks."

Gudewill steered the Lincoln across the overpass to 101. The troops were marshaling. He trusted he was as crafty as the old sturgeon.

eighteen | THE BARN

Magdalena meticulously chiseled the large plaster-and-cement block in front of her. The block was still undefined, although a close inspection revealed hints of a human form in the mass. Dressed in a gray smock, baggy black sweatpants, and a pair of running shoes, she had her hair pulled back in a bun. She was in the Barn, the space the art department had delegated to her. Nestled deep in the woods at the rear of the main campus, the old building had been divided into three studios—the largest one for Magdalena, the other two for her students—and it was here she could usually be found. In one corner were several collages and smaller cement figures, in another a supply of metals, wood, wires, boxes, welding materials, oils, acrylics, brushes, and miscellaneous odds and ends. The south wall was a floor-to-ceiling window that looked out onto the cypresses and pines beyond. A library table stacked with books fronted the window and was flanked by a cushioned sofa and chair. An azure vase blazing with sunflowers sat on the tiled table next to the chair. Along the west wall was a bright blue cupboard, a sink filled with teacups and mugs, and a double hot plate with a teakettle on one burner and a Melitta coffee pot on the other. Magdalena's current project, the nascent human figure, dominated the large studio. She stepped down from the platform.

"Enough! It's teatime. Carlos?" She glanced over to the long table where a tall, brown-haired student hunched over a book on Vietnam. He wore torn jeans, a heavy wool shirt over a white T-shirt, and workmen's boots.

"Great! I'm sick of hawks and doves."

"And what a time it was! All march and protest. Thank God it's over. The fall of Saigon ended the war, but the struggle continues. This afternoon I'm going to the American Fruit Corporation board meeting." She crossed the studio and filled the battered kettle with water. "I have some Ceylon."

"Sounds good." Carlos stretched and looked out the window. "Another foggy day. I'm glad I live in the Mission District. At least we see the sun." He turned and watched Magdalena.

She took two cups out of the sink and rinsed and dried them with an embroidered tea towel. Setting them on the cupboard, she spooned some Ceylon into the bottom of each cup. "How're the projects coming?"

"I've decided on a collage of the sixties. The cause, the war, the civil rights movement, the music, the whole scene. Dorothy's doing a happening. I thought happenings started with Yoko Ono, not the futurists and Dadaists in the twenties and thirties. Anyway, she wants to shock Eliot and Agnes."

"That shouldn't be too hard." Magdalena smiled and checked the kettle. "If the Church went back to Latin Masses, Agnes would be in heaven. Agnes has a difficult time adjusting to change. She's not alone. Many missed the message of Vatican II, the call to social justice. They focus only on the changes."

"You got it."

"Working with Cesar all those years, how couldn't I? How's your uncle feeling?"

"Better, but he's not able to return to La Paz and Cesar yet. He's still at my grandmother's."

The kettle hissed. Magdalena poured the steaming water into the cups. "Do you want anything in it?"

"No, thanks." He took the cup. "What's happening with the union?"

Magdalena followed him to the couch and sat down as regally as if her smock were a velvet gown. She looked at him closely. "So you're worried. And with good cause. It'll probably raise tuition. Eliot's trying to win everyone over. He's talking to the AAUW and USF. He doesn't see the larger picture, only his personal agenda. Has no interest in changing the system. If I learned anything from Cesar, it's the necessity of changing the system. Eliot's like the teamsters who want to control the fields to expand their power. No overview." Magdalena shook her head and put the cup on the table.

"What about the others?"

"Most are in Eliot's camp."

"When's the vote?"

"Probably in the next week or so. Let's see your sketches for the collage."

udewill settled back in his favorite mahogany swivel chair with a cup of coffee and the *New York Times*. Sarajane's chair was back at the decorators'. It was 8:00 a.m., and he and Stein had just mapped out their strategy for the day. Gudewill jerked forward, his eyes wide behind the thick lenses. Shouting out at him from the front page was the headline: "Famed Sculptor Upstages Corporate Board Meeting."

"My God! She's done it again!"

"Who's done what?" Stein turned from the doorway.

"Magdalena. She broke up the American Fruit Corporation board meeting."

He skimmed the article. "Called them bullies, compared them to Simon Legree. Said they're keeping the people of Central America in serfdom. Good God! Has she gone mad?"

"Remember your first encounter." Stein closed the door and returned to the chair across from Gudewill.

"Jail." Gudewill nodded ruefully. "She reminded me of those Bing Crosby nuns, but now she's more like Emma Goldman. Apparently she insulted each board member. You know who's on the AFC board, don't you?"

"Remind me."

"Babcock."

"The plot thickens." Stein chuckled and pulled his cigarettes from the pocket of his blue pinstripe suit. "What did she say about him?"

"Called him an imperialist pig." Gudewill raised his heavy eyebrows so that they rose above his glasses.

"I bet he liked that." Stein laughed out loud. "I can just see him puffing up like a blowfish but not able to say anything because he'd be quoted in today's paper. He must've been ticked off."

"There's not much he can do about it. The last time I heard, freedom of speech was still in the Bill of Rights."

"The celebrated artist from the college where he's a trustee publicly insulting him." Stein couldn't stop laughing. "You'd better stay on Magdalena's good side or God knows what she's got in store for you."

"I know she's against the faculty unionization, sees it as a self-destructive move."

"Isn't Bennett opposed also?"

"Bennett and a few others, but they're in the minority."

"I gather that's the discussion for the dean's meeting."

"Yes, alternative plans."

"I'll check with Charlie and Pete to see how it's going in the trenches. The Russian maids have been giving my office special treatment, so I don't think they're plotting a revolution. Natasha and Marta, wearing their usual white uniforms, even brought me a cake."

"Bribery?'

"More like insurance."

"Insurance," Gudewill sighed. "I wouldn't mind some myself."

Lucy and Noah lounged against the many pillows on her bed, a wicker tray of French bread, cheeses, fruit, and wine between them. Through the windows, the reflected sunset dappled the Oakland hills in vivid hues of red, pink, and orange as they blended into the darkening sky. Noah ripped off a chunk of bread and slathered it with Brie.

"Hey! Save some for me!" Lucy snatched the knife from his hand.

"Give me the knife, I'm not done."

Lucy held the knife out of Noah's reach. Grinning, he grabbed her arm. "The knife, please."

She surrendered it and snuggled back into the pillows. "What did you think of the retreat?"

"So-so. Stein was in my group. I don't like him. He's too observant, watches too closely." Handing the knife back to Lucy, Noah bit into the bread.

"He likes me. Would like to make me laugh. Calls me the ice queen." Lucy quartered an apple.

"I told you that's how everybody sees you."

Lucy smiled. "As they should. Bill Bennett's kids kept interrupting our group until they discovered Katherine's dog. They spent the rest of the day chasing it all over the grounds. Apparently they knocked Gary into the pool."

"I wish I'd seen that. Mr. Cool, wet as a fish. He looks like the last person in the world to go swimming." Noah bit into an apple wedge.

"He doesn't. He told me."

"It was Bill's turn to babysit. Nancy was working. Usually Dorothy does it for him."

"I think you're sweet on her." Lucy sipped the wine.

"Nancy?"

"No, Dorothy."

"No." Noah shook his head. "She's just a friend. But Carlos is." He broke off a chunk of cheddar and popped it into his mouth.

"Your friends are pretty involved in school politics."

"Not me. I'm here to get a piece of paper and move on. My only allegiance is to *numero uno*." He licked a piece of cheese off his thumb and jabbed his chest with it.

"I suppose that's our common denominator."

"You got it." He reached across the tray and tickled her ribs.

"Stop it, Noah! If you do, I'll give you a morsel more savory than these grapes."

Noah stopped and propped himself up on an elbow to look at Lucy. "Shoot."

"Eliot invited me to tea. His flat's filled with goodies that would make an antiques dealer cry, and, if you're a little kinky, even weep."

"What do you mean?" Noah stared at Lucy curiously.

"He has this incredible collection of feet: casts, sculptures, paintings, photos. Eliot's into feet."

"You're kidding me!"

"No, he took me into his study and brought out his pictures. I got the royal treatment so I'd vote with the faculty. Of course, it's all bull. They're only interested in my vote, nothing else. Gary treats me like I'm one of the Russian maids. Eliot put himself on the line by showing me his photographs, his private collection, some of people you know."

"You mean he shot them? That'd shake up the revolution class. Imagine Eliot into feet. I'd heard he had a strange hobby, but I never figured it for feet." Laughing, Noah picked up the tray and set it on the floor. "Meanwhile, I can think of other body parts that interest me more." He edged over to Lucy and began to lick her stomach.

twenty-one | LUNCH AT THE PALACE

Sarajane pulled her burgundy Mercedes up to the Palace Hotel entrance, unfolded herself from the leather seat, and tossed the keys to the doorman who held the door for her. "I'll be in the Garden Court." She threw a blond mink stole over her lavender Castleberry knit suit already draped with a purple silk scarf. Her arms jangled like an armory during an earthquake as she entered the hotel. Outside the elegant restaurant, Agnes perched meekly on the edge of a green velvet chair, in her usual beige and tan tones.

"Sarajane, there you are. I was worried something had happened."

"The traffic was unbearable on the freeway, dear. Why didn't you tell the maître d' you were with me? He'd have seated you. Then you could have had a drink."

"Oh, no, I wouldn't presume."

"Agnes, you've got to become more assertive. You'll never get anywhere being meek. The meek may inherit the earth, but the aggressive are in charge." Taking Agnes's arm, she led her into to the dining room to her usual table. The maître d' followed behind them.

"Your usual, Mrs. Thomas?" Sarajane nodded. "And what would your friend like?" He bowed toward Agnes.

"A bottle of Pouilly-Fuissé for both of us, Pierre, thank you." Sarajane undraped her stole and sat down, her gold clanging across the table. Reaching into the lavender bag, she removed a gold cigarette case and extracted a cigarette. Immediately a busboy appeared with a match.

Agnes asked hesitantly, "Do you think it would be all right if I had one? I feel the occasion calls for one."

"Of course!" Sarajane handed her a Benson & Hedges. Again the busboy magically appeared, match in hand. "You must have had a strenuous morning." She nodded to Agnes, ignoring the busboy but sizing up the diners around them. Seated at the center of the imperial room under the potted palms and large raised glass ceiling, so that everyone who entered was in her line of vision, Sarajane might have been a safari leader plotting her next foray into the jungle. At the side of the great hall, a pianist behind a potted plant played a Schubert sonata.

"And the day isn't half over! There's college council this afternoon and the alumni board meeting tonight." Agnes puffed on the cigarette and coughed. "It's been a long time. I seldom give into my urges."

"Yes, yes," Sarajane said impatiently. "Tell me how the voting's going."

"Most of the votes are lined up. You're sure to be elected chair of the alumni board tonight. The only ones I'm not sure of are the two younger members. They'd like to see Mary continue."

"I bet they would. They're the product of the new Lakeside and go along with all the changes. Thank goodness no men have shown an interest in being on the board. When we're in charge, and the college returns to being an all women's college, we'll be back to the old ways. Once the chair of religious studies is in place, you'll see, Agnes."

The waiter arrived, uncorked the bottle, and handed the cork to Sarajane. She sniffed it, sipped from the glass, and nodded her approval. The white-jacketed man poured them each a glass.

"Have you heard from John?"

"He wrote me a thank-you note for the furniture." She frowned, her blue eyes narrowing. "I expected at least a phone call. Still, there's plenty of time. Once I'm installed as alumni chair, I'm going to give a small dinner party at home for him with key alumni, including you, of course. There's an advantage to meeting in one's home territory." She beckoned to the waiter for the menus.

twenty-two | DRINKS
WITH THE DEAN

Outside the president's office the wind howled, the eucalyptus trees creaked, and the old wooden building shivered under the battering rain. Mallards huddled among the rushes along Lake Merced while inside, Gudewill, Stein, and Dean Marian huddled around the new conference table.

"Maybe the storm means there won't be a drought." Standing up, Gudewill turned to the rain-splattered window. "How about a drink?" He walked over to the credenza. "Thanks to Mrs. Thomas, we have a fully stocked bar. What's your choice?"

"Bourbon and water. Do you mind if I take off my shoes? My feet are killing me." Marian removed her brown Red Cross heels and rubbed the bunion on her right foot. She wore a brown tweed suit and mauve blouse.

Gudewill poured a generous dollop of bourbon for Marian and double shots of Dewar's for himself and Stein. He had supplemented Sarajane's Johnny Walker with his own favorite.

"What beautiful Waterford glasses, John!"

"Another gift from our generous alumna."

"The magnanimous Sarajane of the royal purple." Stein said.

"I see they match the ashtrays." Marian picked up one from the round table. "It must weigh several pounds."

"Royalty doesn't stint, but every gift has its price." Stein nodded over his folded hands. The brass buttons on his blue blazer picked up the light from the chandelier.

"I'm aware of that, Stein. I hope your news is better than Marian's. It's been a hell of a day!"

"And it's not over yet, John. The board meets in an hour to elect a new chairperson, probably Sarajane. Agnes made sure I'm aware of their impending power." Marian settled back in the barrel chair.

"Just what we need, a conservative alumni board. Begin with the college council meeting, Marian." Gudewill sipped his Dewar's.

"We never got past the student demand for equal parking. The students feel it's due to them. They'd also like the back parking lot repaved. Of course, the faculty was incensed, Eliot raving like a madman that the students should not have the same privileges as faculty. After the meeting, he gathered the faculty, to discuss the union, I'm sure. And then the students ranted about the dean of students taking a leave of absence. Everyone left angry." She bent over and rubbed the bunion on her foot.

"More good news," Stein added. "A ring of Volkswagen thieves is operating in the city. They hit campus and took two bugs. And Dooley, the gardener, is inciting the Russian maids to strike. Apparently the retreat triggered off his Marxism. The Russians are afraid of losing their jobs. He's trying to convince them that they have nothing to lose because they're going to lose them anyway." He pulled a pack of True Blues from his jacket pocket and lit one.

"Sounds more like Groucho than Karl. Did the maids get wind of the proposal from XYZ Maintenance to take over?"

"They must have."

"At this point, nothing would surprise me. Tell me more about Eliot, Marian." Gudewill rubbed his chin thoughtfully.

"Eliot thinks he should have been appointed the academic dean. He's never forgiven me for getting it instead. He claims I'm the cause of the college's problems. Says I've created a trade school, where matriculation is all job-oriented. All because my degree is in social sciences, not humanities. Ever since I took this job, he's been undermining me." She held out her glass. "May I have another drink?"

"Of course." Gudewill took all three glasses over to the bar. "And what have you done to ease the situation?" He filled each glass, adding water from the Waterford pitcher, and brought the glasses back to the table.

"Eliot's a traditionalist. He objects to the women's and black studies programs, which he views as an educational smorgasbord without any integration. Students pick a little English, a little math, a little art, a little of this, a little of that. He thinks the new programs have no cohesion, unity, or the structure of traditional education. He doesn't recognize that traditional education, itself, has pigeonholes. By involving Eliot and Agnes in the interdisciplinary classes that grew out of the CORE project, I'd hoped they would see the new programs as more than little pieces. CORE was established to order and revitalize the college classes and is still at its formative stage. At the moment Eliot and Agnes are so caught up in the politics of the union and the chair of religious studies, I doubt if they see anything."

Stein shook his head. "Well, great and terrible wizard, how are you going to handle the latest conundrum?"

*N*oah pulled the white Caddy into the red zone in front of the Go-Go Club. Above the brick-fronted building, scantily clad girls kicked their heels in neon abandon. He rolled out of the car and strolled around it to the entrance of the club. Lucy, in tan gabardine slacks, a white silk blouse, and a brown suede jacket, popped out the other side.

"This is the place, Lucy." Noah grinned. Khakis and an olive green crew-neck sweater covered his large frame. "Unc's number one bar."

The Go-Go Club was in the middle of Broadway's nightclub strip, on the lower end of North Beach, bordering Chinatown, where exotic dancers, the most publicized being Carol Doda of silicone fame, frolicked nightly in various stages of undress. A mustached barker in a striped vest saluted Noah. "How's it goin', kid? Your uncle's at one of the other clubs. Park the car in the alley."

"I'm just dropping something off." Noah motioned to Lucy, who followed him into the smoke-filled club. Disco music blared from the speakers, and on the stage, two girls in brief costumes mimed the motions of dance, their faces blank as fresh canvases in Magdalena's barn.

"Wait here, Lucy. I'll be right back." Noah entered a door

marked "private" at the far end of the bar. In a minute he returned grinning. "Now that that's over with, we can have some
fun. I'll leave Unc's car here and we can go to Spec's for a drink."

In a few minutes they were sitting among the memorabilia at
Spec's, a bar tucked into an alley off Columbus Avenue. "So this
was a haunt of the Beats." Lucy sipped her Scotch and water.

"City Lights, Vesuvio, the whole North Beach scene. I wish
I'd been around. I just finished *The Dharma Bums*. Kerouac based
the main character on Snyder. They all used to hang out down
here." Noah pulled out a pack of Lucky Strikes and lit one. "It all
started with the six poets at Six Gallery."

"I'm more interested in the tapestries. Now that they've put a
guard on duty at night, I'm afraid it's all over."

"Not yet. I was talking to Tim in my ethics class. He's the
graveyard shift guard Charlie hired to watch the tapestries. When
everyone's asleep in the middle of the night, he slips away for an
hour or so to see his girlfriend in Parkmerced. Everyone thinks
he's in the library." Noah crushed the Lucky in the black ashtray
and cupped his hands around his Dos Equis.

"Do you know when he's at the girlfriend's?"

"No, but it wouldn't be hard to figure out. If I watch the
parking lot and see him leave, then I can slip in and out without
anyone being the wiser, and guess who'll get the blame?" Noah
laughed. "Here's to success!" He lifted the beer.

"And ethics." Lucy laughed and tossed down her Scotch.

"Nice necklace." Noah reached across and fondled the heavy
gold chain around Lucy's neck.

"A gift."

"What's the matter? You got your librarian face on again.
Who gave it to you?" Noah's fingers touched her cheek.

"Someone. It has nothing to do with you." She brushed his
hand away.

"From the look on your face, I hope not! And I'm glad I'm not that guy."

"What makes you think it's a man?"

"Only a guy would give you such a gift, and only a guy would make you this teed off. Why don't we go over to City Lights? I promised to show you North Beach. Then we can go to the used bookstore next to City Lights."

"What is this, a busman's holiday?"

"What else do librarians do in their spare time?"

"I can think of something much more interesting." Lucy cocked her head and eased her hand under the table and up the inseam of Noah's khakis, lingering at the crotch.

Noah moaned, then grinned. "You win. It's back to your place." He drained the bottle of beer, removed Lucy's hand, and stood up. Adjusting his pants, he laughed. "It's good these are baggy. Let's go." They skirted out the door and down the alley.

G udewill hummed as he piloted his son's Volkswagen along the Great Highway. The storm had passed and the Pacific shimmered silver under the gray-and-white streaked sky. Commissioned at the same time as Golden Gate Park, the Great Highway was the widest expanse of pavement in the nation at the time it opened in 1929, averaging 180 feet from shoulder to shoulder and spreading to twenty-six hundred feet at the foot of the great park. But the sand was fierce in its proprietorship and engaged the city in an ongoing battle to reclaim the narrowing strip, eventually burying the five-and-a-half miles of pipes and sprinklers. Relentless, the sand continued to inch its way back to total ownership.

"I have a good feeling," Gudewill said to Stein, who was scrunched down in the sheepskin-covered seat puffing on a True Blue. "The bankers' meeting went well, and I expect the campus tour with Eunice to do the same. After the recent rain, it'll be obvious that the new dorms need to be painted and reroofed. The top floor leaked like a sieve. How those crooked contractors got away with watering down the concrete, I'll never know. Eunice will have no choice but to award us the Whitman grant."

"Money speaks, JG, and inspectors are easier than most." Stein stubbed out the cigarette in the small ashtray.

"I suppose you're right. But I still find it hard to believe that Babcock recommended the roofing and painting contractor."

"Your buddy, Babcock, is full of surprises. To change to a more pleasant subject, how long has it been since you've seen Eunice?"

"Several years, but we've talked on the phone occasionally since Julie died. It's lucky for us that she's director of the Whitman Foundation."

"More than luck. How often does the director of the foundation that awards the most grants for building repair turn out to be your college sweetheart?"

Guiding the Bug past the zoo and the east side of Fort Miley, Gudewill turned left on John Muir Drive toward Lakeside's main entrance. As he downshifted, the sound of metal rubbing against metal overwhelmed the loud rumble of the engine.

"Sounds like Johnny's car is the next one to go to the shop." He frowned. "What are all these cars doing double-parked?" The main drive was blocked with cars. "It looks like a funeral. I'd better park in the back lot." He put the car in reverse and backed down the hill.

"I hope the funeral isn't for anyone we know." Stein looked over at Gudewill as they pulled into the mud-filled lot. "Maybe Eunice will give you money to pave this mess." He opened the door and stepped into a giant puddle. "Nice parking job, JG. Great for the Italian slacks." He glared down at his mud-splattered pants.

"You've got a closetful, Stein. Don't worry about it. No wonder the students complain about this lot." The two walked down the hill to the main building.

Outside the president's office, the majority of the faculty

massed, their angry clamor audible from the back entrance of the old wooden building.

"Sounds like it's your funeral, JG." Stein grinned as they climbed the stairs to Gudewill's office.

"There he is!" Eliot shouted when he spotted Gudewill. Flanked by Agnes and Gary, he was at the fore of the rabble thronged outside the office.

"Here comes the lynching party," Stein muttered out of the side of his mouth.

Gudewill strolled nonchalantly down the hall. "What seems to be the problem?"

"Problem! You know damn well. The students have taken over our parking places." Eliot's white face was purple as he stood toe-to-toe with Gudewill. "This is the last straw, Gudewill. I'm warning you! The last straw!"

"So that's why I couldn't park!" The larger man scanned the crowd. "It's probably a student prank. Where are Keiani and the other leaders?"

"In the housing office, I imagine." Gary stepped forward. "Now that the dean's on leave, they're usually there."

"Gary, would you do me a favor and bring them to my office?" Gudewill peered at the crowd. "I'm going to ask the rest of you to park your cars below on the road and then return to your classes and carry on. I'll take care of everything. You'll have your parking spaces again by lunchtime."

Inside the office, Lily chirped like a canary on speed. "President Doctor . . . President Mister . . . Mister Gudewill . . . oh goodness! I called the police to move the cars, and they just laughed at me, and Miss Howard is waiting in the office, and no one will tow the cars, and what are we going to do?"

"Sit down, Lily. It's taken care of. We don't need the police. What did they say?"

"That we're a crazy college and they're too busy to send out tow trucks and can't be bothered ticketing cars over some silly student protest. Then they hung up."

"Did they? Stein, I think a personal visit with the captain is in order. Don't you agree? But before that, would you take Miss Howard on a tour of the campus while I meet with the students?" Gudewill opened his office door. "Eunice! How wonderful to see you, and looking lovelier than ever. You remember Stein."

The sun had long since set. The fog that hovered over Lakeside dampened all it touched. Inside the president's office, Stein and Gudewill relaxed over a Dewar's. "I told you the wizard theory would work, Stein. I knew the car-in was only a gesture. Once I said we'd pave the back parking lot, those kids fell right into the plan. They had some complaints about the food service, so I told them you'd look into it. Check the figures for the past few years. See if this operation is making money. Let's go home." Gudewill buzzed the outer office on the intercom. "Lily, send in Noah."

Noah appeared at the door, and Gudewill tossed him the VW keys. "Get the yellow Bug from the upper parking lot, and take good care of it, Noah. It's my son's proudest possession." He turned to Stein, who was pouring another drink at the credenza. "How'd it go at the police station?"

Stein screwed the cap on the bottle. "Fine. The captain and I had a heart-to-heart about the importance of Lakeside to the community and your long friendship with the police commissioner. There shouldn't be any more problems."

Listening, Gudewill smiled as he nodded approval. "The meeting with Eunice went as I expected, although she couldn't understand the shabby construction either. I assured her it wouldn't happen again. In fact, I'm seeing her for dinner next week."

"Business or pleasure?" Stein sat down in the wing chair.

"A little of both. She's looking good for someone our age. Damn good!"

"So the wizard is paying court to Glinda, the Good Witch. My, my!" He leaned back in the chair and laughed. "And by the way, don't get cocky about your damn Yankees beating the Reds in the World Series, JG; Cincinnati will demolish them! Class always wins out."

"Don't bet on it, Stein." Gudewill stood up and refilled his glass. "I wonder what's keeping Noah." He returned to the desk. "Are the Russians still plotting a revolution?"

"Nothing new on that front. But Donne from XYZ Maintenance is presenting his reorganization proposal later in the week."

"The Russians are right. Some of them are going to have to go. The numbers determine that." Gudewill shook his head.

Noah burst into the room. "John, the car is gone. I can't find it anywhere!"

The two men looked at each other. "The VW ring," they said simultaneously.

A snowy egret soared up from the muddy shore. It perched in the naked buckeye tree on the slope above Lake Merced and surveyed the mallards foraging in the shallow waters. Overhead, the fog drifted. Inside Lakeside's cafeteria, Dorothy slumped over the brown table. Her hands clutched a mug of black coffee and the corners of her mouth drooped.

"What's the matter, Dorothy?" Noah dropped his books and backpack on the table and sat down next to her. He jabbed her on the sleeve of her oversize houndstooth check jacket, her latest purchase from a Mission Street thrift shop. "Come on! It can't be that bad." He poked her again.

Peeking out from under her brown hat, she crossed her eyes. "I don't have money for rent, I hate my babysitting job, and Eliot is on my case. Look how he picked on me the other day when I tried to tell him I was late because Katherine's dog ate my skirt. It's hopeless!"

"Tell me how I can help." Noah leaned against the orange chair and propped his size-thirteen boots on the opposite chair.

"Find me a quick five thousand so I can finish my two years and live without worries until I graduate from here!"

"Why not enough so you can spend the next semester in Italy checking out the Italian men?"

The corners of Dorothy's mouth slowly edged upward, revealing her gap-toothed grin. "Why not enough so you can come over for a weekend and we can have a few laughs? You check out the girls and I'll check out the guys."

"Maybe I can help." He cocked his head. "My uncle has a couple of bars, one in North Beach. How'd you like to be a go-go dancer? It pays better than babysitting, and you make extra on tips. It's weeknights mainly, so weekends you could study."

"A go-go dancer? What would I have to wear?"

"A bikini or bathing suit, no topless stuff. That's down the street at Carol Doda's place. I'll speak to him if you want."

Dorothy grinned. "That'd be great!"

"What are you two plotting?" Jack bounded over to the table and slid into a chair. "Any news on student parking?"

"College council meets tomorrow. We'll hear soon enough. Noah's got a job for me as a go-go dancer at his uncle's place in North Beach. Then I won't have to babysit Bill's brats."

"Those kids would drive me nuts." Jack pulled a couple of apples from his backpack. "I bring my own food. This place is a rip-off." He took a bite and noisily crunched.

"I wouldn't mind one of those. I didn't eat breakfast." Dorothy looked at the apple, then at Jack.

"Here, kid. Lunch is on me." He flashed his jack-o'-lantern grin and tossed her an apple.

"Hey, Jack. Have you ever thought about taking out girls?" Noah leaned back, tipping his chair until it touched the one behind him.

Jack's eyebrows rose. "Me? Not really. I've liked boys since I was a kid in military school. Then when I came to the city, I lived with Roger until we split last spring. How come you're asking?"

"There's a girl in my math class who thinks you're cute."

"Get outta here! Me, cute?" His grin spread from ear to ear.

"You know Tracy?"

"The one with the Farrah Fawcett hair and blue eyes?"

"You noticed!"

"Just 'cause I'm not buying don't mean I can't look. She's a good-looking broad."

"You don't call girls 'broads,' Jack," Dorothy interrupted.

"So she's a good-looking girl. Is that better? And she thinks I'm cute! How about that?" Grinning, he munched on his apple.

"You ought to think about taking her out. You'll never know until you try."

twenty-six | UNION

udewill and Marian sat in the president's office while the fog hovered over the college. Gudewill drained his coffee and put the cup on the tray on the oval table, with its remnants of rolls, jam, butter, and orange juice. The dean cupped her coffee in her hands and stared out the window. She turned to Gudewill.

"The only reason Eliot would call this meeting is to announce that they've unionized. I hope they understand what a mistake they're making."

"People learn from their mistakes, Marian. He'll find out soon enough. The tragedy is that unions have become special interest groups. Labor has turned from its previous role of championing those who face poverty and discrimination. By joining the rank and file, the faculty's doing its students a great disservice. Everyone will lose."

Lily poked her head around the corner to announce the arrival of the faculty representatives. In the distance, Gudewill could hear the guns from the police shooting range on Lake Merced. Lily led Eliot to the conference table. He was followed by Agnes, Carmen, and Lucy. As Lily cleared the table, Gudewill rose and motioned to the chairs.

"Take a seat. Lily, would you please get coffee for the faculty?"

"No coffee for us, Gudewill. We're here on business." Eliot dismissed Lily with a wave of his hand and sat down stiffly on one of the barrel chairs. The others followed suit. "We're here to make our position clear. The college has become a job mill whose only interest is in turning out marketable graduates. The emphasis and selling of graduate programs in order to generate more income has resulted in a decrease in undergraduate enrollment. I see fragmentation where the administration claims there is wholeness." With his frog eyes bulging, Eliot glared at Marian. "An example is the revolution class that Agnes and I are teaching. The students are off doing whatever they feel like. One of the term projects is a happening. My God! What have we come to?" He pulled out a large linen handkerchief and wiped his forehead.

"I agree with Newman, the leader of the Oxford movement. He defined education! The more knowledge tends to be particular, the more it ceases to be knowledge. The university should be a place of education rather than one of instruction. The present administration is bent on the particular, on instruction, not on education. In doing so, it's lost sight of the mission of the college. And what, I would like to know, is a college founded by a religious order doing eliminating religious studies?" Blue veins throbbed on Eliot's head.

"The only way we can protect ourselves from further harm is by unionization. Our salaries and our job security will be protected. There will be a grievance procedure. Lakeside has become impersonal and arbitrary. Decisions are made by a board of overseers with little advice from the faculty. The college is a factory with production quotas and efficiency charts.

"In short, I am here to tell the administration that the faculty has voted to establish the American Association of University Professors as its bargaining unit." Eliot again wiped his pulsing forehead. His flushed face glowed under the fluorescent lights.

Gudewill nodded his head. "I hear what you're saying, Eliot, but I think you are making a big mistake. As part of a union, you'll be losing certain freedoms. There will be no interchange, dialogue, or informal discussion between the two sides. Everything must be taken to the bargaining table. You'll be locked into a position with your hands behind your back. Look what Shanker has done with the American Federation of Teachers."

"Shanker says power is a good thing. It's certainly better than being powerless!" Eliot spat out his words. Agnes, Carmen, and Lucy watched the two men, intent as spectators on the net line at Wimbledon. Marian leaned over the table, her hands folded, her voice even.

"Eliot," she said patiently, "You're forgetting that it was the faculty who made the recommendations for the terminations."

"We were forced by the administration, Marian. It was the administration that led the college astray with false direction and poor leadership. It was the administration that made these decisions. We were merely pawns. No more." Eliot rose, followed by the three women. "This meeting is over."

Silently, the four marched out in single file. The gunshots from the shooting range across John Muir drive echoed in the office.

he first thing Gudewill noticed as he steered the gray Lincoln into the president's parking space outside the main building was the unkempt lawn. He'd have to speak to Stein about it. Image was all-important, especially first impressions. Granted, there was a drought, but Dooley, with his degree from some fancy academy, ought to be able to figure out a way to keep the lawn green and save water. Isn't that why Babcock had recommended him? An intellectual gardener. Shaking his head, Gudewill unfolded himself from the car and shut the door. An early meeting with Sarajane—his first since her election as alumni chair. Thank God he was tightly booked all day. There was no chance of her overstaying the allotted time. The woman made him fidgety.

"Good morning, Lily," he smiled. "Mrs. Thomas should be arriving soon. Just send her in."

"She's already inside."

Gudewill nodded and pressed his lips together. So Sarajane was taking charge and establishing his office as her turf. He opened the office door. Sarajane was posed against the window, her lavender-clad figure outlined by the morning brightness.

"Good morning, Sarajane. You're certainly punctual!"

"Hello, John," she cooed as she turned slowly, making the most of the morning light. She fixed her eyes on his and, after a long moment, dropped them coyly.

"Won't you have a seat?"

She looked at the mahogany chair behind the desk, her eyes narrowing. "This isn't the chair I ordered."

"This one suits me better. I sent the other one back." Gudewill walked around the desk. "Why don't you sit in one of the chairs that you selected? I'm sure you'll be more comfortable." He guided her to the other side and one of the wing chairs. "You did a fine job decorating, a fine job, but I happen to like this one." He strolled back behind the desk and sat down. "I knew you'd understand. What can I do for you?"

"I'm here as the new alumni director." She lowered her head and peeked up at him through long lashes.

"So I heard. Congratulations. I know how dedicated you are. The alumni made a wise choice."

"Thank you, John. My first plan is a small dinner for you and several key alumni." Sarajane paused and tilted her head. "At my house." Another pause. "I think it's essential you meet the important alumni and hear their viewpoint." She opened her purse and took out her gold case, extracting a Benson & Hedges. Gudewill reached across the desk to light it. She touched his hand.

"I agree, but why don't we host the dinner at Lakeside? It would give the alums much more of a feel for the college."

"That's what I'm afraid of."

"Oh?"

"They haven't been pleased with the changes in the college. If they come here, they might be further alienated."

"Really."

"I don't think it's a wise idea at all, John. Besides, my place is much more intimate. I'm sure now that you are alone, there are things you must miss." Her eyes lingered on his as she flicked ashes into the heavy Waterford ashtray.

Gudewill could feel the heat generating off her as if she were a Buck stove on a cold winter day. "Lakeside is a better setting, Sarajane. The food service can cater it right here in my office, and we can show off your new gift to the college." He motioned to the suite of furniture.

"But my home is much more comfortable." Her eyes widened.

"Nonsense, my office is just fine."

"I suppose, if your mind is set on it, John." Sarajane's shoulders drooped.

"Perhaps you can tell me some of the plans the alumni have."

Sarajane perked up. "A return to a women's college."

"A women's college? An interesting concept. Tell me more." Gudewill propped his chin on his folded hands and rested his elbows on the desk.

"It's a winner, John. You can't go wrong. Studies prove that women do better in an all-female environment. It's obvious that Lakeside isn't successful as a coed school. If it returned to its origins, you'd gain alumni support and they'd send their daughters here."

"What about the men students?"

"Phase them out in four years."

"That's certainly an original idea, Sarajane. I'll give it some consideration." Gudewill stood. "My next appointment is due."

Squashing her cigarette, Sarajane gathered her scarves around her shoulders and rose. "Plan the dinner as you see best. You're the boss." She tossed her purple cape around her shoulders and left.

twenty-eight | REVOLUTION

*R*ibbons of sunlight occasionally sliced through the grayness that canopied the quad. The yellow, red, and blue primroses, calendula, and pansies planted in the center flowerbed bobbed in the November breeze, a rhythm in primary colors. Inside the cafeteria, Keiani, Jack, and Dorothy huddled around a table like the 49ers offensive team.

Keiani pushed a mound of red goop around her plate. "Anyone want to take a stab at what the special is?"

"No, thanks." Jack took a bite out of his deli roast beef sandwich. "I'll stick with off-campus food. So the faculty's gone ahead and unionized. They didn't waste any time. Where's that leave us?"

"Fending for ourselves," Dorothy said. "They're so busy with all the negotiation stuff that we're stuck out in left field."

"It doesn't look good. What's gonna happen to governance?" Keiani stirred her fork through the red goop trying to salvage something edible.

"Hey, you've gotta come see my revolution collage." Carlos set his tray down and sat next to Dorothy. "The student-movement segment's almost finished."

"Maybe that's what we should do. Have some sort of student protest and make them aware that we're part of the picture." Throwing his head back, Jack drained his carton of milk.

"You mean like the car-in?" Keiani asked.

"Something like that."

"The faculty and the union." Dorothy brought Carlos up to date.

"Magdalena thinks it's a dumb move." Carlos forked his rice and chicken. "I think the chicken just walked through and didn't stop." He probed the rice, searching for further evidence of chicken.

"Hey, Dooley, how's it going?" Jack greeted the slight man in his Red Sox cap and overalls. "Take a load off your feet. How's the garden growing?"

"OK, because of the big storm. Maybe the drought's over. Have you talked to the chiefs about our plan?"

"Nah, they're too busy duking it out with faculty over the union." Jack leaned forward in his chair.

Dooley pulled up a chair beside him. "That's why I'm trying to get the maids and maintenance to go union. It's the only way to protect ourselves."

"Where does that leave our plan to restore the hill?" Keiani asked. Some student leaders had agreed among themselves to continue planting the west side of campus where erosion was the heaviest, a project started the previous summer under the supervision of the now-departed dean. "After all the time we spent planning this summer, I hate to see it just dropped."

"Me too," Dorothy said.

"We don't need them. If you can get the student labor, I can get the trees donated from a nursery. There's no reason why we can't do it. Can you rally the troops?" Dooley's blue eyes narrowed behind his steel-rimmed glasses.

"A tree-in." Jack's eyes widened, a grin breaking his face, and he looked at Keiani.

"We'll get the students, Dooley. You just get the trees."

"Done. We can set a date later."

"I'll call a student meeting on Thursday. Come by Magdalena's studio after."

"Will do. See ya." Dooley rose and strolled out the door.

"I'm glad I'm working nights," Dorothy said. "I'll be able to make the meeting. Do you think we can plant the whole hill in a day?"

Jack rubbed his chin thoughtfully. "Ya know, planting the hill without going through channels is a good move. They're going to be teed off we didn't bring it to college council and that the big mucky-mucks didn't get to put in their two cents' worth." He grinned. "I like that."

"Yeah, and we're doing something for the school. How can they get upset?" Carlos pulled a turkey sandwich from his jacket pocket and opened it.

"What's everybody smiling about?" Noah plopped down in Dooley's chair.

"We figured out a way to bug the administration by doing something constructive." Jack's ear-to-ear grin threatened to crack his face.

"A tree-in," Keiani said. "We're going to fill in the west side of the campus where there's all that erosion. Can we count on you, Noah?"

Noah shrugged. "I'm not sure. Depends on if I'm working for my uncle. Sounds like a good idea, though. What about the administration?"

"No, they don't know about it. We're finishing last summer's project. Only Magdalena is in on it, and Dooley's working with us. He's an independent agent. We'll show them how to get things done." Jack beamed.

"Not to change the subject, Jack, but have you thought any more about going out with Tracy?" Noah asked.

"She's really interested in you, Jack," Keiani added.

"How do you know, Keiani? You been talking to Noah." Jack's grin vanished.

"Nope, she told me."

"Maybe she really is interested." His grin reappeared.

"I told you, Jack. You ought to think about it. Girls are OK." Noah smiled knowingly. "Take her to the movies. A comedy's good. *Silver Streak* with Gene Wilder is pretty funny."

Keiani looked at her watch. "Time to meet Marian for the educational policy committee meeting. Let's go. Jack, Carlos." The three stood up and headed out the glass doors to the veranda.

Dorothy looked at Noah. "Eliot asked me to come to his office at one-thirty."

"What for?"

"He didn't say. I hope it isn't trouble." She sighed deeply.

twenty-nine | THE BROWN
HOUSE

he Brown House nestled under the dripping pines and cypresses on the east side of the campus behind the other academic buildings. An old garden shed, brown-shingled and pentagon-shaped, it had been converted to office space and claimed by Eliot. Wild blackberries, morning glories, and nasturtiums covered the ground on both sides of the brick path leading to the small building. Ivy climbed the trunks of the sheltering cypresses above. Inside, bookcases lined the five walls; an antique table and chair faced the door with another chair opposite for a visitor. High small pane windows paneled the space above the bookcases, making the room quite bright despite being in the middle of the woods. Atop the bookcases were photographs mounted on easels. Colored shots of Ballybunion and Innisfree and black and whites of Greek and Roman ruins. Eliot hunched over his desk, a stack of papers before him, pen in hand.

Dorothy knocked hesitantly at the door.

"Come in."

She turned the handle slowly. This was her first meeting in the Brown House.

"Hello, Eliot. I'm here at four as you asked."

"I'm glad to see you're punctual." Eliot pulled an antique

gold watch from the watch pocket in his white trousers and motioned her to sit down. "Punctuality is an important quality."

Dorothy eased herself down on the straight-backed wooden
chair and dropped her backpack on the floor.

Eliot removed his glasses; his frog eyes blinked at her across
the polished table. "You're wondering if I want to discuss the
world literature class." He pursed his lips.

Dorothy nodded.

"This meeting has nothing to do with literature. I don't know
if you're aware, but I'm a photographer." Again he stared at
Dorothy.

"I didn't know."

"Good. I'm glad it's not part of the Eliot myth. I'm only an
amateur, although I have received high praise for my work. I
travel each summer to North Africa to take photos of ruins. I'm
interested in certain statuary. I also do live models, and I was
wondering if you'd be interested in posing for me."

Dorothy's mouth dropped open and stayed there.

"You're surprised. Perhaps because I pick you out from the
other students."

She nodded.

"That's a test to see how you do under pressure. And you
passed, my dear, with flying colors. You maintain a coolness under fire that I admire. You're probably wondering what kind of
modeling. I assure you, you won't have to undress. I don't do
nudes. I'm only interested in your feet."

Dorothy looked down at her feet. They seemed quite ordi-
nary.

"Would you mind taking off your shoes?"

Without commenting, she removed her cowboy boots and
wool socks. She was curious to see what Eliot saw in her feet.

Eliot moved around the table. "Please stand up." Dorothy did as she was directed. "Now stand on the chair." Again, Dorothy complied. Eliot, his right hand under his chin, his right elbow held by his left hand, walked around the chair and scrutinized her feet. "What size are you?" He motioned for Dorothy to climb down.

"Six, B." She hopped down.

"That's what I thought. I'd like you to come to my flat on Saturday morning at ten. Of course, you'll be paid. Ten dollars an hour. You may put on your boots and go now. You understand, this is in total confidentiality." Dismissing Dorothy with a wave of his hand, Eliot returned to the desk, picked up his pen, and slashed a red X across a paragraph.

*J*ack and Keiani pushed open the double doors of Room 101. On the landing between the first and second floors, the small, low-ceilinged room was a favorite spot for meetings. The four walls were lined with glass-door bookcases; the two window seats on the east side looked out to the woods, the two on the north to Lake Merced. Four library tables were arranged in a small rectangle, inviting conversation.

"Looks like we're the first ones here," Jack said. "Good. Wait till you hear what Babcock said in his *Foggy Bottom* interview."

"I thought you were talking to him later this afternoon."

"No, he could only meet at ten, so I cut class. First things first." Each pulled out a tall leather chair. Jack sprawled out like the limbs of a willow tree on his chair while Keiani neatly arranged her folder on the table before sitting down.

"What'd he say? I can tell by your voice it wasn't the usual garbage." Keiani lowered her voice and leaned closer to Jack, even though they were alone in the room.

"You're right. Quote: 'There comes a time in the economic life of an institution when it must become pragmatic and ruthless.' End of quote."

"You're kidding." Keiani pulled back and peered at Jack.

"Nope. Those were his exact words." Jack tipped his chair so that his head touched the glass door of the bookcase.

"Did he explain what he meant?"

"That's for us to figure out."

"It sure doesn't give one a lot of confidence, does it? It's scary!"

"What's scary?" Carlos plopped down next to Keiani, who repeated Babcock's quote.

"You're kidding."

Jack shook his head. "He said it, all right."

Eliot and Carmen entered the room and the three stopped talking.

"I won't stand for that woman in my class. She is a menace. She and that dog of hers. What happened to the no-dogs-on-campus rule? Why is she allowed to be the exception?" Carmen dropped her books on the table and nodded to the students. "Are any of you friends with Katherine?" The three shook their heads. "I didn't think so. I don't know why she's allowed here."

"Maybe she's a big donor." Jack laughed.

"She's part of the open-door policy. I told you it would never work. Community outreach, my foot." Eliot sniffed, removed his hat, and placed it on the window seat. "So you're the student representatives on the educational policy committee. I hope it's more successful than the CORE committee." His protruding eyes blinked slowly, and he folded his hands and looked at the three.

"The CORE committee and classes are OK, Eliot. They are helping to revitalize the college. That was the purpose of the committee," Carlos said.

"As Magdalena's protégé, of course you're going to think like she does!"

"Magdalena has nothing to do with it. I'm learning more than art. I'm studying the sixties and the causes of the changes in society. The history, the religion, the sociology, everything."

"You're not studying in depth. It's all superficial."

"What's superficial, Eliot?" Magdalena strode into the room and sat between the students and Eliot and Carmen. Her smock and face were smudged with plaster.

"The CORE class on revolution. There's no depth. It's a pastiche. Carlos finds the class 'OK,' to use his term." He smiled condescendingly. "Of course, that's not surprising since he follows your direction, and you are the biggest advocate of the reorganization, Magdalena."

"We can't stay locked in the past. That's one of the temptations of the ivory tower, to fall into the trap of complacency."

"No one can accuse me of complacency!" Eliot bolted upright in his chair.

"No one's accusing you of complacency. I just said it's a pitfall we need to look out for. That's why I favor the new classes. They broaden our horizons, both students and faculty." She reached into her portfolio and took out a notebook.

"Well, I for one certainly don't need my horizons broadened. They are fine the way they are, thank you!"

"Hello, everyone." Dean Marian breezed into the room and stood at the fourth side of the square by the door. "I'm glad you're all here. I won't be able to meet with you today. As a group we cannot meet, now or anytime, except over the bargaining table. Legal counsel has advised me. Governance and the union might conflict. I'm sorry, but unless there's a change in legal counsel, that is the way it stands." She turned and walked out.

"Marian!" Eliot sputtered to the open door. He turned to Carmen. "She can't do this!"

"My God! It's like Gudewill said. We can't discuss or have any kind of dialogue. What have we done, Eliot?"

"Quiet, Carmen! We'll talk about this privately." He grabbed his hat and briefcase and stalked out of the room. Carmen hurried behind him, her flowered skirt swishing.

Keiani, Jack, and Carlos looked at one another and then at Magdalena. "Magdalena, can we go to the Barn? We need a place to talk."

thirty-one | *FOGGY BOTTOM*
DEMANDS

arian rushed into the president's office without knocking. Outside, the gray November sun poked through the clouds. A line of cormorants on the dock across Lake Merced spread their wings, black flags drying in the breeze. Gudewill sat behind his desk, hunched over a yellow legal tablet.

"John, did you see this?" The well-rounded woman tossed a copy of the *Foggy Bottom* on the desk.

"No." He shook his head. "I'm in the middle of a letter to WASC asking them to postpone the college inspection until next year. There's too much happening now for us to prepare for an accreditation visit." The Western Accreditation of Schools and Colleges committee regularly evaluated and certified the college's eligibility for federal funding.

"Look at the editorial. The paper is demanding my resignation. And that's not all. Richard Babcock was interviewed. He told Jack that it's time for the college to be 'ruthless and pragmatic.'"

"Sounds like the students are following his directive. Sit down, Marian, before you explode, and tell me what it's all about." Gudewill motioned to one of the wingback chairs.

Straightening her brown suit skirt, Marian lowered herself into the chair and leaned forward.

"They're outraged because I won't participate in the educational policy committee. They want me to resign as dean and have the educational policy committee become the sole policy-maker for the college. The students think I have abandoned them and as such am of no use to them at all."

"That's rather extreme."

"It certainly is. They don't seem to understand that I don't have the option to meet with the committee now that there's the union. I represent the administration. The students ought to be demanding Eliot's resignation. They don't understand that if I did resign as dean, Eliot, with his distaste for students, would soon have all students off the committee."

"Those at the top always get blamed."

"I just don't like it. Because the dean of students is on leave, the students feel they have no advocate. I've tried to fill in, but I don't have the time, and the housing director doesn't fill their need in the same way as the dean of students, their spokesperson and champion."

"It's a rough time for everyone. When Dean Tuliver went on leave, no one expected the faculty to unionize. What's this about Babcock?"

"He was quite frank in the interview, probably to prepare them for what lies ahead."

"His timing . . ." The large man shook his head.

"I agree. I'm beginning to dread coming to work. Each day holds a new crisis." She sighed and leaned back in the chair.

"I'm talking to the union consultant later today. Next week at the faculty meeting, I'll tell them we're hiring someone to represent us in negotiations."

"They won't be happy about that, not after the announce-

ment that the administration doesn't want to deal with governance."

They were interrupted by a knock at the door. "What now?"
Gudewill shook his head. "Come in."

Stein popped his head through the door. "You're not going to
believe this, JG."

He nodded to Marian. "My condolences on the editorial."
Sitting down next to her, he took a cigarette from his jacket
pocket, lit it, and tossed the match in the ashtray.

"Enough suspense, Stein. What happened?" Gudewill said in
exasperation.

"A tapestry is missing from the library, and in addition,
there's been a theft in the chapel—a tapestry, the chalice, and
some other things."

"The chapel?" Gudewill's eyebrows shot up.

"The chapel." Stein's head bobbed up and down. "Only
they're two different operations. Two men checked in at switchboard this morning saying they were here to fix the wiring in the
chapel. Sister Agnes took them there. When she left, they helped
themselves. The safe was unlocked. Then they thanked switchboard and walked out the front door."

"No kidding." Gudewill shook his head. "That takes some
chutzpah. As much as stealing tapestries while a board meeting is
going on. How do you know it's not the same people?"

"Different MO. Neither switchboard nor Sister Agnes recognized them. The night thief is probably someone we know. Apparently the extra night man was off campus when the library
tapestry was taken." He flicked his ashes into the crystal dish and
rested the cigarette on the rim.

"Two separate jobs."

"Yeah, Chin thinks so too. He's coming here later to interview Sister Agnes." He bent over to adjust his argyle socks.

"Can the guard."

"It's already taken care of." Stein picked up the cigarette.

Gudewill nodded and folded his hands on the legal tablet. "Not all the news is bad. I met with a real estate group. They're interested in building condos on the west side of the campus. On Skyline up near Westlake. That's a solution to the money problem. Sell off the back forty and pay the bank."

"A good way to raise cash without compromising anyone. Is anyone else interested?" Stein flicked his ashes in the glass dish.

"Not so far, but if the word got out . . ." A smile crept across Gudewill's face.

"I can see the wheels turning. I'll make a few phone calls this afternoon. A little competition is always healthy." He nodded, smiling.

"If the price is right, we can pay off the bank and have change to spare." Gudewill grinned. "Marian, when the nuns sold the property to the college, you're sure the title was free and clear? There're no restrictions?"

"Not as far as I know. It was pretty cut-and-dried. Why not check with the trustees?" She removed her shoes and bent over to rub her left foot.

"I'll take your word for it. I don't want them involved until I know it's final. When the trustees hired me, they gave me carte blanche to do what I could to save this place. Selling off the west side is the best solution."

"It's good to be back in action again." Stein turned to Marian. "Cheer up. Things are getting better."

thirty-two | NOAH'S CONNECTION

orothy, Jack, and Noah climbed out of Carlos's red-and-white '56 Chevy. The silent fog curled over Lakeside's main driveway, muffling the sounds from below and rendering Lake Merced invisible. Dorothy pulled her down jacket tightly around her. Carlos locked the car and joined them on the front steps.

"Deli food sure beats the cafeteria. Next time we have to take Keiani. The food here is ruining her stomach. I should head off to the library. Eliot has some books on reserve for world lit." Dorothy snuggled in her jacket.

"Yeah, and I need to go the prez's office to work." Noah grimaced and laughed.

"I'm interviewing Rick from the cafeteria," Jack said. "I wonder what he thinks of the paper."

"As if he even reads it." Dorothy shook her head.

"After this interview, he'll read it. That I guarantee. Hey, look at that top-of-the-line Caddy coming up the driveway. You don't see many like that." Jack pointed to a white Cadillac. It emerged from the fog like a white chariot and rounded the top of the hill.

"That looks like your uncle's car, Noah," Dorothy said.

"It's like my unc's, but my unc would never come here." Noah stared at the car. "I know who's driving, though. Dominic Cavallo. He's an old friend of my unc."

"Is that the uncle who owns all the clubs?" Jack asked.

"Among other things."

Dominic parked in the visitor zone and opened the door, unfolding his compact frame from the car. Adorned with several gold chains over a white cashmere turtleneck, he wore tailored slacks and a sport coat. Emerald-green eyes highlighted his classic Roman features and wavy black hair. He carried himself lightly, as if he spent a lot of time in the gym. He walked over to the group.

"What're you doing here, kid?"

"Going to school." Noah grinned.

"Really! I didn't think they'd let a palooka like you in the joint."

"What're you doing here, Dom? You going back to school?" Noah laughed.

"No more school for me, kid. Those days are long gone. I have an appointment to see the president. Business."

"I'll take you to his office. I'm on my way there now." Noah led Dominic up the front stairs to the second floor, strolling into the president's office as if he held the deed. "Lily, I've a friend to see the president."

"He has an appointment already, Noah," she stammered.

"No problem. My friend's the appointment." He chuckled and walked into the larger office. Gudewill sat at his desk rewording the WASC letter. He looked up to see the two men.

"John, meet an old friend of mine, Dominic Cavallo. He says he's got an appointment with you." Noah grinned.

Rising, Gudewill reached across the desk to shake Dominic's hand. "So you know Noah."

"His uncle and I grew up in the Richmond District."

"A local man. I grew up in Oakland myself." He turned to Noah. "Thanks for bringing Dom."

Dom turned to Noah. "Stay out of trouble, kid. I don't want to hear any stories about you."

"Don't worry, Dom." Noah left the two to their business.

Magdalena checked the kettle on the burner and arranged some sugar cookies on a blue flowered plate. Outside the Barn, the fog dripped through the cypresses and pines. A squirrel scurried between trees. Wearing a smock and warm-up pants, Magdalena checked the travel clock on the shelf above the sink. Three forty-five. With the dean on leave, Magdalena had unofficially assumed some of the job's responsibilities and opened the Barn most afternoons, giving students somewhere to go. Hearing footsteps, she glanced over her shoulder.

Carlos crossed the large studio to the kitchen area and popped a cookie in his mouth. "Guess what, Magdalena," he mumbled through the cookie. "I got a job in the cafeteria. Washing dishes. No more admissions office screwing up my hours. I'm set till June!"

"Good. You'll have more time for your project." He watched while she prepared the tea. "Any more insights into the sixties?" She set a row of cups and saucers along the blue cabinet counter.

"I want to do something like Larry Rivers's collage *Russian Revolution*. I wish I could see the real thing. Looking at a picture doesn't do it."

"Maybe it's better not to see it."

"You're right." He nodded. "I can create my own vision, not

someone else's. Sort of like listening to the radio instead of watching TV." He wandered over to the window. "Here comes Jack. He met with *Mother Jones* this morning."

"Ah, the internship." She poured the boiling water into the teapot.

Jack danced into the room like a pirouetting scarecrow, angular limbs jutting every which way. "Ain't life grand! I got it! Who knows? You just might be looking at the future editor-in-chief of *Mother Jones!*" He stopped in front of Magdalena, bowed, and held out his arm. "Madam, may I have this dance?" Holding his right arm around her shoulder, he took her right hand, held it in the air, and waltzed the tall woman around the room. Magdalena easily followed Jack's lead, moving gracefully.

When they returned to the sink, she curtsied. "Thank you, kind sir."

Carlos applauded. "I didn't know you danced, Magdalena."

She smiled. "I wasn't always a nun." They were interrupted by Dorothy, Keiani, and Noah.

"Is tea ready? We could sure use some." Dorothy's green hat matched the green vest and striped tie she wore with her oversize khakis. "Would you like some help?"

Magdalena shook her head.

Noah scrutinized the room. "Cool studio. I've never been here before. So this is where you made all those famous sculptures." He continued his inspection.

"This is the place, Noah." She crossed the room and placed a tray with cups, saucers, cookies, and tea on the table. While she poured, Jack and Carlos told the others their news.

"Maybe you can do something about the cafeteria food now, Carlos," Keiani said. "I have some news myself. I ran into Carmen at the copy machine. She was having a hissy fit, going on and on." She paused, waiting for their reaction.

"So tell us, for Christ's sake!" Jack leaned forward over the coffee table. "You're as slow as she is getting to the point!"

"The administration's hired a negotiator."

"I bet it's Dom, Unc's pal. He's an old union man." His surveillance completed, Noah settled back.

"That's not all," Keiani said. "Carmen says the faculty are getting their own negotiator."

"More tea?" Magdalena stood in front of the table with a fresh pot.

"Thanks," Jack nodded. Magdalena filled his cup. "We could sell tickets to the negotiations and probably raise enough to get the college out of debt." He balanced the cup and saucer on his knee.

"I don't like the administration hiring a gun, but I bet the negotiations will get higher ratings than *Saturday Night Live*." Carlos chuckled.

"That friend of your uncle looks like a real pro to me." Dorothy spooned sugar into her tea.

"Yeah, he knows his way around the block. I don't see the faculty hiring anyone like that." Noah shook his head.

There was a knock at the window. Outside, Dooley's face pressed against the glass. The college gardener's flattened nose and round glasses gave him the appearance of an owl.

Carlos beckoned for him to come in. "I don't see the students as winners in this battle, not at all."

"Winners in what?" Dooley asked while shaking the dew off his Red Sox cap.

"Union negotiations," Carlos said. "The administration's hired a negotiator."

"What'd you expect?" The slight man perched on a stool. "That's why I'm recruiting the maintenance staff. We're going union too! It's war."

thirty-four | ALUMNI DINNER

Outside Lakeside, the fog hugged the ground and the wind whistled hollowly through the deserted main building, echoing down the long, dark corridors. Inside, the president's office had been transformed into a formal dining room. A white linen tablecloth set with the college's best silver and china covered the small conference table. Silver candelabras and an arrangement of yellow and white roses graced the center. Gudewill greeted his guests.

"John, I'd like you to meet Margaret Phelan and her husband, Barry, and Terry Shea. Our other alumna has the flu and couldn't make it. She called just as I was leaving." Sarajane threw up her arms in disgust, causing her bangles to jingle like Santa's sleigh on Christmas Eve.

Gudewill shook hands with them and bowed slightly to Sarajane. "A pleasure to see you as always, Sarajane. Let me take your coats." He held out his arm. Sarajane unfastened her full-length blond mink and handed it to him. She was dressed in a magenta-and-pink silk dress that matched her two-tone three-inch heels and handbag. The others handed over their coats. Margaret wore a practical black wool coat with velvet collar over a black velvet caftan, Terry a camel-hair reefer with a navy dinner dress.

"Forgot how cold it is out here." Barry shivered. "Should

have worn my overcoat." He was a wiry man with little flesh on his frame, and his black suit and fixed smile gave him the appearance of a mortician.

"You need a drink to warm up. Let me introduce my right hand and director of institutional services, Stein. He'll take your orders." Gudewill nodded toward Stein. The group sat around Gudewill's desk in the extra chairs maintenance had provided. After filling their orders, Stein, Scotch in hand, joined them.

"Sarajane tells me you're interested in re-creating a women's college. Such a turnabout could be justified." Gudewill settled back in his old office chair. "I've been talking to Mills College. The leadership that develops in a single-sex school is something to consider."

There was a knock on the door, and Carlos wheeled in a covered cart. Lifting the top, he revealed a platter of cheeses, French bread, and crackers. Another platter was filled with vegetables and dip. A chafing dish held an array of warm hors d'oeuvres.

"Quite impressive, John! Is this a sample of the students' daily fare?" Margaret asked as she scooped up a handful of miniature sausages. A round woman with several double chins and deep dimples on either side of her full cheeks, she was quite the opposite of her match-thin mate. "Have something to eat, Barry. They're delicious!"

"No, thanks. Spoils the appetite." He sipped his bourbon and soda.

"What's your line, Barry?" Gudewill asked.

"The insurance business. Family operation."

"Phelan and Phelan?"

"Yep." He nodded and took another sip.

"I know it well. And do you work, Terry?" While Terry told Gudewill about her job as the principal of a large grammar school in the city and the two discussed the number of teachers

Lakeside had produced in its fifty-year history, Sarajane grilled Stein.

"So you and John are longtime friends." She crossed her knees and adjusted the pink scarf around her neck.

"Since our Army days."

"It must be dreadful for him now that he's alone."

"He's not exactly alone. He's got a couple of kids. One is still at home."

"Really? I wasn't aware of that." Sarajane took a sip of her drink. "You do make a good martini, Mr. Stein. It's becoming a lost art." She lowered her false eyelashes demurely.

Stein raised an eyebrow. "Call me Stein. Everyone does. Thanks. Not many people drink them nowadays. Only those of a certain generation."

Sarajane jerked her head upward and glared at him. "What exactly is it that you do here, Mr. Stein?"

"Oversee the buildings and grounds. Troubleshoot for Gude-will. Whatever's needed."

"I'm sure that must be very interesting." She turned and addressed Gudewill. "John, dear," she smiled sweetly, "tell us more about the mini-meetings."

"If you set up alumni meetings around the Bay Area—Marin, the East Bay, Napa, San Jose—then I can talk to the alumni and see what they think about the idea of Lakeside College for Women. It would give me a good idea of what support the college would have if it were to revert to a single-sex college, as well as other things the alumni might be interested in."

"It's a marvelous idea, simply marvelous. Don't you agree, Margaret?" She batted her eyelashes at Gudewill.

"I do! And then you can see what the alumni are truly like. The present students are no example of the real Lakeside." Margaret shook her head back and forth, causing her chins to undulate. "Agnes had better get here soon. The hot hors d'oeuvres are almost gone."

"Now, who's talking about me when I'm not here?" Agnes walked into the room in a beige-and-white ensemble. "I might have known it was you, Margaret." She smiled indulgently at Margaret, who was busy biting into a bacon-wrapped chicken liver.

"She was wondering where you were, Agnes." Gudewill rose and pointed to an empty chair. "Please have a seat. What would you like to drink?" He motioned to the bar and lowered himself into his chair. Stein went to the bar.

"A glass of white wine would be lovely, thank you." She sat down next to Sarajane. "How are you, dear? Do you like my scarf?" Agnes touched the beige-and-white scarf around her neck.

"Fine, fine," Sarajane said without looking at Agnes, her eyes targeted on Gudewill. "John has decided to meet with the alumni to discuss the return to a women's college." She clapped her hands, the bells on her bracelets tinkling.

"How wonderful, John!" Agnes turned her pale face toward John and flickered a smile. Stein rolled his eyes as he handed Agnes a glass of wine.

"I was telling John that then he could meet the real Lakeside products, not the hoi polloi that are here now." Margaret wiped her mouth with a napkin. "The only foreign students then were the girls from Latin America or the Far East, and they were so well-bred. They knew how to dress and behave like ladies. The students today look like they shop at Goodwill or the Salvation Army." Margaret shook her head, creating more undulations. "I'd think twice before sending my children here."

"It's not the fifties, Margaret," Terry said.

"The college should have a dress code like it used to," Sarajane said, looking at Gudewill. "We had to wear stockings and skirts. No trousers allowed."

"Actually, I find slacks quite a boon on a cold day." Agnes smoothed her white skirt. "And when students are sitting on the lawn, slacks are much more modest."

"When is it ever warm enough to sit on the lawn?" Barry held out his glass for a refill.

Gudewill stood up. "Rick is here with our dinner. Shall we move to the table?" The others rose and followed him.

Carlos cleared the table and loaded the dishes and wineglasses on the cart. The alumni were gone, and Gudewill and Stein, in the wing chairs, sipped B & B out of brandy snifters. Stein inhaled his cigarette. Outside, the fog licked the windows, leaving prints of moisture.

"What a group, JG." He released the smoke and watched it curl over his head.

"Terry's OK. She had some good suggestions for reorganization. At least she knows what she is talking about."

"Which is more than I can say for the others. You'd better watch out. Sarajane's got her sights set on you." Stein laughed and threw his head back. "The way she flutters those eyelashes at you. When she said she always wears her jewelry, even in bed, I almost choked. A man could get mauled to death." He shivered and stubbed out his cigarette. "She's serious about the chair of religious studies though."

Gudewill shook his head. "The alumni are unrealistic. They want a hundred thousand dollars for a chair endowment when the college endowment is less than three hundred thousand. They've got the cart before the horse. Even if Sarajane gave fifty thousand, they still have to come up with the other half." He quaffed his drink and refilled the glass from the Waterford decanter. "They're determined to return to the fifties. The white gloves and tea days are gone. Such convention doesn't work today." Gudewill put the brandy snifter on his desk. "I think Terry knows that, but she's the only one."

"Sarajane and Margaret sure don't, and Jack Sprat just came along for the ride. Talk about monosyllabic."

"He's the driver. I wonder what the other alumni are like." Gudewill stared out into the fog as if to decipher the ghosts of Lakeside's past.

Carlos took a bite of apple pie from the plate in front of him. He and Jack sat at a small cafeteria table in the corner. Outside, swirls of gray fog shimmied by the window, causing the garden furniture in the quad to waft in and out of sight. The olive tree in the center danced like a ghostly apparition in the mist.

"Isn't it great? Working on an investigative piece on the American Fruit Corporation? Did I ever luck out when *Mother Jones* gave me the internship." Jack's face was sliced by an ear-to-ear grin.

"You oughta talk to Magdalena, Jack. She knows a lot about them."

"Right. She made that crazy protest at their annual meeting. Next time I drop by the Barn, I'll mention it."

"Set up a time when it's just you two, when no one else is there." Carlos put the last bite of pie in his mouth. "This pie is about the only edible thing on the menu. And that's because it's from an outside vendor. I don't know about this food service. I sure feel sorry for Keiani having to eat their slop every day." He pushed the plate to the middle of the table and sipped his coffee.

"I hear Rick didn't like my satire in *Foggy Bottom*. Has he said anything to you?" Jack scanned the food line looking for the food manager. All he could see were the servers.

"No, he only talks to the girls. The guys he doesn't bother with except to give us orders. He's a real jerk."

"I'd like to do an exposé on the kitchen. Keep your eyes open for anything unusual. Maybe then we'd get some action on the lousy food. We postered the halls with protest signs. Keiani talked to the powers that be. Still, the administration just sits on their duffs. It's time the press took over." Jack picked up a spoon from the tray and started tapping a beat on the table.

"No problem."

"What's no problem?" Dorothy and Noah pulled up chairs and sat down. Dorothy fished a container of yogurt out of her backpack and held it up. "Bringing my own lunch."

"Carlos is going to do a little research in the kitchen." Jack took a bite out of his apple.

"You're really into investigative reporting these days, Jack," Noah said. "How's it going with Tracy?"

Jack grinned. "OK. She's a nice kid, a real nice kid. Sort of naive though."

"Look who's suddenly the expert on women." Noah laughed as he ladled three spoons of sugar into his coffee.

"I mean, she hasn't gone out much. I might not be an expert on women, but I've gone out a lot. Anyway, we're going to the movies over Thanksgiving weekend. A real date."

"You mean you're picking her up and everything?" Dorothy asked.

"Yep, on my steady steed, the Harley. The lady's gonna go first class." Jack polished off his apple. "I gotta go now. Keep an eye, Carlos." He slung his backpack over his shoulder and sauntered off.

Noah stood up. "Me, too. Time to go down to Unc's. Later, man." He followed Jack.

"Jack's into the boy-girl thing, huh?" Carlos said.

"Seems to be." Dorothy smiled.

Carlos hesitated before speaking. "What do you think about us going out? For coffee, after I finish the dinner shift. I could drive you to work at the club."

"I was wondering when you'd ask." She smiled at Carlos, reached over, and touched his arm. "That'd be great. Pick me up when you're through. I'll be at home."

thirty-six | CAMPUS CRISIS

*n*ot far from the Lakeside campus in 1859, Chief Justice David Terry of the California Supreme Court challenged US Senator David C. Broderick to a duel. The two dignitaries met under the Monterey pines overlooking Lake Merced. When Broderick accidentally discharged his Lefaucheux pistol into the ground, Terry showed no mercy and shot Broderick in the chest. So ended dueling in California. Now a plaque commemorates the famous match.

Southwest of the battle site, Gudewill took the front steps of the administration building two at a time. Ignoring the switchboard operator at the front desk, he hurried down the hall to his office. "Get Stein on the phone and tell him to get here as soon as possible. If he's not there, have him paged," he said to Lily. He slumped over his desk and rested his forehead on his folded hands. A knock brought him out of his reverie.

"Yes," he said glumly. Magdalena opened the door.

"Magdalena. We need to talk."

He started to stand, but she motioned for him to remain seated. Lowering herself onto the wingback chair, she settled back into the green plaid as if it were a throne.

She frowned. "I can see this isn't a good time, but I'm here on behalf of the students. They're not happy." She crossed her legs under her black skirt and rubbed her chin thoughtfully.

"The dean and I were discussing that yesterday."

"I have a suggestion."

"Let's hear it."

"Why not have Susan act as their advocate, at least until things settle down. The students liked her at the retreat, and then they would have a spokesperson."

"An excellent idea."

"Good." She leaned forward in the chair. "Nothing's to be gained by them thinking they're pariahs."

"Thanks, Magdalena. You should drop by more often. We can use more of your wisdom. What's new on your own front? Any more board meetings?" He smiled.

"No, I'm busy with my latest piece."

"You mentioned it the night we met. May I ask what it is?"

"You may, but I won't tell you. It's private until it becomes public. And that's not for a while."

"I respect your integrity as an artist, Magdalena. I just hope it isn't something too shocking. You alluded to the fact that it might shake things up."

"Shock is sometimes necessary, John. I have to go to a meeting in Berkeley." She stood up and bowed delicately. "Thank you for hearing me." She turned and left.

Gudewill slumped over the desk again. Stein appeared a few minutes later. "What's the problem, JG? The bankers foreclosing?" He shut the door and sat down.

"They're calling in the markers on the two-hundred-thousand-dollar deficit. I managed to talk them into giving us an extension until fall."

Stein reached into his jacket pocket for a cigarette. He lit up and tossed the match into the ashtray. "What's the plan?"

"Thanksgiving weekend gives me a chance to work on the real estate deal. I want you to see what you can generate from rentals. That could be a big moneymaker. Also, find out how many empty dorm rooms there are. We could rent them out to the Arab students who are studying at some of the other colleges in the city. They're big business, and they've got money."

"Haven't some colleges had problems with them?"

"Yes, but we won't have any. The Arabs were paying for college credit. We're selling rooms, not diplomas."

"Not yet." Stein chuckled under his haze of smoke. "How big do you want to go in rentals? Isn't the college closed in January?"

"For intersession. There's a college workshop on missions and goals, but they won't be using more than a few rooms. Why?"

"Some front man for Luz Gabriela Fumando-Seer came to see me last week about holding a retreat here. I was going to talk to you about it."

"Is she the evangelist?"

"I don't know about her, but they're willing to pay. They want the theater, classrooms, cafeteria, even dorm rooms." Stein stubbed out the cigarette. "It could mean a lot of money."

"Sounds good to me. Check with the housing office and Marian." Gudewill leaned back in the chair and put his index fingers in a steeple position under his chin.

"Have you told the board about the bank or the real estate deal?"

"No, I met with the bankers earlier today. The board was already aware of the deficit, something Babcock forgot to mention when he offered me the job. I'm sure that's why I was hired." He breathed deeply and leaned forward. "I'll tell them about the real estate deal when it's a fait accompli. I don't want false expectations."

"Good idea. I met with Rick again. He wasn't happy with the cafeteria article in *Foggy Bottom*. He's not a fan of satire, especially when he's the butt of the joke."

"The important thing is for him not to go into the red."

"He's not, and the college is actually making a little profit on the food service. Any place we break even or better yet make something is definitely a win. It was a good contract negotiation. Have you heard from Eunice about the grant from the Whitman Foundation to reroof and repaint the library? It's lucky California's in a drought; otherwise we'd have to rent the top floor out as a swimming pool. The place is falling apart."

"Given the deficit, it's no wonder they put off maintenance. But that only increases the final costs. There should be a letter soon from the foundation about the grant."

"What other tricks do you have hidden behind the screen, wizard?"

"I'd settle for selling off the unused land. That at least would buy time to keep the bankers at bay." Gudewill swiveled around when the door burst open and Katherine rushed in, pulling her dog Gladys behind her. Lily followed, wringing her hands.

Gudewill rose. "It's OK, Lily. What can I do for you, Katherine? Please sit down." He walked around the desk and guided her into the chair next to Stein. Upon seeing Stein, Gladys bared her teeth and growled. Katherine glanced from Stein to Gladys and back to Stein and glared.

"What's he doing here?" The spindly woman jerked her head toward Stein.

"We're in the middle of a meeting, Katherine. What's bothering you?"

"I don't want to tell you in front of him. Gladys doesn't like him."

"You can trust Stein. He's on our team." Gudewill patted Katherine on the back of her green-and-orange plaid sweater.

"I want him out!" Katherine glared again at Stein. He stood up and buttoned his jacket.

"I'll get the figures for you, JG. The meeting's over anyway."
He looked down. Gladys had edged over to him and was squat-
ting on his polished cordovan loafers. Stein looked from Gladys to
Gudewill to Katherine to the dog and back to Gudewill. His eyes
widened incredulously. "The creature is relieving herself on my
shoes!"

"I told you she didn't like him. She thinks he's a fire hy-
drant." Katherine let out a high, thin laugh. Gladys turned her
mournful eyes up at Stein and ambled back to her mistress.

Speechless, Gudewill and Stein looked at each other. Stein
removed a handkerchief from his pocket, bent over, wiped the
loafer, and dropped the handkerchief disgustedly in the wastebasket. "I'm leaving." He walked out the door.

"What's the problem, Katherine?" Gudewill sat next to the
distraught woman while she knuckled the palm of each hand
rhythmically as if she were kneading bread.

"Jerry Lee Lewis tried to kill Elvis last night."

"What?" Gudewill peered over his glasses at her.

"He showed up at Graceland with a .38 Derringer and asked
to see Elvis. He went there twice. He wanted to kill him."

"Are you sure?"

"It was on the news, and I phoned the president of my Elvis
fan club. She told me it was true."

"Was Elvis hurt?" Gudewill patted her on her sweater sleeve.

"No, no. Jerry Lee didn't get in. The police arrested him. He
was drunk."

"Then everything is all right, isn't it?"

"No. There's a conspiracy to kill Elvis. I know that. They
want to kill the king."

"How do you know that, Katherine?"

"I know. I have a source. I can't say any more." She pressed
her thin lips together.

"This is quite serious, Katherine. Have you told anyone else?"

"The police, but they told me to go home and have Gladys talk to the little green men. They laughed at me. And I know that's what your friend would do. Laugh at me. Gladys knew too. That's why she peed on him." Katherine laughed again.

"Katherine, do you take medication?"

"Sometimes. How do you know?" she asked suspiciously.

"I just know. What is it you want me to do about Elvis?"

"Stop the conspiracy." She smiled at him and narrowed her yellow-tinged eyes.

T he faculty lounge, formerly the student lounge, was on the ground floor of the main building. It had changed hands when the new cafeteria was built in the early sixties. Bridge tables and chairs were clustered around the room, and two pairs of French doors with a writing table between them opened onto the quad. A typewriter sat in a corner. Groupings of rattan sofas and chairs covered in fabric displaying oversize flowers were placed around the perimeter of the room. Watercolors of Hawaiian wildflowers hung on the cream-colored walls. Faded hydrangeas and budding camellias peeked through the small pane windows.

Eliot hurried across the tropical-themed room to Carmen, Agnes, and Gary, who huddled on a sofa. "Do you believe this letter from the banker?" He spat out the words and threw himself down on one of the chairs. "The nerve to send us this the day before negotiations! He's jerking us around like puppets. Announcing there's been a two-hundred-thousand-dollar deficit for three years. I'd like to know why he chose today to make his announcement." The pale man took a large print handkerchief from his back pocket and wiped his dripping forehead.

"The timing is definitely odd," Gary nodded. "Maybe he just received the information."

"Poppycock!" Eliot roared. "He planned it this way, to undermine our negotiations. He knows exactly what he's doing, the same as he knew when he wouldn't let Marian attend the educational policy committee meetings, and the same when he informed us that governance was over."

The others in the lounge turned to stare at the group. Carmen half rose from her seat and smiled wanly, announcing, "We're discussing tomorrow's strategy." She turned to Eliot. "Get hold of yourself. You need to remain calm. Tomorrow's the first day of negotiations, and we need to review. Has Lucy gathered the necessary information? Have you been in touch with USF? They are familiar with the process. Have you checked everything you need to check? The image we present is very important."

"Don't you think I know that already, Carmen?" Eliot clicked the lock to his leather briefcase back and forth. "I just received very unsettling information and don't need you to tell me how to behave. For Christ's sake! We have to rethink what we're negotiating."

"The fact that the college is heavily in debt does affect our demand for salary increases." Gary leaned forward and scrutinized his fingernails, apparently searching for an imperfection in his manicure. His yellow hair, dampened, ringed his head like a halo. "It affects all our demands regarding money."

"But it doesn't affect our demands to have a voice in who makes the decisions. Obviously the banker isn't aware of what we really want: control. So his ploy to intimidate us with figures and lack of funds has nothing to do with what we really want." Eliot's face relaxed as he listened to his own words. "Yes, the banker's latest trick won't work." He smiled grimly at them all. "In fact, he's outsmarted himself." The pale-faced man laughed.

"And what have we decided on?" Agnes asked.

"Admission and recruitment are the main issues. We demand that we have a say in what the college is selling," Eliot answered.

"Speaking of selling, what about PR?" Gary asked.

"There's no publicity as far as I can tell," Carmen said. "The public relations office sends out occasional press releases, but the press never seems to receive them until the event is over. I know from my Spanish plays. It's dreadful, simply dreadful. I agree with Gary. We need to do something about PR."

"And don't forget about the administration's emphasis on graduate programs," Agnes added. "The administration claims they save money with part-timers and contract people in the graduate programs and by eliminating undergraduate departments and classes that are not cost-effective. I believe my colleague is seeking a hearing regarding her having been cut to a half-time position."

"She's discussed it with me." Carmen nodded. "She nearly had a nervous breakdown when her position was cut. I was on the phone with her every night. The poor woman! She wants to prove that the college acted negligently in eliminating the religious studies department."

"Of course, if the changes that the alumni want take place, the religious studies department will be reinstated." Agnes smiled and straightened her brown skirt.

"That won't be for a long time, Agnes, believe me!" Eliot snapped. "We have to worry about tomorrow right now! And the administration is using part-timers and contract people so they won't have to pay benefits. It's the bottom line." He unclasped the briefcase and pulled out a leather-bound tablet and gold pen.

thirty-eight | STEIN AND LUCY

T he office of institutional services was down the hall
from the faculty lounge. The walls of the narrow room
were covered with floor plans, public safety and maintenance schedules, rental activities, and a large master calendar
for the college, an innovation Susan Wood had suggested at the
Valhalla retreat. Several filing cabinets stood in the corner next to
the small pane window facing the quad. The wall adjacent to the
door held a bookcase with neatly stacked files and shoeboxes la-
beled "Rooms." On the wall directly behind the desk hung one of
the smaller college tapestries, a scene of St. George and the
Dragon.

Bent over a government-issue steel desk purchased at auction,
Stein perused a contract. The desk held three small monkey figures—one with its hands over its eyes, one with its hands over its
ears, and one with its hands over its mouth—a pen-and-pencil set,
and a large metal ashtray. Stein signed the contract, placed it in
the out file, and breathed deeply. The contract contained arrangements for the January rental of the college to "the Way,"
Luz Gabriela Fumando-Seer's organization. When Bernie Levin
returned the signed contract, he would post a sizable check. That
should get the college through December. And the second, even
larger check, to be delivered at the end of the January conference,

would help with the coming year. The rental business was proving to be a boon to Lakeside. Yesterday an outfit called Language Studies Exchange had called about renting space on a permanent basis. Life was looking up. There would even be a new man in the White House in January, Jimmy Carter, the peanut farmer from Georgia. Things were changing!

He smiled and checked his watch. Nine o'clock. Time for the night man to begin his shift in the library. Stein crossed the room, switched off the light, and closed the door behind him. Down the hall, in the covered corridor that connected the buildings around the quad, he could see the security guard. He quickened his pace and caught up with the student. Reaching the library, the two pushed open the heavy oak door. A four-story addition had been added to the original two-story building, constructed in the thirties. The addition was the building that leaked and was in need of the grant from the Whitman Foundation. Behind the front desk, Lucy, in a navy suit and white silk blouse buttoned primly to her neck, was checking out books for a student. She nodded to them.

"You can secure the library," she directed the night man. "Be sure the basement windows are shut." She stamped the return date on the inside of a book.

"I'm surprised to see you here so late, Madame Librarian," Stein said as he raised an eyebrow.

"I told you, we're understaffed. Believe me, there are better things I could be doing." She handed the stack of books to the student.

"You look like you could use a drink." Stein leaned on the desk.

"Is that an invitation?" She closed the inkpad and smiled coyly.

"I'm going out to the Cliff House, if you'd care to join me." He grinned.

In a short time, the two were seated at a table overlooking the ocean. Below them, the waves crashed on the shore, creating an eerie glow, and Seal Rocks glistened under the moon, but Stein was more interested in the view across the table. Several of the buttons on Lucy's blouse were unfastened, and the soft silk parted just enough to reveal a very attractive cleavage.

"A Scotch on the rocks and a tall Scotch and soda," Stein told the waitress.

"How . . .? Ah, the retreat! You have a good memory."

"That's part of my job, madam, to notice things."

"How's the investigation going?" Lucy folded her hands on the table and leaned toward Stein, causing the blouse to gap more.

"Not much is happening. Inspector Chin's working on it, but so far nothing's turned up. The thieves seem to have gone underground."

"What about the things that were taken from the chapel and cloister?"

"Two separate jobs. Completely different MOs."

"Really." Lucy brushed a strand of blond hair off her forehead. The blouse gapped to one side, revealing ecru lace.

"That's what Chin says."

"You must find the police aspect of your job fascinating."

"It has its moments, Ms. Stuart." Stein pulled his cigarettes from his pocket and offered her one. She shook her head. The waitress appeared with the drinks and set them down in front of them.

"Call me Lucy. I suppose I shouldn't be meeting with you." She cupped her glass in her hands and bent over the table confidentially.

"You mean because of the negotiations? I'm not part of the team. In fact, I have very little to do with it. Cavallo's handling it all. Are you involved?"

"Careful, you don't want to violate any of the regulations."

"You mean, ask you who's on the negotiating team?" Stein laughed. "I hope it's not the queen of Babel. Lord only knows what you'll end up with."

"I'm not at liberty to talk about it." Lucy's back straightened and the gap in the blouse closed. "Why don't we change the subject? You must have other interests than Lakeside."

"Art and ballet."

"Really? I love the ballet." She leaned forward again.

"I have season tickets." Stein grinned. "Perhaps you'd like to go with me sometime." He was interrupted by a young man with a bouquet of roses in his hand.

"Would you like to buy the lady a flower?" His unlined face was devoid of any expression except for a half-moon, cookie-cutter grin. Dressed in a brown suit, white shirt, and green striped tie, the man wore shoes so polished they appeared lacquered.

"What's the gimmick? Are you working your way through college?" Stein asked, turning toward him.

"No, it's for my church, the Unification Church."

"Oh?" Stein squashed the cigarette out in the ashtray.

"At night I visit different restaurants and bars and sell roses."

"What do you do during the day?"

"The church has a commercial carpet-cleaning business."

"Why don't you give him your card, Stein? The college could use someone to do the rugs. The maids are so busy polishing and scrubbing, they don't have the time." Lucy smiled and leaned a little closer to him.

Stein laughed. "Maybe you're right. What's your name, kid?"

"Eric."

"Well, Eric, why don't you come out to Lakeside College and ask for Pete Johnson. He's in charge of maintenance. Talk to him. Do you know where Lakeside is?"

"No, sir, but I have a map of San Francisco."

"Find Lake Merced. The college is on the south end. You can't miss it."

"Thank you, sir." Eric flashed his cookie-cutter smile. "What about the flowers, sir? Do you want to buy one for the lady?" He thrust the bouquet in front of Stein.

"What the hell. Give me the bunch." Reaching into his pocket, he pulled out a silver money clip, unrolled a twenty, and gave it to the young man. "Go have a good time, kid." He handed the bouquet to Lucy.

thirty-nine | REVOLUTIONARIES

THE HAPPENING
PICK YOUR REVOLUTION
HELP YOURSELF TO A COSTUME
Courtesy of the DRAMA DEPARTMENT

proclaimed the sign outside the art gallery. A coatrack packed with costumes stood next to it. Another sign on a table covered with cardboard strips, strings, and marking pens asked:

WHO ARE YOU?
IDENTIFY YOURSELF
DRESS AS THAT REVOLUTIONARY

Inside the gallery, members of the revolution class and their invited guests, arrayed in outfits from raccoon coats and flapper dresses to tie-dyed shirts and hippie beads with signs indicating who they represented, chatted and sipped wine. Along the far wall, Carlos's mixed-media collage jumped out at the crowd, overshadowing the colorfully costumed rebels. In the center of the wall-size work, a triumvirate of John F. Kennedy, Martin Luther King, Jr., and Cesar Chavez popped off the wooden frame in faux-naïf three-dimensional figures of wood. They were surrounded by smaller figures of Malcolm X, Bobby Kennedy, and Pope John XXIII. Fabric motifs of peace slogans and signs, grape vines, and bombs were woven over a song-sheet background of Joan Baez and Bob Dylan works. Hovering overhead were a giant hawk and a dove made of papier-mâché.

Huddled in a corner, Carmen, in a flowing gown and long scarf wrapped around her neck, talked to Agnes and a white-suited Eliot. Carmen's flowery script proclaimed "Isadora Duncan"; Eliot's neat block letters said "William Butler Yeats." In the opposite corner, Dooley chatted with Keiani, who wore a slinky blue dress, a white gardenia in her hair, and a sign reading "Billie Holiday." Facsimiles of Dorothy Day, JFK, John L. Lewis, Bessie Smith, John Ford, Joan of Arc, Mario Savio, Neil Armstrong, Ken Kesey, and Margaret Sanger clustered about the room.

"Goodness. Look at all the people," Agnes said to Carmen and Eliot as she adjusted her white miter. She carried a staff and wore white clerical robes, and her sign said "John XXIII."

"They've invited half the college," Eliot sniffed. "I invited my own guest." He paused. "Katherine," he smirked at both women.

"Good grief! Why, Eliot?" Carmen asked, stepping back to look at him and almost tripping over her long scarf.

"Because Lakeside is going through a revolution, and Katherine is a perfect example."

"But Eliot, she's crazy," Agnes said, her gray eyes wide under the pointed miter.

"Exactly." He smiled smugly. "As is the whole idea of a class on revolution and as are all the other changes that Lakeside has undergone. Just listen to the music. The Beatles. Can you imagine?"

"I'm surprised you even know who the Beatles are."

"I don't live in a vacuum, Agnes. Of course I know who they are. A bunch of upstarts," he snapped and glared at her.

"As I recall, Eliot, something similar was said about Shakespeare," Carmen said. "And I know for a fact that many musicians think that someday the Beatles will be as important as Beethoven and Bach." She tossed her scarf around her neck.

"Poppycock! I don't believe a word of it. My God, what's the cacophony on now?"

"'Revolution,'" Carmen said.

"'Revolution'? It's chaos. A discordant, formless distortion that reveals some sort of perversion on the part of its admirers." He threw back his head and drained the glass.

At the other end of the table, Magdalena, swathed in white robes with a "Gandhi" sign, talked to Dooley. He sipped a glass of apple cider. Attached to his Red Sox hat was a mushroom sign that read "The Bomb."

"Are we saying the same thing?" Dooley asked Magdalena, who looked more like a queen who had just stepped off a dhow in the Indian Ocean than her ascetic hero, Gandhi.

"I believe so. We're both for peace. We just have different ways of expressing it."

"Gandhi revolutionized revolution."

"And the bomb revolutionized the world. It will never be the same. Which is all the more reason for Gandhi's form of revolution."

"I agree, Magdalena. Speaking of peaceful revolution, are you coming when we finish the west slopes with a tree-in?"

"My gardening clothes are in the studio. I'm ready whenever you give the word."

Jack and Marian walked in the door at the same time. "I'm surprised to see you here, Marian," Jack said, adjusting his "Ginsberg" nametag.

"As dean, Jack, it's part of my job to see how the new classes work out."

"I thought you were too busy playing war games with the faculty and issuing proclamations to have any interest in student projects. Watch out, Marian. Power can be a dangerous thing. You're beginning to act like the Queen of Hearts. I gotta go see my friends. Do you have any, Marian?" Giving her a searching look, he turned and headed over to Carlos and Keiani.

"Hey, Cesar!" Jack slapped Carlos on the back. "Where's the beer? I could drink a whole keg!"

"Down by Eliot and Carmen. You missed Bill the Breeder. He came as a light bulb. Says the coming of electricity to the farm was the biggest revolution in this century." Carlos laughed.

"Everyone's got their own definition." Keiani looked around the room.

"I'm gonna get a brew. Either of you want anything?" Jack arched his eyebrows questioningly.

"I'll have another one." Carlos handed him a plastic cup. Keiani shook her head. Jack cut through the crowd to the bar, where Dooley was refilling his cup with cider.

Marian had joined Magdalena. "If numbers are any indication, the happening is a success. I think the class is too. Do you agree?" Marian shifted from one foot to the other and rubbed her instep against her ankle.

"Definitely. Of course, Eliot wouldn't, but Agnes and I both find that the students and faculty have benefited. Look at Carlos's collage. It's a marvelous expression of the sixties. And I know the effort he put into it. He's not alone. All the students immersed themselves, and it is continuing here and now. People are actually discussing revolution."

"What's fascinating is the variety of interpretations. Everything from Nijinsky to John Ford."

"The variety is fascinating. And I'm glad you dropped in, Marian, given the anger on campus due to the administration's ruling on governance."

"That couldn't be helped. The administration's acting on the advice of our counsel."

"I understand, but others don't. The students are restless. When is Susan going to begin working with them?"

"After the Christmas break. In fact, she'll be facilitating the January workshops. John got the green light from the trustees to go ahead." She rested her foot on its side.

"I hope so. Lakeside needs something!"

Dorothy, her brown cloche hat, jersey dress, and long brown coat evidence of her "Emma Goldman" sign, joined them. "Thanks for coming, Marian. Now that you have seen how the revolution class worked out, I hope you'll let classes like it continue."

"The administration has no intention of stopping them, Dorothy."

"Good!" Dorothy grinned. "Isn't Carlos's project great?"

"We were just talking about it. It's very impressive. He's certainly captured the sixties vibe. I especially like the papier-mâché hawk and dove."

Dorothy beamed. "You want something to drink? There's wine and cider and beer."

"No, thanks. I have a meeting. Thanks for inviting me. Your happening's a real success."

Noah passed Marian as she was removing her "Eleanor Roosevelt" sign. He sported a chartreuse velvet jacket with red braid similar to Sergeant Pepper's, with an elaborate gold sign proclaiming "John Lennon." Following not far behind was Katherine, her hair swept up in a sleek pompadour, a guitar slung over her shoulder, dressed in her blue satin Elvis costume. She didn't wear a sign.

Noah approached Keiani and Carlos. "How's the real revolution? Everything set up for the tree-in?"

"The students are ready. You can ask Dooley about the rest." Keiani nodded toward Dooley and Jack, who were returning from the bar. Just as the two reached them, Katherine jumped in front of Noah and glared up at him from under her pompadour.

"It wasn't the Beatles who revolutionized music. It was Elvis. You shouldn't be allowed at this party."

Keiani wedged herself between Noah and Katherine, her gardenia falling down over her ear. Noah's jaw hung open as he stared at Katherine. She stepped back and twisted her left arm behind her back to protect the guitar.

"Katherine, it's OK," Keiani said, pushing the gardenia in place.

"But the Beatles only copied Elvis. They weren't revolutionaries." She looked from Keiani to Noah, shaking her head frantically. The pompadour bobbed up and down.

"That might be true, but Noah can be John Lennon if that's who he wants to be."

"That's not fair!"

"It is fair. Who invited you to the happening, Katherine?"

"Professor Blanc. He told me to come in my Elvis outfit."

Keiani looked across the room to Eliot, who was watching the scene intently. He crossed the narrow gallery.

"I invited Katherine. Is she not a result of the administration's own revolution, the new face of Lakeside?" By now the whole gallery had stopped talking and was focused on the small group.

Eliot turned to them. "I wonder how many of you know the origin of the word 'revolution'? The word first referred to the motion of the sun, moon, and stars around the Earth. In 1600, a new meaning evolved that meant a replacement with a new ruler or form of government. Lakeside is presently going through a similar revolution. The administration has replaced the old form of governance, declared it obsolete, and substituted a new form of governance, all because the faculty decided to unionize. Thus, there is no communication between the administration and faculty. I find it entirely appropriate that this gathering represents rebellion through the ages.

"It is time for faculty and students to revolt, to unseat the present administration. They have played themselves out. By declaring governance a thing of the past, they have written their own history. Marian was quite prescient when she suggested that Agnes, Magdalena, and I teach a class on revolution. Little did she know that the revolution would be against her and her cohorts upstairs. We are the new government! I propose a toast."

He raised his glass. "To revolution! And I propose Katherine as its poster child with her proposed opera about Elvis Presley and the havoc that Elvis's music brought to the twentieth century."

Magdalena stepped to the center of the room. "Revolution is necessary, but a revolution of peace, of nonviolence, such as Gandhi, Martin Luther King, Jr., and Cesar Chavez have shown us. It's important to listen to both sides and try to reach an agreement. Lakeside has crossed the line. Revolution is here, but let us not lose sight of the kind of revolution we want. Don't be manipulated."

"Peaceful revolution will never happen! Chaos is necessary!" Eliot interrupted vehemently.

"But what about John Lennon?" Katherine stepped in between them, her gaunt body vibrating with tension.

"He can stay, Katherine," Magdalena said gently. "That is what we mean by reaching an agreement. You must coexist with John Lennon." She dismissed Eliot with a glance.

"That's right, Katherine," Dorothy said. "Lennon acknowledged Elvis as the beginning. He said that before Elvis there was nothing. You can both be here at the same time. It's only a party." She took the frantic woman's arm and led her over to the hors d'oeuvres table.

forty | THE GIFT OF GIVING

*L*ucy rolled off Noah to her side and looked over at him. Outside the apartment, thin shards of light pierced the cumulus clouds, brightening the dull day. Noah stretched and propped himself against the embroidered pillowcase. Lucy pulled the down comforter over her shoulder and shivered.

"Turn up the thermostat, Noah. I'm freezing."

"Aren't I hot enough for you?" He slid his hand under the cover, down her hip to her inner thigh.

Lucy raised a perfect eyebrow. "That's not the problem, Noah. It's freezing out." She pulled the comforter higher. "I've been thinking. We should make a move over the Christmas break. No one's going to be around. With only a skeleton staff, it's the perfect time."

Hopping out of bed, Noah crossed the room and raised the indicator to seventy degrees. He dove back under the comforter and rested his head on his elbow. "Sounds good to me. Unc mentioned that his client's interested in more tapestries." His hand rubbed her belly.

"How about Christmas Eve?"

"I like that. A Christmas gift from the college to ourselves. Nice touch! No one will be expecting anything to happen that night." His fingers traced concentric circles on her smooth skin. "Maybe your boyfriend Stein can tell you if they're gonna put on extra security."

"Stein's hardly my boyfriend, although I'm sure he'd like to be. But he can be useful. I still can't believe he bought that bouquet of roses from the Moonie. Speaking of which, how is your little friend Dorothy?"

"Lay off, Lucy. I told you she's going out with Carlos. They're out planting trees this morning. But if you want to get jealous, I think that Tracy, the kid who likes Jack, might be competition. Somehow I don't think Jack is ready to switch to the boy-girl world, so maybe when he discovers that, I can console Tracy."

"Isn't she a bit young for you?" Lucy asked crisply.

"Less difference than between you and me. And what about the difference between you and the old man?"

"There are definite advantages to old men, as you call them. They treat women with a certain respect, give them gifts."

"Like flowers or that necklace you sometimes wear?"

"Something like that."

"I bet they don't give as good gifts as I do, Lucy in the Sky with Diamonds." His hand edged between her legs and his mouth closed over her breast.

"You're right, of course, Noah." Laughing, she arched her body and fanned her legs. "You can give me your gift whenever you're ready."

forty-one | THE TREE-IN

G udewill guided the gray Lincoln along Lake Merced. Stein rode shotgun. In the back were Bert Connor and Jim Miller from the Eureka Corporation. They traveled the scenic route from downtown, through Golden Gate Park, along John F. Kennedy Drive, past Rainbow Falls and the lakes that bordered the road: Lloyd Lake, Spreckels Lake, Middle Lake. At the Dutch Windmill and Queen Wilhelmina Garden Gudewill steered the Lincoln onto the Great Highway. December waves glistened offshore. At Sloat Boulevard, he turned east and followed the edge of Fleishhacker Zoo until it reached Lake Merced. Sentinel-like eucalyptus lined the road to the college.

"That's Lakeside to the left." Gudewill pointed to the south end of the lake. "You can see the old convent on the rise."

"Looks like the Hotel del Coronado," Connor said. He was a long, angular man in a navy blazer and gray flannel slacks.

"Built at the same time. Same architect. A real gem." Gudewill followed Skyline at the intersection with John Muir Drive. "The area you want to see is the west side. It has a beautiful view overlooking the Pacific. It's the perfect location for condos. You can't go wrong. You're close to Stonestown, Westlake, and the downtown freeway, yet removed enough to have a country feeling. And you're overlooking the Pacific. It's ideal."

"So you've been telling us. What about the adjoining college property?" Connor asked.

"Nothing to worry about. It's just what you say. College property. Lakeside has no intention of doing anything with it except maintaining it the way it is."

"We'll need something in writing. A guarantee," Miller said. He was stocky and tanned like a golfer.

"Not a problem. The west end is just up ahead to the right of the gate." Gudewill clicked the turn indicator to turn left.

"What are those people doing?" Miller leaned forward and pointed over Gudewill's shoulder. On the west side, a miniforest of young pines was grouped behind the gate. Along the slope, twenty or more people were in various stages of planting the pines. Gudewill could see Magdalena's tall figure at the top of a knoll. She wore dun-colored trousers and jacket. A broad-brimmed straw hat covered her head. She was talking to a wildly gesturing Dooley. Carlos and Keiani were visible digging on the hill below her.

Gudewill's head darted from the hill to Stein and back to the hill. "They're putting in trees to protect against erosion. Isn't that right, Stein? Buildings and grounds are Stein's areas."

"That's right! Our students are so dedicated that they're giving up their Saturday to improve the campus."

"If you're selling the property, why the hell are they planting it?"

"They're not aware of our negotiations, Jim. It's not our policy to involve the students in business dealings. You understand that."

"I understand all right. Who else isn't aware of your dealings? Does the board know?"

"Not a problem. They've given me carte blanche to do what I want with Lakeside." Gudewill smiled. By now the car had stopped outside the gate. "Perhaps today's not the best time to look at the property. It might be awkward with so many students around. Stein can find out when they'll be finished planting." Gudewill glared at Stein.

"I'll check with the gardener, Dooley. It's quite unusual for him to rally such support on a Saturday. It must be some sort of student project. You know these college kids." Stein shrugged his shoulders."

"Why don't we head back downtown and have lunch at the club. It's on me. What's your take on the new man when he gets to the White House? How do you think he'll compare with Gerry? From Michigan football great to peanut farmer! That's a switch!" Gudewill turned the car around and headed north.

oah whistled as he opened the door to Lily's office. It was the day after Christmas, and Gudewill had called from Sea Ranch. He wanted Noah to pick up some papers and mail them to him. Noah was feeling quite pleased with himself. So far no one had noticed the missing tapestries from the theater. Tapestries hung throughout the college, reminders of when it was Lakeside College for Women. His Christmas Eve visit to the college had passed unnoticed. He had dropped by the public safety office on the pretext of seeing Jack to check in about any new developments. Jack had even remarked how quiet the campus was, especially on Christmas Eve.

Stealing tapestries was as easy as stealing candy bars from Safeway, one of Noah's favorite pastimes as a kid. He still copped the occasional candy bar or razor to stay in practice. Noah chuckled to himself. The best part of the Christmas Eve job was that Lucy had gone with him to the president's office. She was something else. Wanting to do it in Gudewill's office. What if someone had walked in with her buck naked on the conference table, her legs wrapped around him while he pumped her? They'd used her fancy raincoat as a blanket. After, draped in the raincoat, she sat bold as a blue jay in Gudewill's chair, toasting their partnership with Gudewill's B & B. There weren't many like Lucy!

He flipped on the light switch by the door in Lily's office and stopped. Something was different. He looked around and did a double take. The tapestries were gone. He blinked to make sure his eyes weren't playing tricks on him. Sure enough, the walls were bare. Holy shit, he thought. He and Lucy had competition. It was good they'd already taken the ones from the library and the theater. He walked over to Lily's phone and pushed nine for an outside line.

"Lucy. I'm in Lily's office." Propped up on the edge of the desk, he switched the phone to his other ear and told her about the tapestries. "You're right. It does divert attention. I'm gonna call right now. Talk to you later." He clicked the phone and dialed public safety.

"Jack, Noah. You'd better get upstairs. The tapestries from the secretary's office are missing." On the other end, he heard Jack yell. "Yeah, lots of balls is right. I'll wait here for you." He hung up the phone.

In a matter of minutes, Jack burst through the door, his lean frame engulfed in a green fatigue jacket. "Didja touch anything?" he said, examining the empty walls.

"Just the phone. I haven't even gone into Gudewill's office."

"We'd better check there. You want to open it? I don't have a key."

"Sure." Noah pulled a ring of keys from his pocket, found the right one. Inside they scanned the room.

Then Jack turned to Noah, shrugging. "I don't know what's here. Anything gone?"

Noah shook his head. "Not that I can see. I don't know about files and stuff, but they probably didn't get in here. This office's got a different key. Lily's is on the regular master."

"You'd think that changing all the locks would have prevented this." Jack grimaced. "I'd better call Stein and the police."

He settled into Gudewill's chair and dialed. "Stein, Jack from the college. Thought you'd like to know that someone's ripped off the tapestries in Lily's office. You want me to call the police? You'll do it? OK. I'll be down in public safety." Jack put down the receiver. "I guess they figured with just one man on duty and nobody else around, the joint's an open invitation." He looked around the room. "Nice space." He tipped the chair back and propped his feet on the desk. "How do I look?" He laughed. "President Harrison. You can call me Jack."

forty-three | INTERSESSION

With her brown wool skirt swirling about her legs, Carmen marched across the faculty lounge, tossed her briefcase on the flowered sofa, and collapsed beside it. It was intersession and supposedly a time to regroup, but already she felt overwhelmed. She needed to prepare for her new drama classes and for a French tutorial for a transfer student completing his coursework. The mission and goals workshops, scheduled for all of January, would consume the few hours left in the month. And to think some people said teaching was easy. Obviously they had never taught. The lounge was empty, and outside in the quad, the fog crept over the building like a silent thief. An eerie light penetrated the fog, creating strange shadows that bounced off the faculty-room walls, sending cryptic signals. Carmen removed a tablet and gold Sheaffer pen from her briefcase and opened the pad. As she was jotting notes, two maintenance men ambled into the room. Carmen glanced over at them as they paced off the distance between the French doors and windows. "You, you in the green suits, what are you doing? Are you planning to redecorate the faculty lounge?"

They looked at her, then at each other, and laughed. "Just getting some measurements for the boss," the shorter one said and laughed again.

Carmen narrowed her eyes and returned to her notes. Within minutes, Agnes and Eliot had joined her, passing the workmen on their way out. Eliot wore a white fedora and a bulky camel-hair coat over his white suit.

"What time did Gary say he'd be here?" Eliot said as he put his coat on one of the bridge tables. He pulled a large linen handkerchief from his pocket and wiped the minuscule beads of perspiration glistening on his brow.

"Ten o'clock, but you know he's always late," Carmen answered. "I wonder if it's true what they say."

"What's that, dear?" Agnes asked.

"That being late is a controlling behavior. If so, it's rather an amusing habit for the school psychologist."

"What's that about the school psychologist?" Gary appeared in the doorway.

"That he seems to have the habit of being late," Eliot sniffed. He was sitting on one of the print chairs. "Or so Carmen says. And that it's exercising control."

"That's not true, Carmen." Gary's blue eyes rounded dolefully. "I'm usually tied up with a student or in a meeting." He sat down next to Carmen.

"Forget this nonsense and let's get on to business. Have you done your homework on the mission and goals?" Eliot mopped his brow again.

"Are you all right, Eliot?" Agnes asked. "You seem really tense today. Why don't you take off your hat? You might feel cooler." She leaned over and patted him on the arm.

"Leave me alone, Agnes. I'm fine," he snapped. "What does bother me is the fact that the college has forgotten its mission as a Catholic institution."

"You're quite right, Eliot." Agnes quickly withdrew her hand. "Dropping religious studies is certainly not in line with the mission and goals. The administration has drifted from the Judeo-Christian foundation of the college."

"I also agree, Eliot. We need to get the college back on the right track." Carmen straightened her skirt. "But I do feel that the changes in the college have allowed a greater atmosphere of free inquiry."

"Poppycock, Carmen!" Eliot barked. "Inquiry? Is that what you call some of the new classes? They're nothing but platforms for students to pursue whatever they feel like. It's all feeling, no intellectual discipline. Look at the CORE classes, especially Revolution in the Twentieth Century. Pure nonsense."

Carmen's eyes narrowed. "Eliot, is something the matter with your head? Why is your hat on? We're inside!"

Eliot reddened and muttered through tightened lips, "Everything is fine." The others fixed their eyes on the white fedora. Ignoring them, Eliot continued, "I'm concerned about the facilitator. She's acting as an advisor to the students and, of course, is in the pocket of the banker." He snarled the word "banker." "If she's in league with Gudewill, then she'll attempt to turn the students against the faculty. I can see the writing on the wall." He paused and wiped his brow.

"You can't be serious, Eliot. She's quite reputable. My friends at Stanford tell me how respected she is." Carmen laid her notebook on the table.

"What have I told you all along about the banker? Beware of Greeks bearing gifts. Our facilitator qualifies. She's a gift from Odysseus himself."

"I agree with Carmen. Because the dean is on leave, the students need someone to turn to. I know I certainly don't have the time, nor do you." Gary bent over and adjusted his Earth shoe.

"Nor the inclination," sniffed Eliot.

"So there you are. I think Gudewill did the right thing in

bringing in Susan for the students." Carmen continued to stare at the fedora.

"I don't care. She's in his camp. But back to the meeting. Do you think we can incorporate any of our other demands into the mission and goals?"

After the meeting, Gary and Carmen crossed the quad to the cafeteria, where the fog had completed its descent to the ground. "Don't you find it odd that Eliot wouldn't remove his hat?" Carmen shook her head and tightened her cape around her. "I wonder what he's up to. It's very peculiar."

*T*he gray Lincoln edged hesitantly north along Skyline Boulevard. The fog hugged the ground; the lakes and forested hills to the west were invisible, as were the sparsely covered rolling hills to the east. The road traced the San Andreas Fault, the tectonic division of the North American and Pacific plates, with different landforms and flora on each side of the fault. Offshore, a pod of gray whales bobbed up and down on their annual Alaska–Baja pilgrimage. Stein glared over the dashboard as if the venom in his stare could dissipate the murky soup. Gudewill glanced across the seat and shook his head. "Relax. There's nothing you can do to lift the fog."

"I told you we should have taken 101." The small man sat up even straighter. "The new public safety man's supposed to meet us at ten."

"He'll wait."

"I know he'll wait. I wanted to make some phone calls before the appointment."

"You didn't have to go to the alumni breakfast."

"You needed someone there to protect you from the wolves, or should I say Sarajane." A smile played at the corner of Stein's mouth. "She's something else. The way she was all over you, JG, you definitely needed me. It's going to be your pound of flesh she gets for the fifty thousand she's gives the college." He grinned and lit a cigarette, creating his own curtain of fog inside the Lincoln.

"I thought I'd get a hernia," he continued, "when Agnes suggested before the meeting that we pray for that rich alumna from Atherton, and you asked if it was 'prey' or 'pray.'"

"The breakfast went well. The alumni approved of the possible return to a women's college. I think we can count on their financial support, something new in Lakeside's history. The mission and goals meetings begin tomorrow. Maybe we can achieve a little harmony there also."

"Susan can bring it off if anyone can." Stein reclined against the gray seat. "Your Stanford contacts are quite useful." He flicked the ashes in the tray.

"And we still haven't tapped into the important ones. I'd like to get an advisory board going. Maybe sometime this summer. See if some of the old Army buddies can put Lakeside on the map. By then the union business should be settled and things should be back to normal."

"Lakeside, normal?" Stein snorted. "Isn't that an oxymoron? How go the negotiations?"

"Dom knows what he's doing. By the end of the month, both sides should have reached some agreement. Governance should resume before the new semester begins. When Sister Clark, my predecessor, established governance, her plan was to set up an egalitarian system whereby all the divided factions in the college work together. Right now we need people working together! How about the rental business?"

"The Grand Hotel? Luz and the Way arrive tomorrow. The front man, Bernie, has it under control. He's working with maintenance and public safety. I hired a new public safety officer, Larry Preston; Bernie is meeting Larry today, and we'll have more officers on duty. I've looked into space for the Language

Studies Exchange group. It looks like the only thing available is the faculty lounge. Pete's men checked it out this morning. And I put the kibosh on renting to Arab students. We don't need them. The Language Studies Exchange students will fill the dorms. That deal should be finalized by the end of the month."

"Sounds good." Gudewill turned into the west entrance to Lakeside, the fog drifting around the gray car. The upper parking lot was empty except for a few cars. He pulled into a spot next to the wooded staircase leading down to the main campus.

"I can't understand why you don't park in front, especially after Johnny's Bug was taken by the VW ring. You've got your own space."

"To set an example, to set an example." Both men climbed out of the car and headed down through the grove of cypresses and pines.

Pacing the corridor in front of Gudewill's office was a short, square man in crisp khaki pants and shirt with a heavy leather belt and a holster at his waist. Barrel-chested and low to the ground, he had a broad forehead with deep horizontal creases, and his cheeks hung like dewlaps.

"Larry, I'd like you to meet the chief." Stein motioned to Gudewill. The bulky man extended his hand.

"Glad to have you on the team, Larry. Stein says you're highly recommended. He'll take you into my office while I have a word with Lily." The two proceeded into the inner office.

Lily smiled nervously. "Mr. President, Mrs. Eunice Howard phoned. It's very important for you to contact her."

"I bet I know what it's about. Dial her for me," he grinned. Lily punched out the numbers and handed the phone to her boss, whose grin broadened as he talked to Eunice. He raised his eyebrows at Lily and gave a thumbs-up sign. He handed the phone back to Lily. "We got the grant, Lily, we got it! Now we can reroof and paint the library." He did a little jig right into his office. "We did it, Stein. Eunice's foundation awarded us the grant!"

"Congratulations! Luz and the Way, the grant, Dom. Maybe the wizard's magic is working, but I'd hedge my bets just to be sure." Outside, spears of light threatened to dispel the overhanging fog.

forty-five | DOROTHY AND NOAH

*L*ake Merced shimmered in the bleak afternoon sun. Along the shores, the sleeping blackberries, morning glories, nasturtiums, fennel, and lupines gathered their resources in preparation for spring. Perched on a log, two cormorants air-dried their wings while three black-and-white buffleheads dove for dinner.

"Hurry up, Noah, before that VW gets you," Dorothy yelled as she darted across the road circling the lake. She pointed to an approaching green Bug and laughed.

With a few broad strides, Noah bypassed Dorothy and waited for her on the path. "Maybe that's the Bug thief in disguise, casing the campus." He smiled down at her. "Which way you wanna go?" He nodded in both directions.

"The boathouse. Then we can sit and eat my apples." She pointed to her backpack.

"Sounds good. I have a couple of candy bars in my bag, so we can trade. Then I won't be in debt to you." He laughed.

"We couldn't have that, could we?" Dorothy nudged Noah as they headed west. "I'm already so obligated to you, I'll never be able to even the score."

"Don't worry about it. How's the job going?" Noah adjusted

his pace to Dorothy's. Gunshots resounded as they passed the police-academy shooting range.

Dorothy pulled a long wool scarf over her ears and quickened her pace. "Too noisy!" They hurried beyond the blast of the gunfire. "The job's fine, though I was wondering if your uncle does other things than the bar. I mean, a lot of weird people come in to see him. Of course, it's none of my business." She looked up at Noah and grinned.

"Unc's a man of the world, but he's OK. No one's bothering you, are they?" Noah frowned.

She shook her head. "Nothing like that. I was just curious." Dorothy released the scarf from her ears and let it hang over her tweed jacket and jeans.

"Don't worry about it. It's nothing that concerns you. How's your job with Eliot?"

"Weird." She raised her eyebrows and then scrunched up her face. "What more can I say? I went over to his flat during Christmas break and he had this turban on. I didn't say anything, but I guess he saw me staring at him. He got real upset and asked me what I was looking at. I said nothing, but, of course, it was the turban. If the turban had been taller, he could have one of the Coneheads on *Saturday Night Live*." Have you seen them yet? They're hysterical!" Dorothy shifted her bag. "Slow down a minute. I think I'll eat my apple now. Would you get it for me? Help yourself to the other one."

Noah unfastened the green pack and pulled out two apples. "Where's Carlos this afternoon?" He handed her an apple and closed the pack.

"With Magdalena and Jack. Something to do with Magdalena's sculpture and Jack's research on the American Fruit Corporation. Those three are thick as thieves these days. I'm seeing him later, before I go to work." Dorothy took a bite out of her apple. "I haven't told Carlos about Eliot. You're the only one who knows." She grinned.

"Don't worry. It's our secret. Don't you think Carlos would approve?"

"Not exactly, even though he's an artist. Eliot taking photographs of my feet is weird."

"That's all you do, right?"

"That's all. He has all these shoes in size six, an entire closetful. Floor-to- ceiling shelves of shoes. You know how he zeroes in on some girl in class each year? Always calls on her, gives her a bad time? If she can take it without cracking, then she passes his test. Of course, he picks only size sixes."

"Yep, it's weird." By now the two were walking on the west shore of Lake Merced. "Look at the coots." Noah pointed to the drifting birds beyond the boathouse.

Eliot steered the cream Mercedes up the main drive to Lakeside. Mallards and coots dove in the waters below, and tips of green poked through the ends of the pine branches. It was the first day of the mission and goals workshops. He pointed to the cars, trucks, and vans that crowded the road. "What is this? A bloody Shriners' convention?"

"It must be an outside rental group," Carmen said as she scanned the driveway. "I don't see any spots here. Try the back lot."

"One would assume, since it's intersession, there'd be an abundance of parking. It just shows that one can never count on anything at Lakeside." He circled the driveway, turned, and headed to the back entrance, where he edged up and down the parking rows. Every row was packed. "The banker had better be getting good money," he fumed.

"Park on the road, Eliot."

"Where do you think I'm going to park? At the beach?" He glared at Carmen and pulled out of the driveway, narrowly avoiding Katherine, who was dragging Gladys. The string-bean woman and squat dog teetered precariously between the asphalt and the ditch next to the road. "That woman should watch where she walks," he said as he drove back to the entrance and parked the car next to a brick pillar. Grabbing his briefcase, he locked the car.

Carmen hopped out of the passenger side, and the two trudged up the stairs.

The entrance to Lakeside was impressive, with formal terraces of English flowers climbing up to the top. A horseshoe driveway outlined the gardens and ascended the hill to the imposing white building overlooking Lake Merced. A boy of about seven dodged in front of Eliot and Carmen, immediately followed by several other children in pursuit.

Eliot clutched his briefcase to his chest. "Who are those brats?" At the next level, they came upon a child relieving himself on the primroses. "I can't believe my eyes. What's happened to Lakeside?" He flattened his nostrils in disdain.

A woman at the top called, "Children! Time for snack! Let's go to the meeting room."

"I told you," Carmen said. "A rental group. We can discuss our goals for the meeting in the faculty lounge."

"We did that yesterday!" Eliot snapped, returning his briefcase to his side.

"I know. But it won't hurt to go over it again." They squeezed through the first-floor door. The halls overflowed with people, mostly in their twenties and thirties. Edging their way through the crowd to the faculty lounge, Eliot and Carmen found a young woman leading a group of children in a dance. The chairs and sofas had been shoved to the side, and the tables were lined up against the wall. Pitchers of juice and plates of fruit and crackers were arranged cafeteria-fashion.

"I don't believe this," Carmen said, eyes wide. Breaking through the circle of children, she marched over to the fresh-faced woman in a T-shirt and denim skirt.

"Excuse me, miss, but you can't be in here. This is the faculty lounge." She repeated the words slowly as if talking to someone with limited understanding.

"I don't think so." The girl smiled sweetly. "Bernie said this room was perfect for childcare."

"It might be perfect, but it's not for rent. This is faculty space!" Eliot spat out.

"Then you'd better talk to Bernie. Excuse me, but I have to get back to the children." She turned, took the hands of the two children on either side of her, and resumed the dance.

"Well, I never!" Carmen put her hands on her hips and glared.

"We're going to the banker's office. He's the one responsible for this." Eliot stormed out of the office and upstairs to the president's office.

"I demand to see Gudewill!" he roared at Lily.

"He's not here. He . . . he's at a meeting downtown," Lily sputtered.

"Then we'll see Stein. He's in charge of operations." Eliot left with Carmen in his wake. When they reached Stein's office, the door was closed. The secretary informed them he would be in later. "What kind of administration is this? No one's minding the store. No wonder the college is in trouble!"

"Surely security can do something about removing those children from the faculty lounge," Carmen said.

The two crossed the quad to the public safety office. Inside, behind the cleared desk, Larry Preston, the new public safety man, was reading the file on the tapestry thefts. He eyed Carmen and Eliot suspiciously. "What do you want? Are you part of the Way group?" He put the file aside and folded his hands over his stomach.

"No, I'm Doctor Blanc and this is Professor O'Doyle. We've come to register a complaint. The faculty lounge is crawling with children." Eliot shook his head in disgust. "We want public safety to get rid of them. And who are you?"

"I'm Larry; I was hired to help public safety. The people in the lounge have use of that room. It's in the contract."

"Contract, poppycock! I want them out of there. Immediately!" Eliot's eyes bulged behind his glasses as he reddened.

"Sorry, Doc, but I can't do anything until I talk to Stein. I take my orders from him. As far as I know they have full use of the campus except for rooms designated for college meetings."

forty-seven | KATHERINE
AND LUZ

atherine pushed open the door to the lower entrance to the main building. Gladys, tired from
climbing up the terrace steps, panted heavily and
shadowed her owner. Walking over to a bulletin board, Katherine
squinted and read the day's schedule for the Way conference. Luz
Gabriella Fumando-Seer would be appearing in the auditorium.
Katherine nodded her head. Luz must be on campus now. The
white Rolls-Royce parked outside would be the kind of car owned
by a woman who had been visited by an angel. A car fit for kings
and prophets. Katherine approved. She had been following the
rise of Luz since she read of the prophet's visitation by the angel
Gabriel. When Katherine wasn't busy with her Elvis club and
singing, she was in the library reading. A small item about an
Oregon woman's encounter with Gabriel had captured her attention. There had been some trouble with the law. Something about
weapons and coercing people. Katherine had watched the growth
of the Way from a small commune to a large organization that
held recruitment meetings all over the West Coast. Katherine was
thrilled that Luz had chosen Lakeside as a mission site. That
meant she could finally meet the woman she admired so much. A
woman in contact with the angel Gabriel would know about the
Elvis conspiracy. Of this, Katherine was quite sure.

She sat down on the ornate wooden bench beneath the bulletin board. Gladys lay next to her, her head resting on Katherine's boots. Where on campus would such an important person as Luz be staying? Katherine mentally checked off possible locations. The president's office would be the most fitting, but she doubted President Gudewill would vacate it. He would be involved with those other meetings, the ones about the college's mission, something that held little interest for her. Her narrow face lit up. Of course! The dormitories! Because it was between semesters, they were nearly empty. Tugging on Gladys's leash, she stood up. "Come on, girl! We're off to meet the prophet!"

The two made their way through the groups milling about the halls, across the quad to the dorms. Several large men in black uniforms stood at the entrance and were talking to a dumpy middle-aged man in a Dodgers cap. Katherine could tell he was someone important.

"Excuse me, mister." Katherine planted herself in front of Bernie Levin, Luz's front man. "I need to see Luz. It's very important. In fact, she's probably expecting me."

"Oh?" Bernie eyed Katherine inquisitively. "And who, may I ask, are you?"

"Katherine. Katherine Wright. I've come about the Elvis conspiracy. Luz will know why I'm here."

Bernie looked from Katherine to the men encircling her and rolled his eyes. "Really! I have to check with her before you can see her. Besides, she's not receiving anyone today. It's too exhausting on the day of an appearance."

"I'm sure when she hears I'm here . . ." Katherine looked at him hopefully.

"OK, Miss Wright. I'll see what I can do." Bernie winked at the men and turned to go into the dorms.

Katherine watched him enter the building and turned to

Gladys. "She'll know who I am, old girl. Just wait and see." The men started to laugh. Katherine whipped around and glared at them. "Stop that! Stop that laughing! You'll see." Gladys bared her teeth and growled.

Within minutes, Bernie returned. "I'm sorry, Miss Wright, but Luz is unable to see anyone. She did send her blessings."

Katherine's face dropped. "Did she say anything about the conspiracy?"

"I'm afraid not." He turned his back on Katherine and walked over to the men, who laughed again.

She stomped over to them. "Stop it, I say! Stop it! Stop laughing at me!" Gladys, sensing her mistress's distress, howled and then squatted on the foot of the man closest to her and re- lieved herself. The man jumped back and started swearing.

"Miss Wright, call off your dog. This is entirely unnecessary." Bernie stepped forward, his eyes narrowing.

Katherine glared at the uniformed men. Pulling Gladys along, she marched off across the quad.

forty-eight | CONVOCATION

The chapel was on the south side of the campus under a grove of pine trees. Unlike the college's other recent additions, the chapel incorporated both the traditional and the modern. From the outside, it appeared to be a conventional stucco building with a peaked roof. Once inside, however, one was struck by the floor-to-ceiling glass wall behind the altar. It opened out to the woods and contrasted sharply with the three white stucco walls. The cathedral ceiling's heavy beams echoed the brown trunks of the trees, and the overall feeling was one of peace.

Faculty and administrators were gathered for the mission and goals convocation. The meeting had opened with a short prayer led by Agnes. Now Gudewill stood before the group.

"It is important for us to set forth our mission and goals in the coming weeks. Lakeside is at a crucial place in its history. The college has received national recognition. Only yesterday, I was notified of a grant the college received to reroof and repair the library."

A murmur of approval ran through the crowd.

"As the outside world affirms Lakeside, so we—"

He was interrupted by Larry running down the aisle waving a gun. "Chief! Chief! We got a crisis. Some nut with a dog cut the video cables of the Way. The dog bit one of the guards, and she and the guards are fighting. I want to know if I can shoot the dog."

Before Gudewill could respond, Eliot jumped up and turned to the audience. "It's just like I've said all along. The college is running amok. The faculty has no rights! Only today we were driven from the faculty lounge by this same obstreperous rental group, some woman who claims to be a prophet. Looking at her Rolls-Royce parked in the parking lot and the masses of people paying to see her, I'd spell 'prophet' p-r-o-f-i-t. She's nothing but a charlatan. We cannot allow this to continue." He looked at the audience, his pale face shaded by the white fedora.

Carmen stood up. "Eliot has a point, but I think we should give the administration a chance. I'm sure the college must be making a tidy sum off the group, which is all well and good. We're here for the more important task of establishing the college's mission and goals. Let's not get hysterical."

Susan rose. "Carmen's right. Focus is all-important. I think John should take care of the crisis while we go about the business of the mission and goals."

"Thank you, Susan and Carmen." Gudewill's strong voice resounded through the chapel, drawing all eyes back to him. "You're right on target. We are here for a purpose. The mission and goals. Why don't we go to our individual meetings and I'll take care of the emergency. The convocation is over." He strolled down the aisle to the back of the chapel to Larry, who still clutched his revolver. Gudewill motioned for him to return the gun to his holster, and the two headed for the auditorium.

forty-nine | ELIOT'S SURPRISE

liot walked from his office with Carmen to the main building. It was the second week of the mission and goals workshops. Drops of water from the overhanging pines showered down on them. A stellar jay hopped from branch to branch and cocked his head. "It's good you have your hat. It's almost raining," Carmen said, glancing up at the white fedora that Eliot had been wearing since the beginning of the year.

Ahead of them, some of the Way children, ranging in age from nine to fourteen, dodged and darted among the trees. Eliot shook his head. "I suppose those brats are going to be sequestered in our faculty lounge again."

"The college is making a lot of money, Eliot." Carmen pulled her black cowl-neck sweater tighter around her neck. It matched her black raincoat and boots.

"That still doesn't give them the right to our space."

"As Gudewill pointed out, it's intersession, not the semester, and we're just here for the mission and goals meetings."

"I can't understand why you always stick up for him, Carmen. Whose side are you on, anyway?" Eliot stopped.

"Don't be ridiculous! Of course, I'm on our side, but sometimes you're unreasonable as far as the administration goes. After all, these meetings are going quite well."

"Not due to the administration, let me tell you. It's the faculty that's doing all the work."

"Now, Eliot . . ." Before Carmen could continue, one of the Way boys, playing a game of tag, jumped up and grabbed Eliot's hat as they passed him and sprinted off. Eliot's eyes popped wide, and he threw his hands over his head. As Carmen's eyes followed his hands, her eyes grew round. "What have you done? What are those things sticking out of your scalp?"

Eliot glared at her. "I have no idea what you're talking about." He peered into the woods where he could hear the boys laughing. "This is outrageous!" Turning, he stormed down the path after the boys who had disappeared in the direction of the main building.

"Wait, Eliot!" Carmen said, running to catch up with him. "Where are you going?"

"To public safety!"

At the office in the dorm building, Larry looked up from the *Chronicle*'s "Sporting Green." He was checking the stats for the Oakland Raiders and the Minnesota Vikings, who were facing off that week in the Super Bowl. "What can I do for you?" Recognizing them, he said, "Oh, it's you. I thought it might be someone from the Way."

"That's why I'm here," Eliot sputtered. "One of their brats stole my hat."

Larry eyed the plugs on Eliot's head. He nodded knowingly. "Looks like you're trying one of those transplants."

Eliot reddened. "I don't know what you're talking about."

"I can recognize a transplant when I see it. I was thinking of getting one myself." He rubbed his bald dome.

Carmen's eyes darted from one head to the other and she blurted out, "Why, of course, Eliot! That's why you've been wearing that hat. You had it done over Christmas. My goodness, there's nothing to be embarrassed about. After all, Diana from the art department had her eyes done." She stretched to look at the top of Eliot's head.

He turned to her. "Mind your own business, Carmen. I'm here to get my hat back and have the brat punished!"

fifty | REARRANGING THE DECK CHAIRS

udewill leaned back in his chair and watched a lone oarsman row across Lake Merced. Thank heavens the mission and goals meetings were over. The faculty and administration had finally reached an agreement. Opening day had been a nightmare, with Katherine sneaking into the auditorium to cut the Way's cables. Then Luz's bodyguards and security came to blows, and Bernie threatened to pull out of the whole deal. An obnoxious man, he seemed to have a sixth sense about the college's precarious position. Luckily Stein had talked him out of it. Despite his caustic manner, Stein could sweet-talk people. Gudewill chuckled at the image of Stein and Bernie negotiating. The administration and faculty had signed an interim agreement on internal governance. He swiveled around. Stein was standing in the doorway.

"I just talked to the Language Studies Exchange man. It looks like they're ready to sign the contract. Have you talked to the faculty about the lounge?"

"Not yet."

"It seems the Queen of Babel and Eliot have been asking some questions about why maintenance measured the faculty lounge."

"Um. Then I'd better be prepared." He was interrupted by the phone. "Gudewill here. Hello, Jim. What can I do for you?" He leaned back in the chair and raised his eyebrows to Stein. "What? You're not serious?" He turned the chair so he faced the window. "Who told you? He did." Gudewill nodded, his head drooping a little lower with each nod. "I had no idea, Jim. Obviously my information was wrong. What can I say? Thanks for letting me know, and sorry about the inconvenience."

Gudewill turned around and hung up the phone. "That was Jim Miller from the real estate group. He played golf with the money man from the archdiocese." He shook his head. "It seems the property was given to the order on the condition it not be divided. Otherwise it reverts to the original owners' heirs. We can't sell off the west side." He slumped in the chair and looked at Stein. "Do you have the feeling we're merely rearranging the deck chairs on the Titanic?"

"So it seems. At least Bernie and the Way are putting money in the coffers. And there's the Language Studies Exchange deal. Don't jump off the bridge yet."

"You're right." Gudewill stretched his long body up and out of the chair. "Let's go over to the dean's." The two left the office. In the hallway, they bumped into Eliot and Carmen.

"Just the person I want to see," Eliot said. "The banker."

"Hello, Eliot, Carmen. Ready for the new semester?"

"We're ready for the takeover of the faculty lounge. That's what we're ready for." He smiled smugly.

"What do you mean?"

"You know what I mean. Renting out faculty territory to some sophomoric language school. I know all about your scheme. You're not going to get away with it. If you think negotiations are going well, think again. You're setting yourself up for an impasse." Eliot pulled a handkerchief from his pocket and wiped his forehead. The fedora once again covered his brow. Larry had found it in the east garden.

"I've no idea what you're talking about."

"You're not bargaining in good faith." He leered at Gudewill.

"Eliot's correct. Your intention is to change our working conditions. By taking away the faculty lounge, you're changing our working conditions, and therefore you're breaking faith." Carmen smiled triumphantly. "I saw those maintenance men taking measurements in the lounge."

"When maintenance is working, it's time to be suspicious." Eliot looked knowingly at Stein.

"I made some inquiries. You're planning to turn the college over to another rental group." Carmen tossed her head, her long hair swinging over her shoulders.

"As if that 'profit' woman weren't enough. We sacrificed our lounge for the month believing it to be in the best interest of the college. But no more! What we give up this time is our decision. The faculty lounge belongs to the faculty. You can file that in your depository, Banker. You'll find it's not negotiable." Eliot jerked himself around and headed down the hall with Carmen at his side.

Coming out of her office, Marian wasn't sure what Eliot was alluding to. Something about rights and negotiations. Nothing direct, of course, because that would be in violation of the bargaining rules. He definitely had something up his sleeve. And he was still wearing the white fedora. The rumor about a hair transplant must be true. She smiled to herself. The vanity of middle-aged men.

"Come in," she said to Gudewill and Stein. You look like you've seen a ghost, John."

"Only Eliot and Carmen." Gudewill sighed. "They're adamant about the college taking over the faculty lounge. I hate to

concede, but they're holding the trump card. Have you any suggestions for alternative space for the Language Exchange group?"

Marian thought for a moment. "We could rent a building.
School districts do it all the time. A portable bungalow. It would
cost us, but it would solve the problem of where to house the
Language Studies Exchange offices."

"Brilliant, Marian! I knew I could count on you. That's not
the only news. The information on the west side of campus was
wrong. The property can't be split up, so the deal is off."

"Oh, John! I'm really sorry."

"Shall we move the deck chairs to section A or section B?"
Stein asked.

fifty-one | LUCY'S SECRET

*T*hrough half-veiled eyes, Lucy watched her reflection in the bathroom mirror. Her legs and arms were wrapped around Noah as she straddled him. He stood, his back against the bathroom wall, and rocked her back and forth. Absorbed in his own pleasure, his eyes were closed. "Stop, Noah. I have to go."

"Not now," he moaned.

"Yes, now."

Opening his eyes, he smiled wryly, and with Lucy still straddling him, he walked into the bedroom. The midmorning sun flooded the room. A few minutes later, propped against the white pillows, he watched her brush her hair. Dressed in a gray skirt and a white silk blouse, she wove her long blond strands into a French twist. "I still say wear it down. Give them something to think about, especially Stein," Noah said. "So what's the faculty up to today? Any more tricks, like last week's elimination of students from the educational policy committee?" Eliot's announcement had caused a student uproar equivalent to the eruption of Mount Davidson.

"Not that I'm aware of, but you never know with Eliot."

"I hear he didn't like Jack's article about the January meetings, so that's why he got rid of the students."

"Who knows? Time to go, Noah. Eliot abhors anyone who is late." She rose and walked to the door. "Be sure to lock up," she called over her shoulder.

Noah heard the front door close. He wondered if Lucy had anything to eat. Probably not. He threw her green silk robe around him and walked to the kitchen. The refrigerator was almost empty: some yogurt, several bottles of soda, some crackers. Luck! Some cheese in the meat drawer. He took out the cheese, crackers, and a Coke. On the counter in a bowl were some grapes and bananas. Cramming them onto a plate, he carried them into the living room. Too bad Lakeside didn't get the Marina sunshine. Noah plopped himself on the settee. The crackers and cheese hit the spot. He'd had doughnuts and coffee before he arrived, but the morning's sport had made him hungry. If only Jack could see him now! If any of them could! They didn't have a clue about him and the ice maiden. Even more, he wished Stein could see him in Lucy's dressing gown. He laughed out loud. The cocky little guy would have a stroke. Lucy was really leading him on. And Stein actually thought he had a chance. Noah polished off the last grape and set the dish on the table. Lucy's desk was across the room. Maybe it held something interesting. There was only one way to find out.

The desk was locked. Noah remembered seeing a key in Lucy's jewelry box. He found it; it fit the desk. He sat down. An excursion through someone's private papers could be quite revealing. Lucy kept her cards close to her chest (nice chest that it was) and didn't let on much about herself, never mentioned anything personal. Noah knew there was the guy who gave her a gold necklace. Lucy came unglued every time he brought it up. He rifled through the drawers. Nothing much, the usual bills, but nothing personal. Noah checked one of the pigeonholes, and found a packet of gift cards tied with a ribbon. He opened one; it was signed, "Your Dickie." Noah went through the bundle. They were all signed the same. Interesting. Very interesting. Most of the cards were from Podesta Baldocchi, the florist. Dickie must be a good customer. Another one from Gump's. One from Shreve & Co. Dickie was a guy with bucks. Noah smiled. Now, who could Dickie be? He replaced the cards and locked the desk. He'd have to find out. This could be fun.

fifty-two | ROMEO AND JULIET

he Opera House was filled with the usual crowd circulating in the spacious foyer. Dowagers in long evening gowns mingled with pale-faced women layered in black. Inside, the grand hall sparkled under its resplendent chandelier, and the plush red seats accented the gilt rococo of the elaborate theater. Stein held Lucy's elbow as he guided her up the marble stairs to the grand tier. They passed the bar on the mezzanine, already set up for the intermission crowds, and continued on to the next level. At the entrance, he showed his tickets to the usher, a gray-haired woman in a simple black dress and practical pumps. She escorted them to the midsection of the first row.

"I'm impressed," Lucy said as Stein helped her remove her black coat. Her aubergine velvet dress clung to her curves. Stein watched approvingly as she lowered herself into the seat. The square neckline was cut just low enough to be interesting. "How did you manage to get such fine seats?" she said.

"Years of practice." He grinned. "I've been a subscriber since I first moved to the city." He settled down in the seat and handed her the program for *Romeo and Juliet*.

Directly below them, in box seat Q, Eliot was busy arranging the straight-backed chairs. A bottle of champagne, a bowl of chocolate-dipped strawberries, and a box of Swiss chocolates waited on the table in the anteroom. Eliot reached into a large satchel and removed his camera and a half dozen pairs of ballet slippers, methodically lining up the slippers along the side of the wall. As he completed his task, he heard a knock on the door. He opened it. Dorothy stood in the passageway.

"Come in, come in! You're running late." Eliot glanced at his pocket watch. He wore a white dinner jacket with a white tie and cummerbund, and his hair was covered with short plugs of white fuzz.

"Sorry, but the Fulton bus was late as usual."

"Then you should have taken an earlier bus. Never mind. Here are the ballet slippers. Do you remember what I want you to do?"

She nodded and removed her trench coat. She wore a black leotard and skirt as directed. He wanted a picture of her feet in a different pair of slippers for each scene of the ballet. That was fine with Dorothy. After all, Eliot was paying her good money, more than she made at the Go-Go Club. Besides, except for *The Nutcracker*, she'd never been to the ballet. That was a treat in itself. Eliot handed her a pair of blue slippers. She sat down on one of the brocade-covered chairs, kicked off her black Chinese slippers, and eased into the ballet shoes.

"I'll signal when I want you to get into position." Eliot had discussed the positions she was to assume at their last meeting. She had been practicing. When she was little, she had taken ballet and tap from Madame Genevieve. Eliot poured himself a glass of champagne. "Help yourself." He nodded to her and walked out to the front of the box.

Dorothy poured herself a glass and joined Eliot. "Do you come to the ballet often?"

"I have season tickets." He sipped from the glass.

"The only ballet I've seen is *The Nutcracker*."

"What you experienced, my dear, is the worst of European culture, endlessly recycled white trash." Eliot curled his lip in disdain. "Anyone who is a true balletomane knows that *The Nutcracker* is low-class entertainment. I assure you, you shall see something entirely different tonight."

Dorothy's eyes widened as she considered her own plebian background. In one of her sociology classes, she had learned that if your family had only two servants at the turn of the century, you were lower middle class. At the turn of the century, her immigrant Irish great-grandparents were the servants. She shook her head, returned to the anteroom, and popped a chocolate into her mouth.

Above them in the grand tier, Stein's head bobbed around as he looked for familiar faces. His mouth turned up as he leaned over to Lucy. "We're honored tonight with the presence of one of Lakeside's more illustrious trustees."

"Oh?" Lucy raised a neat eyebrow.

"Tricky Dick."

Lucy flinched slightly, but since Stein was whispering in her ear and checking out the crowd at the same time, he didn't notice.

"That's what I call Babcock, especially now that Magdalena has targeted him for her hit list with her American Fruit Corporation meeting protest that made the front page of the *Times*." He chuckled. "We'll probably see him at intermission." The orchestra finished warming up, and the conductor took his place. Smiling at Lucy, Stein turned his attention to *Romeo and Juliet*.

The curtain closed, ending the first act. Stein took Lucy's elbow and guided her down the stairs. He had reserved his usual table at the mezzanine bar. As he had predicted, they ran into Babcock and his wife. Stein smiled broadly. "Well, if it isn't the chairman of the board, Mr. Babcock. Up to any new tricks, Dickie Boy? Why not join us?"

Babcock hesitated for an instant, nodded, and pulled out a chair for his wife, a willowy blond in her early sixties. Her hair was elegantly swept up in a chignon, and she wore a simple black dress decorated with a large emerald brooch.

"Are you acquainted with Lakeside's librarian, Lucy?" Stein asked.

"I'm sure we've met at one of the college functions," Babcock answered curtly, and he sat down.

"I haven't seen your chief admirer, the fighting nun, lately." Stein chuckled and looked at Lucy. Her face was as composed as a Japanese mask. He looked at Babcock, who ignored his comment and was lighting a cigarette.

"I didn't know you smoked, Dick."

"Occasionally." He inhaled and turned from Stein to Mrs. Babcock.

Lucy carefully lifted her drink and took a sip. "How sweet of you to remember my order." She smiled and turned to Stein as if Babcock and his wife were on another planet. "What did you think of the first act?" She leaned over confidentially.

Despite the sugar in her tone, Stein could feel the shield of ice that Lucy had girded around herself. It swept across the table with such force that he felt physically chilled. If he didn't know better, he'd say that Lucy and Babcock were more than just acquainted, but that wasn't possible. They traveled in different circles. Or was it? He took out his cigarettes and offered one to Lucy. He glanced from Lucy to Mrs. Babcock, and as he lit one, he noticed the strong resemblance between the two. Mrs. Babcock was Lucy in thirty years. He chuckled to himself. The plot thickened, like a good Russian soup.

After the ballet, Stein and Lucy walked down the stairs to the main floor of the opera house. "The production's totally void of drama," Stein said of the ballet. As Lucy nodded her head in agreement, she noticed Eliot and Noah's friend Dorothy ahead of her. There was no mistaking Eliot in his white dinner jacket, especially with the new crop of hair across the top of his head. So Dorothy must be Eliot's shoe model. Funny, Noah hadn't said anything. But maybe he didn't know.

fifty-three | KEIANI RESIGNS

T he ground glowed an eerie green, almost as if it were phosphorescent. Jack and Dorothy hurried down the path to the Barn, ducking to avoid low-hanging branches. Chickweed, miner's lettuce, and other signs of spring popped out of the damp earth. Dorothy quickened her pace.

"Hey, Jack! Slow down. My legs aren't as long as yours."

The gangly man halted. "Sorry. It's just that I'm so pissed off. I'd like to . . ." He shook his head and clenched his lips together, grimacing.

"I know." The slight girl caught up with him, and they proceeded down the trail. "Can you imagine how Keiani must feel?"

"We'll know soon enough." The Barn shimmered ahead of them, its lights a welcome beacon in the fog. Through the window in Magdalena's studio, they could see Keiani and Carlos talking to Susan. The plump psychologist perched on a chair next to the window; Keiani was curled on a beanbag chair. Carlos sprawled on the opposite chair. Dorothy and Jack cut across the woods and the glowing grass and burst into the studio.

"I'm glad you're here." Keiani nodded, her glow gone, vanished like the flame of a burnt-out candle. "I've decided to resign as student body president." The others looked at her silently. "Eliot's plan to eliminate student representation from the educational policy committee is too much. I've had it. After spending all last summer and fall organizing and planning . . ." She sank deeper into the chair.

Dropping down next to her, Jack hunched forward and hugged his knees. "I'm with you, kid. Their plan stinks. After all we've done, they screw us. We got the students involved. My God, we even planted the west campus, and what does the faculty do? Cut us off at our knees. What recourse do we have? None! What options do we have? None! It stinks."

Susan nodded sympathetically, her dimpled hands folded on her lap. She had been meeting weekly with the students since January. On her drive up from Woodside, she had pondered this most recent action of the faculty. Eliot had pulled the carpet out from under the students and further alienated them. What a shame. The students' desperate attempts to rejuvenate Lakeside weren't even noticed. But what could one expect? The students were as isolated from the rest of the college as the Farallon Islands hovering off the San Francisco coastline, what with the dean of students on leave and the faculty embroiled in battle with the administration over union negotiations. Her weekly meeting was little better than a Band-Aid on a gushing major artery. "I know it seems hopeless, but there's still student government," she said.

"It's essential for us to be part of the educational process!" Jack unlocked his arms from his knees and leaned back against the couch, his bent arms like egret legs. "They're butchering us, piece by piece. What'll they chop off next?"

"Since you're the vice president, will you take over, Carlos?" Susan asked.

"Yeah. I'm too stubborn to resign." His face hardened, accenting his Aztec bones. "What about *Foggy Bottom*? Are you two still in the game?" He looked at Jack and Dorothy.

"That's what they'd like, for us to quit, but no way. I'm hanging in to spite them." Jack turned to Dorothy.

"Me, too. We've stuck it out this far; I'm not giving it up now!" She looked at Keiani. "Sorry. That's no reflection on you. I back your decision 100 percent. But Jack and I are in a different position. Someone has to let the campus know what they're up to."

"Your resignation will show them we're fed up," Jack said grimly. "The editorial's already written." He tapped his forehead.

Susan nodded approvingly. "It sounds to me like you're moving in the right direction. It's important that student government remains in place. Very important. And also that *Foggy Bottom* stays on press. Keeping lines of communication open is essential. You're on the right track." Her face dimpled as she smiled at them, but her eyes were thoughtful.

"Thanks, Susan," Keiani said. "You don't know how much you being here means for us. I just can't do it anymore." She shook her head.

"Don't worry about resigning, Keiani. If you feel it's time to step down, then you should. Your first duty is to yourself." Susan reached over and patted her arm.

Dorothy jumped up. "Would anyone like some tea? I'm sure Magdalena wouldn't mind." She crossed the studio to the kitchenette. Carlos joined her.

"That would be lovely. May I help?" Susan gathered herself up from the chair, but Dorothy waved for her to sit down.

"Thanks, but Carlos and I know where everything is." She filled the kettle with water and removed cups and a tea canister from the blue shelf.

"How's Magdalena's project coming, Carlos?" Susan said.

"Great! The warehouse is a much better space for her to work in."

"Hey! Look outside. Isn't that the new cop, Larry, hiding behind that pine tree?" Dorothy pointed out the window.

"What's he doing? Spying on us for the administration?" Jack said.

Carlos peered through the window into the fog. "I thought he was hired to find the tapestries."

"Maybe he thinks Magdalena has them hidden in one of the studios," Keiani said.

"I don't see him." Carlos turned away from the window. "Dooley warned me to watch out for him."

"He's an odd duck. A real throwback to the fifties." Jack shook his head. "And a fanatic about commies on campus. You ought to hear him in the public safety office."

"Commies? You're kidding. If anything, the college's gone reactionary," Dorothy said. "Look at Eliot's latest move to take away student power."

"Maybe the administration thinks we're something to be afraid of." Jack's eyes narrowed. "Maybe they're right."

fifty-four | LUNCH OFF CAMPUS

Gudewill eased into the Lincoln. Stein slid into the passenger seat and lit a cigarette. The two avoided looking at each other. Turning the ignition, Gudewill put the car in reverse and slowly backed out of Lakeside's parking lot. At Highway 1, he pointed the car south. Stein turned to him. "We're not going downtown to the club?"

"Down the coast. Lunch at Nick's."

The two rode in silence past the toy houses that ribboned Westlake. Gudewill turned the Lincoln down the grade to Pacifica and Rockaway Beach. Neither man spoke.

"Looks like we're early." Stein waved his arm to encompass the nearly deserted parking lot at the restaurant.

"Fine with me."

Inside, the maître d' escorted them to a window table and took their orders. "A double Dewar's on the rocks," Gudewill said.

Stein ordered the same. The two stared out at the Pacific. "Rough today." Stein motioned to the churning ocean.

"Storms in Japan. But nothing to compare with the storms at Lakeside. It looks like the tempest has outgrown the teapot. Larry might have found the tapestries in a student's room, but he opened Pandora's box with his illegal search. Wasn't he aware of student rights? He needed permission to enter a dorm room. And now the student's called in a lawyer and is threatening to sue."

Gudewill rested his hands into a "here's the church and here's the steeple" position.

"When you took this job, you said you wanted a challenge."

The waiter set the Dewar's on the table and handed them each a menu.

"I wasn't expecting to be broadsided by my own team. Larry's a loose cannon. You'd better keep your eye on him." Gudewill slumped in his chair, his large frame crumbling like the sandstone cliffs that held back the Pacific. "Give me a cigarette."

"You're sure?"

"Yep."

The small man shrugged and handed Gudewill the cigarettes and matches. Gudewill extracted one from the pack, put it in his mouth, and carefully lit it. Inhaling deeply, he leaned back in the chair and closed his eyes. Exhaling, he opened them and looked across at Stein.

"This is a surprise."

"Life is full of surprises." Gudewill lifted his glass and took a sip. "Nothing like Scotch and a cigarette to put things in perspective."

"Speaking of perspective, how was your meeting with the anointed one?"

"Sarajane of the royal purple? She's becoming a royal pain in the ass. I made up some cock-and-bull story about being involved with someone. She's the least of my problems. Besides, she's already committed her money for the religious studies chair and can't back out or she'll lose face with the alumni. No, it's the lawsuit that worries me. It's not the kind of publicity the college needs."

"Larry didn't find all the tapestries. Only the ones from Lily's office."

"The student probably got rid of the rest."

"I wonder if he's the only student involved."

"What the hell are students doing stealing from their own school?"

"Maybe they figure everything is up for grabs and they'd better get theirs while they can."

Gudewill shook his head and inhaled. "At least the faculty seems copacetic."

"It's all about power. Now that they have the educational policy committee back in their hands, they think they're sitting in the catbird seat. That is, until they decide they want more power."

"Dom should be able to handle that. The faculty doesn't stand a chance against an old union man like him. Thank God we have Dom and Susan putting out fires." Squashing his cigarette in the ashtray, Gudewill sighed again. "Susan accepted Keiani's resignation. Carlos will be the new president. The faculty can expect a lashing in the *Foggy Bottom*."

"Lakeside seems to be passing through the deadly poppy field."

Gudewill ignored the remark and lit another cigarette. "At least the income from the Language Studies Exchange students is keeping the bank at bay."

"For the moment."

"Your optimism never ceases to amaze me, Stein." He picked up the menu. "The halibut looks good."

"I saw the chairman of the board at the ballet the other night."

"What's unusual about that?"

"I think he and Lucy know each other." He grinned and unfurled his menu.

"They do have the Lakeside connection."

"They ignored each other too deliberately. And Lucy is a dead ringer for Mrs. B. thirty years ago."

Now Gudewill grinned. "Are you saying Babcock and the librarian had an affair?"

"That's what my gut says."

"Which makes the librarian even more attractive." He leaned back in his chair and laughed.

"Somehow I can't see the two of them together."

"The same could be said of you and Lucy."

The waiter appeared, and the two ordered.

fifty-five | CATCH-UP TIME

$\mathcal{S}$un sheared the sheet of fog above Lake Merced, and several sailboats flickered in the gray light. A bright green tipped the pine branches, spring grasses feathered the path around the lake, and the white flowers of miner's lettuce and milkmaid danced under the eucalyptus. Red-winged blackbirds flitted above the willow catkins along the east shore. Dorothy examined the red apple she had pulled from her backpack, rubbed it against her sweatshirt, and took a bite.

Noah watched her. "Does it taste better polished?"

She laughed. "I guess it does."

Noah shrugged. "Food is food. Just so long as it fills you up." He opened a package of Hostess cupcakes.

"Not the cafeteria food." She took another bite of the apple. "Carlos has been negotiating with Rick to serve more vegetables."

"How's he doing?"

"Not so good. Rick's making a big deal of it. You'd think Carlos was asking for New York steaks, not fresh vegetables."

"That must be pretty tricky for Carlos, acting on behalf of the students and also working for Rick."

"It is."

"If he doesn't get the green stuff, is he gonna do anything?"

"He has this great idea for a food-in."

"Food-in? Like the car-in we're planning?"

"Exactly, only on a larger scale. We'll completely close down the college and block the driveways so no one can get in."

Noah grinned and nodded his head. "There should be no problem getting everyone behind you. The food is so lousy nobody eats in there except the poor saps with meal tickets."

"I know. Poor Keiani's stomach is always upset. An all-starch diet can't be very healthy. That's why I don't see why Rick won't agree to Carlos's demands."

"Because it cuts into his profits."

"I guess you're right." Dorothy shook her head. "Sometimes I have a hard time figuring people out. Like the student who's been stealing the tapestries." Dorothy took the last bite of her apple. "How can he rip off the school like that? Poor Lakeside, it's falling apart." She threw the core and watched it disappear into the bushes, unaware of the sheepish look on Noah's face.

"Maybe he figures that it's public property and belongs to him."

"Give me a break. Stealing is stealing. Paying his tuition doesn't give him the right to take them."

"Obviously he has a different philosophy. If you're so principled, how come you work for Eliot after what he did to the students and the educational policy committee?"

"I'm not. I quit. After I went to the ballet with him." She grinned.

"You went to the ballet?" Noah raised his eyebrows, making his hound-dog face even more elliptical.

"*Romeo and Juliet*. It was really cool. Eliot had a box right in the middle and these great chocolates and strawberries and even champagne."

"What did you have to do? Anything kinky?" Noah leered at Dorothy.

"Nothing like that," she laughed. "He just took pictures of me in different ballet slippers for each scene."

"Were they in color?"

"I don't know. It'd seem sorta dumb to take them in black and white when I wore different colors in each scene."

"Maybe the colors show up differently in black and white."

"Who knows? Anyway, I'm glad it's over. I've made quite a bit of money between that and the job at your uncle's club. I should be able to quit working before finals in May, and then it's summer and I can get a different job. I can't wait."

Noah nodded and bit into his second cupcake.

"So have you been taking Tracy out since Jack stopped seeing her?"

"Yeah, but we're just friends. I feel kinda responsible since I set her up with Jack. Hey, Dooley, how's it going?"

Dooley climbed the stairs lugging a burlap bag. "Collecting the usual weekend debris from Friday's dance. Beer cans and empty Thunderbird bottles from the front of the school. You'd think the students would take care of the place. It's their college." He dropped the bundle and parked himself next to Noah. Removing his glasses, he wiped them on the tail of his flannel shirt.

"Dorothy was just telling me that Carlos has another plan up his sleeve if Rick the cafeteria manager doesn't agree to give us vegetables." Noah laughed. "He's going to shut down the school like we did for the park-in, only really shut it down."

"I like Carlos's line of thinking. A little anarchy keeps the administration on their toes. Count me in." He put his glasses on and adjusted them. "Have you seen Larry around? He's making my life miserable. Stalks me like I'm a felon. The guy's a real wacko."

"I know what you mean. When I'm working public safety on his shift, he rants and raves about how the perverts and commies are taking over, specifically at Lakeside. Says the college thinks it's so 'hip' with its dancers and prancers. If he only knew that Jack likes guys." Noah laughed. "I thought I'd split a gut the day the Moonie came in looking to make a deal to clean the carpets. Larry told him Lakeside didn't need any of his kind. He equates Lakeside with thirties Berlin and its kinkiness. Like the movie *Cabaret*."

"Don't worry too much, Dooley," Dorothy said. "You heard that Larry broke into that student's room to search for the tapestries, so the administration has reined him in. He really blew that one."

"I understand the student is suing." Dooley looked over at Dorothy. "Did you hear that?"

"Yeah. Jack interviewed him for the paper. He's hired an attorney. There's some question about whether the search was legal."

"It looks like Lakeside loses on that one." Dooley stood up. "Keep me posted on the revolution." He picked up his sack and sauntered toward the main building.

fifty-six | THE BUST

ords, Chevys, Plymouths, VWs, Volvos, a Buick, an old
Caddy, sedans, coupes, a Model T, clunkers, a limou-
sine, buses, vans, trucks, convertibles, and even an old
school bus jammed the road in front of Lakeside. The driveway
leading up to the top of the hill also brimmed with cars—big ones
and little ones—and other vehicles—Harley-Davidsons, Hondas,
mopeds, bicycles. Students congregated on the steps and along
the driveway, making Lakeside look like Candlestick Park on the
day of a doubleheader with the Dodgers. The back parking lot
and the gardeners' entrance on the west side of campus were also
blocked.

"I didn't know that many students had cars." Jack tied a blue
bandanna around his forehead. He and Carlos stood at the top of
the steps surveying the traffic jam.

"They don't. You're looking at a lot of loaners."

Jack slapped Carlos on the back. "Good job, Carlos. Wait
until the administration gets a load of this." He laughed. It was
seven forty-five in the morning; Gudewill and Stein usually sauntered in between eight and eight-thirty.

"It's a much better turnout than I expected," Carlos said.

"It looks like the entire school's here. Where are Dorothy and
Keiani?"

"With Dooley in the back making sure everything is OK there. Did you help him last night?"

"Yeah, Noah and I lent a hand. It's the least we could do."

"I know what you mean. Dooley's OK."

As the two looked down the steps, Larry's green Ford Fairlane pulled up in front of the college. The square man jumped out of the car and looked wildly around at the traffic jam. His beady eyes scoped the hill until they lighted on Carlos and Jack. He charged up toward them, sputtering like an industrial coffeemaker gone haywire. "I knew it was you two, the minute I saw this mess, you commies." He jabbed his stubby finger toward Carlos. "And don't think I don't know about your connections with that other pinko, Chavez." He glared at Carlos. "You're undermining the country, and this is what I'm talking about." He pointed to the cars.

Larry reached the top of the stairs. As he paused to take a breath, Dooley appeared around the side of the building, followed by Dorothy and Keiani. Turning a bright shade of red, Larry lashed out at Dooley. "And you, you Bolshevik anarchist. Where are all the other members of your cell? Out in your greenhouse?" He started to laugh. "And don't think I don't know about the greenhouse. You're not pulling any shenanigans on me. I've called in my buddies. They'll soon take care of you and your funny business, Mr. Bolshevik in a Red Sox hat. You'll see!" Larry looked at the crowd assembled around him. "And you students! You're part of the lunatic fringe." He winked one eye knowingly. "And your faculty's no better. That crazy Eliot won't admit he got a transplant. What's he think? The Blessed Mother came down from heaven and gave him hair? And the administration is just as nuts. Students stealing from the college, crazy nuns making statues I wouldn't let my mother see, gardeners corrupting American youth with illegal substances. You all deserve each other. I've been hired to do a job, and that's what I'm going to do."

Two blue squad cars screeched to a halt at the bottom of the stairs. Larry pulled out his gun and fired into the air. "Up here, boys! They've used barrier tactics to thwart the plan." He gestured manically to the cars blocking the driveway. The four patrolmen looked at one another.

The leader shrugged and said, "What else can you expect? We're back at the funny farm." Snickering, they mounted the stairs.

Larry jumped up and down in excitement. "To arms, boys, to arms! Let's up and at 'em!" He waved his gun in the air.

"Hold it, Larry. Put the gun away. You can't go shooting it off here. The police range is across the street." He laughed at his own joke.

"But the students are an obstruction to justice."

"All I see they've done is block the driveway. It's a protest, and, since the sixties, pretty much par for the course."

"But what about the days when we washed them down the steps at City Hall?"

"It's 1977. Besides, this is private property."

"But I'm in charge. I'm the head public safety officer."

"Not anymore," Stein interrupted Larry. He and Gudewill had quietly joined the circle. "What's the problem, Sergeant?"

"Larry gave us a call about a big bust." The burly officer grinned, obviously enjoying the situation.

"Yeah, boss. This Bolshevik gardener is growing dope in the greenhouse. I saw it myself, in flats. Rows and rows of it. And I don't need no search warrant to go into the greenhouse. I checked it out. It belongs to the college."

"OK, Larry. We'll take a walk to the greenhouse and see."

Gudewill leaned over to Stein. "I told you he was a loose cannon. He's finished. Get him out of here as soon as the cops leave."

Stein nodded and turned to the policemen. "To the green-house, officers."

Gudewill faced the students. "What's the problem, Carlos?"

"The food. We've tried to negotiate better food quality. Fresh vegetables, maybe even salads, but all Rick serves us is canned food. When half the school got food poisoning last week, that was our signal to mobilize."

While Gudewill and Carlos discussed the food situation, Stein, Larry, Dooley, and four of San Francisco's finest trudged through the woods. They passed Eliot's office and Magdalena's empty studio in the Barn. When they reached the greenhouse, Larry shouted, "In here, boys!" He rushed ahead and threw open the door. Inside the glass structure, long tables stood in military precision. Flats of marigolds topped the tables, tiny green plants filling each one.

The sergeant burst out laughing. "What's the matter, Larry? Can't you tell the difference between marigold and Mary Jane?" The others joined him.

"The officers are right, Larry. All that's here are marigold plants." Stein shook his head. "Sorry for the inconvenience, Sergeant. Larry, I want to talk to you in my office." The group headed back toward the main campus. Mumbling to himself, Larry trailed behind them.

fifty-seven | LUCY IN THE SKY WITH DIAMONDS

$\mathcal{S}$tein guided the Buick into the parking space in front of Lucy's apartment. He hoped she was home; he glanced up at the bay window. Good! The shades were open. So she was up. Pulling forward, he banked the wheels and let the car settle into the curb. Lucky to find a spot on a Saturday morning. He grinned and reached over to grab the LP on the passenger seat. A recording of Bach's Unaccompanied Cello Suites. Lucy would like it. If his luck continued, her enthusiasm would outweigh the surprise of his dropping by. Still, she couldn't be but pleased. When he had extolled the record's praises, she seemed keen to hear it. The small man pushed open the door and climbed out of the green sedan, adjusting his tan Italian slacks and black cashmere pullover.

The upstairs activities would have floored Stein. Noah sprawled on the settee with his head thrown back against the plush mauve velvet while Lucy knelt before him pleasuring him. The doorbell jarred the two of them.

"Damn! Who can that be?" Lucy pulled her head off Noah.

"Don't. They'll go away." Noah's fingers fondled Lucy's head.

Her blond hair cascaded down her shoulders, and Lucy shook her head. "Who would ring my bell at ten on a Saturday

morning?" Jumping up, she crossed the room and peeked around
the drape. A smile edged its way across her face. "Well, well!
Stein. What do you know?" She strode over to the intercom and
buzzed. "Yes?"

"Stein here. I have something for you."

"Come up. I'm not dressed yet, but you can drop it off." Lucy
turned to Noah and pointed to the bedroom. "In there. This
shouldn't take long."

Noah followed her into the bedroom and plopped down on
the white eiderdown comforter. "I hope not. I liked what you were
doing."

"Patience, big man. I won't be long." She pulled a gossamer
green robe from the closet and wrapped it around her like a second skin.

"You're not leaving much to his imagination. He ought to like
that." Noah leaned back against the pillows and rested his head in
his clasped hands. His elbows jutted out like the wings of a glider.

Lucy ran a silver brush through her hair.

"Even better, your hair's down. He'll really get off on that.
Does he stop by often on Saturdays?" Noah grinned and ducked
to avoid the flying brush.

"None of your business. Just stay put. I'll be back soon." She
closed the door behind her. A moment later, Lucy was peeking
from behind the front door. "Good morning, Stein."

"I hope I didn't interrupt anything, Lucy." He smiled sheepishly.

"Nothing that I can't resume. Come in." Slowly Lucy stepped
from behind the door with the expertise of the famed stripper Lili
St. Cyr peeling off her long white gloves. Stein's mouth hung
open as he clutched the package in his hand. Lucy raised an eyebrow. "Won't you come in?"

She turned and sashayed across the room, pulling the robe

tightly around her, aware that Stein was watching her every movement. She sat down on the settee, carefully settled one knee over the other, and adjusted the silk robe around her, displaying just enough breast and thigh for Stein to take a deep breath. She patted the seat next to her. "Sit down."

Stein followed her directions like an eager puppy. "Sure, Lucy!" He stumbled over the coffee table leg and fell down next to her. Suddenly aware of the gift, he gingerly handed it to Lucy. "I bought this for you. After our chat, I thought you might like a copy."

Lucy tossed her hair back over her shoulder. As she took the offering and removed the ribbon, the robe shifted. She paused to rearrange it and exposed a little more flesh. Stein watched her, eyes wide. "How sweet of you! I really don't know how to thank you." She leaned over to put the record on the table and the front of the robe gapped. Stein looked like a kid at a candy counter the last week of Lent. Leaning against the settee, Lucy cinched the robe around her. Stein relished every move, noting the hardness of her nipples pushing against the silk. Unexpectedly, she leaned over and kissed him on the cheek. The robe fell open, this time revealing breasts round and firm as ripe melons. She looked down and, raising her eyebrows, looked at Stein. His eyes were riveted on her breasts, his face a combination of pleasure and pain. Performing a reverse of her Lili St. Cyr routine, she closed the gown, gradually covering each breast just enough to veil the taut nipples which now played peekaboo every time she inhaled. Stein quietly moaned. Lucy rose from the settee.

She raised an eyebrow and strolled back to the door. "Thank you so much. I know I'll enjoy the recording. I have an engagement, so you really must go."

Stein shook himself as if waking from a dream. "Do you mind if I use your phone? I want to check in with the college, see if everything is OK. After the food-in, I'm in close contact with public safety."

"Help yourself." Lucy pointed to the phone resting on the secretary. "Maybe you should carry one of those beepers." She stood by the door, the draped robe accenting the fullness of her body.

As Stein dialed the college, he said, "You should wear your hair down all the time."

Lucy flung her head back and laughed, her body arching. "I don't think so. It's not the librarian image."

"You can say that again." He sighed and turned toward the window. "Public safety." A pause. "Jack? Stein here. What? No, no, he's not resigning nor is Marian nor Gudewill. They're forgeries. What? A letter attacking *Foggy Bottom* also? I'll be right over." He turned to Lucy.

"Trouble?"

"Someone's posted forgeries of resignations all over the college. Babcock, Gudewill, and Marian. Which reminds me. Are you sure you don't know Babcock?"

Lucy's body stiffened, the curves hardened. "Of course I know who he is. He's the chairman of the board, but other than those large social events the college hosts, like the Christmas party and graduation, I don't know him." Her voice assumed its librarian tone, and she adjusted the robe to cover herself fully.

"Odd. I'd think he'd seek you out. You have such a strong resemblance to his wife, Frieda."

Lucy flushed. "I wouldn't know. Goodbye, Stein." She opened the door.

Stein surveyed her from her blond hair to her pedicured red toenails and sighed. "It was my pleasure, Lucy." With his shoulders stooping, he left.

Lucy closed the door and hurried into the bedroom. Noah

lounged on the many pillows like an eastern potentate. "It sounds like someone's up to no good," she said. "There are forgery letters posted around campus saying the chairman, president, and dean have all resigned." Standing at the foot of the bed, she deliberately lowered the silk robe inch by inch off her shoulders, gradually revealing herself until the robe dropped to the ground.

Noah grinned. "So Stein came bearing gifts. You seem to bring that out in men, Lucy in the Sky with Diamonds. I suppose even I fit into that category, though all I ever gave you were roses I stole from the east garden. Still, we all fall under your spell, even Dickie Babcock."

She stiffened. "What did you say?"

"Dickie Babcock." Noah watched her carefully.

"Where did you ever get that idea?" Lucy was now as rigid as a Greek statue of Venus.

"Knock it off, Lucy. Some guy gave you all that jewelry and stuff, and it wasn't one of the maintenance guys. His name is Dickie. I heard your conversation. Stein thinks you know him too."

"That's ridiculous!"

"Look how you're reacting. The lady doth protest too much." Noah laughed. "Now I understand why you were so keen to take the tapestries. Revenge of the woman scorned."

Narrowing her eyes, Lucy folded her arms and lowered herself to the foot of the bed. "That's right, Noah. And since you brought it up, I'd like to discuss the rare books that need to go to your uncle."

fifty-eight | KATHERINE'S DREAMS

The cafeteria was empty. It was Wednesday, and no classes were being held on campus, so most of the college community was elsewhere. Outside the floor-to-ceiling windows, the fog glowered angrily. Gary Wright crooned "Dream Weaver" over the PA system. With heads together, Gudewill and Stein hunched over a corner table, their empty dishes shoved to the side and stacked on brown plastic trays. Gudewill cradled a mug of coffee in his large hands. "I'm not at all surprised the faculty planted those letters, and I'll give you odds it's the frogman." He shook his head. "They're choking on their own petard. I warned them they'd lose everything they had, and now Eliot is acting out of frustration. He's losing his power."

"And more each day." Stein nodded.

"What's amazing is they had the audacity to use the faculty-lounge typewriter, and even more amazing, the typewriter hasn't been stolen yet."

"It's not an IBM, that's why." Stein's mouth grinned sardonically.

"What's the latest on the summer rentals?" Gudewill reached into his suit pocket and extracted a pack of cigarettes. He pulled out one and lit it.

"Back to old tricks?" Stein pointed to the cigarettes.

Gudewill shrugged and inhaled. His eyes narrowed as he exhaled. "If I can keep it to a pack a day. Never thought I'd go back to smoking."

"The college is too late to recruit conference groups for summer rentals. That should have been done last summer. At least we'll save on the utilities." Stein lit up also. "Lakeside is going to need every penny it can get, especially now that it has to make a settlement over the tenure hearing." He tilted his chair back. "How's it going with Eunice? Are you still seeing her now that her foundation has awarded us the grant to reroof? You haven't mentioned her lately."

"Not as much as I'd like. The job takes up more time than I anticipated." He scoped the room. "I don't see the ice queen." He turned to Stein. "I still can't believe she flashed you. I wish I could have seen the expression on your face." He laughed.

"If only you could have seen them! They were perfect." Stein groaned.

"It will be interesting to see what the lady's next move is." He stubbed out the cigarette and ascended through the smoke gathered overhead. "Time to get back to the office. See you at five."

Rounding the corner to his office, Gudewill collided with Katherine and Gladys. As he bent down to untangle Gladys's leash from his ankles, the hound eyed him plaintively and began to howl.

"There, there, girl. It's all right." He patted her head. The sad-eyed dog stopped and lay down on the polished wood floor.

"See, even Gladys is upset, Mr. President. I told her about my dreams. In fact, that's why I came to see you. Your secretary told me you were at lunch, and I was coming to find you. And here you are." The spindly woman brightened, then frowned. "But I must tell you about my dreams."

Gudewill motioned to the carved wooden bench next to them. "Sit down, please, and do tell me, Katherine. You're obviously bothered. How can I be of help?" Avoiding Gladys, he sat down next to Katherine.

"It's the conspiracy, Mr. President, the conspiracy. They're after him. Elvis. I know it. More and more people. My dreams keep telling me."

"What people?" Gudewill asked gently.

"Why, the Colonel and Elvis's girlfriend, Linda Thompson. They're conspiring to do away with him. They've locked him in Graceland. And the government is part of it. They're poisoning him. My dreams tell me all about it. Did you know that I'm going to Graceland in September, making a pilgrimage with some of the other members of our Elvis fan club? I want you to stop this conspiracy. I know you know people. My dreams told me. It's up to you. That's what my last dream told me." She stared intently at Gudewill, her olive-black eyes boring a hole through him to the tapestry hanging above the bench.

He sighed. "I'll do what I can, Katherine. Thank you for your information." He stood up and, nodding to her, strode down the corridor to his office.

fifty-nine | DOROTHY'S DISCOVERY

*T*he shoebox-sized tables clustered in front of the stage at the Go-Go Club were empty except for a few businessmen ogling the dancer. The disco music blared Abba's "Dancing Queen" hollowly in the empty space. Dorothy sat at the bar sipping a Coke. It was a Monday night and pretty quiet. If it were Thursday or Friday, there would have been several girls dancing. The more customers, the more dancers: it was Louie's policy. Dorothy didn't really care, just as long as her paycheck was on time. And soon she wouldn't have to think about the club, period! With the money she'd saved from dancing and posing for Eliot's photos, she'd be able to quit before finals; in fact, she had already lined up a job at a summer day camp. A few more weeks and so long show business, if one could call go-go dancing show business. Louie had taken her notice pretty well. Probably Noah had clued him in. Noah sure had been a pal the past year, listening to her problems, helping her out with the job. A true friend.

Eddie tossed her a bag of chips from the display rack behind the bar. "Hey, Dorothy, would you grab a case of these from the storeroom? You can have one as reward."

Dorothy jumped off the stool and walked past Louie's office to the back of the building. Frowning, she hesitated. Which room held the bar food? The one closest to the alley? That made sense. Then the delivery guy wouldn't have to walk so far. Opening the door, she switched on the light. The room was a jumble of boxes, stacks of chairs, and broken tables. Cases of soda and mixers were heaped along the wall. In front of the mélange, she spotted the chips. She shook her head and pushed her short henna bob off her face. Louie ought to get someone to tidy up the place. As she bent over to pick up the box of chips, she noticed some books in the back corner. Old leather-covered books. Odd. They didn't fit in with the mishmash of bar paraphernalia. She squeezed between two tables and grabbed a book. A history book, in French and part of a set. She opened it. Inside was a bookplate. The Monsignor Delaney Library. Dorothy jerked. One of Lakeside's private collections! What was it doing in Louie's storeroom? Along the back wall, she saw a small rolled-up rug. Should she open it? She didn't want to. Suppose it turned out to be what she thought it was. Shuddering, she unfurled the four-by-six carpet. Her stomach dropped. It was one of the hangings from the music-room alcove. Her legs wavered, and she collapsed into one of the chairs. Yikes! Along the baseboard, she recognized several etchings from the college. Her stomach twisted. Noah. She knew he didn't have many scruples, but stealing from the college? Why? Poor Lakeside had so many problems. Why add to them? Her shoulders drooped, and a chill crept over her. She really couldn't blame Noah. His parents had never cared, so what could you expect? That was immaterial. The question was, what was she going to do about it? Eddie was waiting for the chips and her break was almost over. There must be some way she could fix this. She pulled herself out of the broken chair and maneuvered her way back to the box of chips. Adjusting the fringe on her red corset, she hoisted the box to her cinched-in waist, flicked off the light, and closed the door behind her. She'd figure something out.

A shroud of fog covered Lakeside. A handful of students gathered on the broad steps leading up to the administration building. Carlos stood at the top holding a drum. Next to him, Keiani carried a basket of daylilies. Behind them were Jack and Dorothy. All wore black. Carlos began to beat a dirge on the drums and marched into the white building, trailed by the ragtag band of students. As the procession passed the switchboard, the operator waved to them, and they stopped. Dorothy handed her an "In Memoriam" card while the others hummed a requiem to Carlos's drumming.

Inside the president's office, Susan leaned forward in one of the wing chairs. "I'm sorry, John. I can't continue any longer." Her hands were folded in her lap, and a frown had replaced her trademark dimples. "The administration's latest decision to halt all governance is more than I can take. Not being able to work together with the other members of the college . . . the students are in a vacuum. The situation is impossible."

"The students and faculty leaders wouldn't accept consultation roles in governance. Our interim governance agreement expired. We didn't have a choice. Are the students aware of your resignation?" His eyes narrowed as he peered over his glasses.

"No, you're the first. I do know that Jack's resigning from

Foggy Bottom as a result of your action. I imagine there will be other consequences."

Lily popped her head around the door. "President Gudewill! Come outside. There's a group of students. Susan should come too!"

"We'd better see what it's all about." Gudewill stood up, and they hurried past the outer office. The procession waited in the hall. Keiani handed them each a lily while Dorothy gave them each an "In Memoriam" card. Chanting, the four students continued down the hall, followed by the crowd.

"Another student protest. Will it ever end?" Gudewill asked.

"That's why I'm leaving. The students are in a no-win position. They consider me a dupe of the administration. It's better that I go. You'll have to figure out a solution, John. Good luck." Swinging her blue cape around her, Susan left Gudewill holding the card and flower in his hand. He examined the black-bordered card.

IN MEMORIUM

TO

THE SPIRIT

OF

LAKESIDE

Causes of Demise

Elimination of Departments

Unionization of Faculty

Dearth of Communication

Plethora of Bureaucracy

Vacuum of Administrative Leadership

Cessation of Governance

Eradication of Student Representation

Around the corner, Stein and Marian huddled over a chart comparing room-and-board costs for Bay Area colleges. Stein jabbed his thumb at the chart. "There's no way we can avoid raising fees. Look at the competition. Even with an increase, we're still at the lower end of the scale."

"I suppose you're right. We don't have a choice, do we?" She brushed back a strand of graying hair from her forehead. "The students won't like it."

"The students have to come to terms with the real—" He was interrupted by Marian's secretary.

"You both better come outside."

Marian struggled to slip on her shoes. She looked at Stein. "What's wrong now?" They crossed the room to the waiting students.

After delivering cards and flowers to all the administrative offices, the procession marched down the stairs and outside to where Dooley, with a black plastic raincoat covering his overalls, stood in the middle of the quad. In one hand, he held a scarecrow dressed in jeans, a Lakeside sweatshirt, and an orange-and-black Giants cap. In the other, he held a silver cap pistol. The four students gathered around Dooley, who propped the scarecrow against the olive tree in the center of the quad. Students flowed out of the surrounding buildings like hornets emptying a nest.

Peering through the faculty lounge French doors, Carmen watched the growing crowd. Katherine stood on the opposite side of the quad, Gladys in tow. Eliot joined Carmen. "They're at it again."

"Quiet, Eliot! I want to hear what they're saying."

Carlos stepped in front of the scarecrow. "Now that the semester is ending, we've gathered to commemorate Lakeside, once a college with a vision, now only a ghost. Sadly, the spirit of

Lakeside is not quite dead, so today, in the interest of compassion and humanity, we will hasten her demise. Dooley, if you will hand me the gun."

Dooley stepped forward, and Carlos took the gun. Carlos aimed at the scarecrow and fired, then passed the gun to the others; each shot the dummy.

"The coffin, please," Carlos said.

Dooley pulled a cardboard coffin from behind the olive tree and removed the cover. Keiani, Dorothy, Jack, and Carlos placed the scarecrow in the box.

Carlos replaced the cover and turned to the crowd. "We will now take the spirit of Lakeside and bury it in the woods by the Barn." The four lifted the coffin by the corners and, humming the funeral dirge, marched between the buildings to the woods. The mourners followed, with Katherine and Gladys at the end. The basset hound's bays were muffled by the fog.

sixty-one | THE GO-GO CLUB

The traffic on Broadway was unusually light as Carlos eased the '56 Chevy into the alley next to the Go-Go Club and turned off the ignition. But then it was Monday. The matador-red and white car gleamed under the streetlight. He checked his watch. Ten-thirty, time for Dorothy's break. She should be opening the side door to the club any minute. He must be crazy letting her talk him into stealing back the tapestry and books. What if Louie showed up? If so, he didn't even want to think about what could happen. He checked his watch again, 10:31. The metal door edged out toward the alley, and Dorothy thrust her head around the corner. She wore her red corset outfit, black net stockings, and a red bow atop her henna bob. Waving for Carlos to come in, she put a finger to her lips and disappeared into the building. Carlos hopped out of the car and followed.

"In here," she whispered.

Seconds later, the two were inside the storeroom. Carlos looked around at the maze of chairs, tables, cases of mixer, whiskey, chips, and beer. "We could have some party!"

"Right! And have Louie come looking for me because my break's too long."

"You mean he's here?" Carlos's voice rose an octave.

"Yep."

"Why didn't you tell me? We could have done it another time."

"No. The stuff has been here too long. I'm afraid he's going to sell it or do whatever he does with it."

"This is crazy. What if he comes in and finds us?" He touched her arm. "Do you know what he could do to us?"

"So we have to move fast. You take two of the cartons. They're over there." She pointed to some boxes in the corner. "I'll get the tapestry. It'll only take us two trips." Sliding behind a stack of chairs, she reached behind a broken table, struggled with the tapestry, and returned to Carlos, who balanced a carton of books under each arm.

"Sh!" She opened the door and stuck her head out. "OK."

Carlos followed her, his eyes darting back toward the bar as he sucked in his breath. They tiptoed down the hall. Dorothy pushed open the exit door, and they hurried down the alley. Carlos set the two boxes next to the Chevy and rummaged in his Levi's pockets for the keys. Finding them, he thrust a key into the trunk, picked up the boxes, and dropped them inside. Dorothy carefully laid down the rolled tapestry. Just as Carlos closed the truck, the door to the club opened.

"Louie!" Dorothy put her arm around Carlos. "I'd like you to meet my boyfriend, Carlos."

Carlos looked from Dorothy to Louie and extended his hand. "Nice meeting you, Louie. I've heard about you from Dorothy and Noah."

"So you're the boyfriend." Louie gave Carlos the once-over. He was a big man who appeared to enjoy his pasta. His large face extended to his gold-chained chest, his neck buried beneath huge jowls. A snakeskin belt girded his protruding belly. "I saw the door open and wanted to make sure no one was runnin' off with the joint." He eyed Carlos again.

"He came by to say hello while I was on my break." Dorothy smiled.

"Can't keep away from her, eh? Don't stay out here too long. It's only a fifteen-minute break." He headed back into the club.

Dorothy's grasp on Carlos tightened.

"My God! We almost got caught," he said, and he leaned against the car.

"But we didn't." Dorothy danced on the tips of her red high heels.

"Forget the rest of the stuff. I don't want to take any more chances."

"But I'm sure he's in his office."

"No, Dorothy. It's too risky. I don't like the way he was checking me out. I'll get these to Magdalena."

"We have to, Carlos! Somebody has to do the right thing. There're just the two boxes and the etchings. Come on! We've got five minutes!"

Carlos hesitated. "I suppose the most he can do is beat the shit out of me. Let's go!"

They dashed down the alley. Dorothy checked the hallway and they crept back to the storeroom. Carlos grabbed the cartons while Dorothy seized the etchings and then surveyed the hall. The coast was clear! The two raced back to the exit and the car. Carlos opened the trunk and tossed in the boxes. Dorothy set the etchings in the backseat and, after kissing Carlos goodbye, ran back into the club. Carlos gunned the Chevy and took off for Lakeside.

O n the hills overlooking Lake Merced, lupines, red Indian paintbrush, and yellow monkey flowers thrived in the June fog. Rattlesnake grass rustled in the late afternoon breeze, and mallards and coots swam in the gray waters below. In Lakeside's art gallery, Dorothy arranged clusters of grapes between wedges of Brie, Camembert, block cheeses, and imported crackers. Rings of vegetables circled dips on large platters. She stepped back to survey her work. Dorothy's sienna-colored jumpsuit was accented with a black striped scarf. She wore high tan boots and a jaunty brown beret.

Keiani set several bottles of white wine on the table. "The college is sure going all out for Magdalena." She fanned the cocktail napkins around the wine glasses. "Fancy cheese and all these great crackers!"

"They expect a big press turnout. Sure there's enough wine?"

"Plenty, and not jugs either. Have you seen it yet?" Keiani, in a magenta caftan and matching turban, pointed to the floor-to-ceiling curtain that sealed off Magdalena's sculpture from the rest of the gallery.

"No, and Carlos won't tell me a thing. Magdalena swore him and Jack to secrecy."

"Well, I, for one, can't wait," Keiani said, and she popped a cracker into her mouth. "Golly, this is more exciting than the opening of *Star Wars* at the Coronet!"

The gallery was empty, with the exception of the refreshment tables on the side of the room. The low-hanging fog outside created the effect of a luminous white cloud, which was intensified by the white walls, white woodwork, and white oak floors. The only spots of color were the food and bursts of sunflowers on the white linen tables. Carmen and Eliot appeared in the doorway and headed for the hors d'oeuvres. "The last time I saw food like this was at the party for the banker," Eliot sniffed, "and we all know the outcome of that." Attired in summer whites, Eliot held his Panama hat in hand, displaying a mat of white hair. Carmen wore a navy blue linen dress and jacket and sling-back heels.

"I wonder where everyone is. I hate to be the first person at a party. You shouldn't have insisted on picking me up at four." Carmen rearranged her silver bracelets while Eliot poured them each a glass of wine.

Strutting, Stein escorted Lucy into the gallery, a proprietorial smile on his face. She wore a black figure-hugging silk sheath and green bolero jacket buttoned at the throat.

"Magdalena's opening ought to put Lakeside on the map. All the old Army buddies will be here. Gudewill figured it's a good time to show off the place," Stein said.

"Especially since it's summer and there aren't students around."

"Exactly. Care for a glass of wine?"

Swathed in purple, Sarajane sailed into the gallery like a frigate on a mission. She was flanked by Margaret Phelan and her husband, Barry. Sarajane's lavender-tinted eyes scoped the room. Without looking at her companions, she said, "He's not here yet. Let's get a drink."

Stein handed Lucy a glass of Chablis. "Would you hold it for a minute, Stein, while I remove my jacket?" Lucy tossed her blond hair over her shoulder as she unfastened the buttons.

"My pleasure." Stein's eyes feasted on Lucy as she shrugged off the wrap. Under it was a low-cut strapless dress that revealed almost as much as it covered. Stein whistled. "My pleasure, indeed!"

Lucy smiled at him. "My wine, thank you. Now tell me about the Army buddies."

The white spaces in the gallery were soon splashed with dashes of color. Everyone had donned his or her brightest and best apparel for the grand event. Clusters of faculty, bands of students, and pockets of alumni scattered about the room, each group contributing its own hue to the canvas. Members of the press, pens and pads in hand, circled the crowd. The board of trustees arrived en masse, providing grays and browns that completed the palette. Babcock, his arm encircled by his blond wife's fur-clad one, a protection against the June fog, was the immediate center of attention. By the time Gudewill arrived with the Army buddies, the room was packed. Only Magdalena was missing. But not for long. Dressed in a long blue caftan, her brown hair braided and circling her head in a crown, she swept into the room. Carlos and Jack, in Levi's and starched white shirts, escorted her through the crowd to the small podium in front of the curtain.

"Good evening, friends, students, staff, faculty, and trustees. It is both an honor and a pleasure to see so many of you here for the unveiling of my latest work." Magdalena paused and sipped water from the glass on the podium. "It is my belief that art should question society, be both subjective and objective. But enough. You shall judge for yourselves." She turned to Carlos. "The curtain, please. The piece is called *The Emperor's New Clothes*."

Carlos and Jack pulled back the curtains that covered the

work. As the curtains parted, there was silence and then a long, collective gasp.

Gudewill blinked his eyes several times as if to better focus. "My God! It's Babcock!" His eyes darted to Stein and Lucy, who had joined the Army buddies.

Stein's eyes bugged. "It sure is!"

Lucy smiled and agreed, "That's Babcock."

The artwork was a multimedia construction with the emperor standing with his back to the room. Facing him, a wall of found art and various collages was superimposed on a background of banana boxes. Magdalena seemed to have studied and collected all the chapters of Babcock's life and created a giant three-dimensional jigsaw puzzle. Banners from his schools; ballet, symphony, and opera posters; models of sailboats; and pictures of his office buildings were all there. The front end of a Mercedes projected out of the center of the wall. The figure itself was a life-size sculpture in a plaster, cement, and sand mixture evocative of Michelangelo's unfinished sculptures. Upon further inspection, one could see that the setting was a dressing room where the figure stood smiling at himself in a mirror. He was naked except for a strategically placed banana bunch and a plastic cape over his shoulders. The clear plastic cape and was embellished with the names of the corporations with which he was associated. Under each corporate logo were photographs of starving or impoverished people.

Eliot leaned over to Carmen. "Good God! That's the chairman of the board. Why does Magdalena have to bring her political agenda into the college now, of all times? She'll gum up the works!"

"Really, Eliot, isn't a university a forum for freedom of expression?" Carmen asked, tilting her head to get a better view of Babcock. "I think Magdalena's done a remarkable job."

"Lakeside is hardly the ideal university, Carmen. We're fighting for our existence."

"Calm down, Eliot. It's just a work of art." She looked at Agnes, who stood next to her, tittering. "You, too, Agnes. You're behaving like an adolescent."

"I can't help it," Agnes giggled. "It's so . . . so scandalous." She covered her mouth with her pale hand.

"Get hold of yourself, Agnes!" Sarajane said on her other side. "Once again, Magdalena has overstepped herself. Can't the order control her?" Sarajane raised a painted eyebrow. Until the unveiling, she had been watching Gudewill. It was difficult to tell if he was with anyone, but he didn't seem to be. She intended to go over and stake her claim once the hullabaloo calmed down.

Margaret, who was engrossed in the plate of hors d'oeuvres she held in her chubby hand, bobbed her head up and down on her layer of chins. "Now maybe the order will send her off on an extended retreat. She's an outrage. Isn't that right, Barry?" He nodded and sipped his wine.

All eyes turned to Babcock, who was holding up Mrs. Babcock. Upon recognizing the emperor as her husband, she had fainted. Luckily, Babcock had caught her just before she hit the floor. One of the trustees was splashing soda water on her face. She fluttered her eyelids and looked up at Babcock. "Richard, how could you allow this to happen?" Silence washed through the gallery like the diffused light of the fog as everyone strained to hear the conversation.

"Frieda, darling, it's only an art piece."

"Art, my foot!" She pulled herself up and glared at him. "That woman has a vendetta against you. You'd better do something about it." She turned and stormed out of the gallery, her Gucci pumps clicking on the white oak floors. Babcock looked at the other trustees, shrugged his shoulders, and followed.

Lucy burst into uncontrollable laughter. Stein looked from Lucy to Gudewill, who strode across the gallery, the crowd parting as he approached Magdalena.

"Well, Magdalena, your latest work should win Lakeside some kind of acclaim. Your combination of politics and art is truly unique. Do you have anything to say?"

"Thank you, John. No. The emperor speaks for himself."

*N*oah climbed the steps to the upper parking lot and adjusted the walkie-talkie on his hip. Public safety was a breeze. The campus was practically deserted. Everyone was off for the summer except for the administrators and staff, and they were buried in their offices. All he had to do was make rounds every hour or so while Charlie played cards with Pete. Noah didn't mind the quiet. It gave him time to read. He was still caught up in the Beats. He wasn't sure if he'd return to Lakeside in the fall. Maybe he'd head south to Mexico and check out things there. Maybe even travel down the Pan-American Highway. When Noah reached the top of the stairs, he noticed an unfamiliar gray Ford pulling up the driveway. He checked the parking lot. There were only a few cars, one a VW belonging to Dave, the tech from the theater. It couldn't be what he was thinking. No VWs had been stolen in at least two months. He stepped behind the cypress at the top of the stairs. The Ford pulled over next to the VW, and a guy in a gray sweatshirt and black cords got out. He tried the driver's door, opened it, and gave his partner a thumbs-up. Then he bent over and put his head under the steering wheel. Noah grinned. It was the Volkswagen thieves. He pulled out his walkie-talkie.

"Charlie, Noah. Come in."

"What is it?"

"Call the police. The VW thieves are in the upper parking lot. They're trying to hotwire Dave's Bug. Their license is . . ." He gave the number to Charlie. "Ten Four."

What luck! The VW ring had been plaguing the college for as long as he'd been working for Gudewill. Almost a year. He watched the sweatshirted man fiddle with the wires. Should he confront the guy? Why not? The cops would be arriving any minute. He tucked the walkie-talkie under his leather jacket and casually strolled across the parking lot as if he were going to his car. Looking as casual as possible, he approached the VW. The Ford idled next to it. "Need any help?"

The man pulled his head back from under the steering wheel. "I lost my keys and was trying to get my car started." He looked over at the driver of the Ford.

"I used to be pretty good at this. Did a little joyriding in my younger days." Noah pulled himself up to his whole six feet four inches.

The man looked at him. "Yeah?"

"Yeah. Out in the avenues. Instead of going to school."

The man smiled and nodded to the driver of the Ford. "This guy says he can help us."

Eyeing Noah, the driver nodded. "Sure, go ahead."

The sweatshirted man moved aside. As Noah bent over to check the wiring, a siren sounded in the driveway.

"It's the cops!" the driver yelled. The sweatshirted man ran for the Ford. Sprinting, Noah tackled him. The driver put his foot on the gas and peeled out, veering around the squad car. As the car screeched down the driveway, it collided with another police car.

"Guess you weren't expecting the cops," Noah said. The man groaned.

❀✂

From his office window, Gudewill watched Dooley, a sack over his shoulder, cross the deserted lower parking lot. The wiry gardener had just fertilized the plants in the east garden. Because it was the summer hiatus, a skeleton crew staffed Lakeside. Was it less than a year since he'd come on board to set the college right? He shook his head. The college had gotten its fifteen minutes of fame, but not in the way he'd intended. Copies of *Time* and *Newsweek* lay on his desk. Photographs of *The Emperor's New Clothes* stared back at him with the headlines "Politics and Art" and "Art as Judge and Jury."

Stein popped his head through the door. "I see you're checking the reviews." He walked in. "Magdalena's done what none of us could do. Put Lakeside on the map. It started in the fall with the *Times* article on her American Fruit Corporation protest. She hinted then she was up to something more." He eased himself into one of the wing chairs.

"Who would have thought? It seems Babcock is her nemesis due to his chairmanship of the American Fruit Corporation. Babcock is generating his own brand of publicity." He pointed to a copy of *Mother Jones*. "Corporate corruption isn't exactly the proper image for the chairman of a floundering college."

"At least he resigned from Lakeside's board. What gets me is that a Lakeside student was interning on the investigative reporting." Stein shifted in his chair.

"Yes, Jack, the former editor of the school paper. Poetic justice."

"Perhaps. By the way, I understand Sarajane's name has been proposed as Babcock's replacement on the board."

"From boardroom gray to passionate purple." Gudewill reached into his jacket for a cigarette. "Yes, I heard from one of the nuns on the board. They think it'll placate the alumni."

"I'm glad I'm not on the board."

"Don't worry. You're not on the shortlist. There is one bright spot on the horizon. The dean of students is returning at the end of August. God knows we need someone to keep the students in line. And we've reached another interim agreement with the faculty. I'm off to Tahoe for a few days with the boys. Care to join us?" He lit the cigarette and inhaled slowly.

"No, thanks." Stein grinned.

"What's up?"

"A date with the librarian."

"Ah, the lascivious Lucy. Any more flashing?"

"I'll know after the weekend."

The intercom buzzed. "What is it, Lily?"

"The police are here."

"Send them in." He sighed and smashed the cigarette in the ashtray. "What next?"

The door opened, and in walked two patrolmen, a sergeant, and Noah. Gudewill rose from the desk. "Gentlemen, how can I help you? I'm surprised to see you, Noah." Then he noticed the walkie-talkie on Noah's waist. "Public safety business?"

"Yes." The sergeant stepped forward. "Your man here caught the Volkswagen ring thieves. Red-handed in the upper parking lot. They were in the act of hotwiring a '63 Bug. Noah here called Charlie, who called us, and we arrested them." He nodded toward Noah. "He even tackled one of them."

Noah's grin threatened to eclipse the overhanging fog.

"Well done, Noah. This calls for some sort of commendation. Thank you, Sergeant, and you officers too. It's good to have such cooperation between the police and Lakeside. Noah, I'll talk to you later."

Gudewill and the sergeant shook hands, and the policemen and Noah left, closing the door behind them.

Stein spoke. "And I thought they were here to tell you Noah was the tapestry thief."

Gudewill turned and stared at Stein. "Noah?"

"Why not? He's as likely as any. And he has access to your office. But I guess now that he's a hero, he's beyond reproach."

sixty-four | HAIL THE HERO

o the conquering hero!" Lucy raised her champagne glass.

"Aw, shucks, ma'am. I was just doing my job." Noah said in his best Jimmy Stewart voice. He lounged next to her on the bed like Alexander after his conquests.

"It's too bad the *Chronicle* didn't take your picture when they interviewed you." She sipped from the fluted glass. "And what does Gudewill propose to give you as a reward for single-handedly catching the VW thieves?"

"Didn't say." He grinned.

"If Gudewill and Stein only knew." She smiled. "And now you're getting accolades. Isn't it marvelous?" She reached over, picked up the bottle from the nightstand, and refilled their glasses.

"I almost forgot to tell you. Unc has another guy interested in rare books."

"The last ones disappeared from the club's storeroom around the same time your friend Dorothy conveniently quit the club." Lucy's eyes narrowed as she set the bottle on the nightstand.

"If Dorothy did it, it's no big deal. With all the people in and out of the club, you can't be sure."

"You're too soft on her."

"So what. What about you and Stein? At least I'm not screwing Dorothy."

"Who said Stein and I are anything other than friends?"

"Friends? I'd say he's a suitor. I see a new toy." Noah pointed to a jade bracelet on the dresser.

"Just because friends give me presents doesn't mean anything. And it has nothing to do with you. Remember, no jealousy, Noah. Our relationship is strictly business. Nothing else. No emotional involvement." Lucy's chiseled features hardened, and she drew the down comforter up over her breasts and folded her arms.

"I'm not jealous, Lucy. I'm just giving you a hard time." He looked over at her.

After a moment of silence, she turned to Noah. "I'll get the books for your uncle." The mask loosened, and she smiled. "In fact, Stein adds a new dimension. He can even help us." She unfolded her arms and rolled over on Noah. Her body covered him like a snug cashmere throw as she contoured herself to fit him. "Now let's get down to business. I can tell you're ready."

Carlos whooped when he spotted a narrow space on Page Street.

"Good parking karma," Dorothy said, squeezing his arm. Finding a parking spot in the Haight could be an all-night adventure.

Carlos maneuvered the Chevy between a green Bug and a pink Pinto. "Lucky they're both small, or we'd never make it."

The two climbed out of the car. Dorothy wore a white sailor's outfit, the jaunty cap perched at an angle. Carlos was in jeans and a flannel shirt under his down vest. They were headed for the Winged Monkey, a small club on Haight Street where Dooley and his blues band had a gig, the group's debut. The Monkey was an old store converted to a coffee house. They passed the funky sixties shops and turned into the club. Psychedelic monkeys in all stages of flight patterned the plate glass windows. They were serenaded by "Hotel California" as Keiani and Jack hailed them from a table near the stage.

"What's happening, Carlos?" Keiani asked after he gave her a hug. "I miss seeing you, now that I'm working downtown."

"Not much. I've been busy with the October show. Magdalena's letting me use her studio while she's back East, so I spend all my time in the Barn."

"I don't even see him some days," Dorothy said.

"When the muse calls, I gotta follow." Carlos smiled and chucked Dorothy under the chin. "When does Dooley come on?"

"Pretty soon." Jack sipped his beer. "Dorothy, did you interview Gudewill yet?"

"Next week. You sorry you're not editing *Foggy Bottom* with me?"

An aproned waitress appeared with pad and pencil in hand.

"I'll have an apple juice," Dorothy said.

"A Bud," Carlos added.

"No regrets." Jack pulled out a pack of Lucky Strikes and tapped it on the table. After carefully removing the cellophane and top covering, he shook out a cigarette, lit it, inhaled, and leaned back in his chair. "It'll be strange not to be so involved in Lakeside, but *Mother Jones* will keep me busy. It's a cool gig."

"The information you came up with on Babcock sure helped Magdalena with *The Emperor*." Carlos said. "She's back East lecturing because of it."

The waitress set the juice and beer on the table. Carlos reached into his jeans for his wallet.

"Can you believe the effect the *Mother Jones* article and Magdalena's *Emperor* had, getting rid of Babcock? Maybe now things will turn around." Keiani cupped her mug of coffee in her hands.

"Don't bet on it." Jack flicked his ashes on the floor. "I heard they have an alum coming on the board."

"That's good, isn't it?" Keiani asked.

"Depends on the alum." Carlos put a couple of dollars on the tray and waved the waitress away.

"Is it that woman who wears purple all the time?" Keiani straightened her Guatemalan blouse.

"Yeah, Sarajane Thomas. I'm interviewing her for the paper," Dorothy said.

"Aren't you the busy one!" Jack jabbed Dorothy in the arm.

"Listen, anytime you want to come back, you're welcome, Jack. That is, when you get tired of big-time journalism."

"Who's tired of what?" Noah asked, joining them.

"Take a load off, man." Carlos grabbed a chair from a nearby table and made space next to him and Dorothy. "So how's the hero of the Western world?"

"Isn't it 'playboy'? I think I like that better."

"And who are you playing with?" Jack leered across the table. "Anyone I know?"

"Wouldn't you be surprised?" He grinned and settled back in the chair, his long legs reaching across to the other side of the table.

The waitress reappeared and took Noah's order.

"Hey, Noah, if they make a sequel to *Rocky*, you can try out for the part. You KO'd the Bug thief," Carlos said.

"I was thinking more of stepping in for Roger Moore. He's no Sean Connery. *The Spy Who Loved Me* was weak. They need a new 007," Noah laughed. "Seriously, I might take the semester off and do a little traveling. Like down to Mexico and points south." Noah waited to see their reaction.

Dorothy broke the silence. "Why?"

"To see the world. I've been reading a lot of Kerouac and the Beats, and I think it's time to move on."

"But Noah, you've got only a year left. Isn't it sort of dumb? You may never finish." Dorothy pursed her lips.

"One semester's not a big deal. I can always come back."

"Mexico will always be there, Noah. But who knows about Lakeside?" Jack's long face was thoughtful.

"Wait a minute, Jack. You know something the rest of us don't?" Carlos said. Everyone's eyes riveted on the angular man.

"No, but Mexico ain't going nowhere. Who knows about financially shaky colleges?" Jack stubbed out his cigarette.

"That doesn't sound good!" Dorothy shook her head.

"At least we'll all graduate next June. Then we won't have to worry about it," Keiani said. "Hey, here comes Dooley!" They turned and joined the applause as the gardener and his band, all sporting Red Sox caps, paraded onto the stage.

tein opened the trunk of the Oldsmobile, put a carton of books on the curb, and locked the car. Lucy was already headed for her apartment. Picking up the carton, he turned and watched her shapely bottom undulate as she walked up the stairs. He sighed and followed her. The things one did for women. Lucy waited for him at the front door.

"Won't you come in, Stein?"

"I should hope so. After carrying these all the way from the college, I think a drink's in order." He grinned. "Where do you want me to put these?"

"Over there." Lucy pointed to the desk. "I'm exhausted. Why don't you make us both a drink? I'm going to change into something more comfortable. Help yourself. There's some cheese and bread in the kitchen." She turned and walked to the bedroom.

Stein's grin expanded. Lord, he liked to watch her walk. She moved like a sleek tigress, all action from within, nothing awkward or sharp. Everything flowed. He went to the kitchen. The liquor was in a cabinet next to the stove. Dewar's. Wondering if it was a coincidence, he poured himself a double. On second thought, he added an extra shot to Lucy's. In the refrigerator he found a decent Brie. He checked out the dishes. Royal Doulton. Lucy liked nice things. Good taste all around. He sliced the

French bread and put it on a plate with the Brie, placed it with the drinks on a silver tray—sterling, not plate—and carried it into the living room. Lucy was still in the bedroom, but the door was open and he could hear the bath running.

Lucy called. "Stein, come in and bring the drinks. I'm in the tub." He grinned even broader. The evening could prove to be quite interesting. He walked through the bedroom. It was nicely furnished with several antique pieces and good prints on the wall. He stepped over Lucy's stockings, silk chemise, and panties. He could hardly wait to get into the bathroom. Lucy lay in the tub, her eyes closed, her full breasts just covered by the bank of bubbles. As she breathed, her pink nipples rose to the surface through the cloud of foam and then disappeared. She opened her eyes slowly, smiled as if waking from an erotic dream, and looked at Stein. "God, there's nothing like a bath to relax you." She breathed deeply, her breasts rising above the bubbles.

Stein wet his lips. "I can think of some things."

"I'm sure you can. Why don't you give me my drink and sit down on that stool. Just put the goodies over there." She pointed to the sink, her breast fully revealed.

He placed the platter as instructed and handed her the Scotch. "I see you have Dewar's."

"Do I?" " She looked at him and dropped her eyes demurely as she sipped the drink. "Would you fix me something? I'm famished!"

Stein spread Brie on several slices of French bread and handed her one. "Here, madam. Is there anything else you'd like?"

"I'm fine." She put the glass on the edge of the tub and took the bread from Stein, who was intently watching the bubbles disappear.

Lucy finished the bread and took another sip of Scotch.

"Do you usually have company when you bathe?"

"It depends."

"Oh?"

"If I'm not alone or not."

"I'm certainly glad you aren't alone tonight."

"I imagine so." She sat up and, taking soap from the tray, started to wash herself. Stein's mouth opened as she raised her arms and carefully soaped them, working up a foam. She massaged each arm and then moved to her breasts, massaging each one. She continued soaping her entire body. Stein had stopped drinking and just stared. When she finished her feet and toes, she carefully cupped water in her hands and rinsed herself. Then she rose from the tub. Her body gleamed luminescent as Tuscan marble. Stein moaned.

Looking over as if just realizing he was there, she smiled. "Would you hand me a towel and get my robe from the closet?" She took the towel and proceeded to dry herself. Moaning again, Stein went into the bedroom to find the robe. There were several at the front of the walk-in. He chose the green gossamer one she'd worn the day he brought her the Bach. He returned to the bathroom. Lucy stood in front of the mirror smoothing lotion on her face. She smiled.

"Is there anything else I can get you, Lucy?" He stood directly behind her, holding out the robe. She dropped the towel wrapped around her and backed into the green silk that he held, brushing against him as she draped the wrap around her. He could feel the warmth of her body through his shirt.

"No, that's all. I'm going to bed now. You can let yourself out." Turning, she kissed him on the cheek and walked into the bedroom.

sixty-seven | FACULTY RALLIES

$\mathcal{S}$treaming into Eliot's flat, the sun highlighted his collection of Imari china. A sterling tea service with silver pots of water and tea, a creamer and sugar bowl, a bowl of lemon slices, and a tea strainer rested on the mahogany sideboard. Two platters, one with petit fours, éclairs, and other delectables, the second with tiny cucumber, egg salad, and watercress sandwiches, were placed next to four porcelain cups and saucers. Eliot arranged four damask napkins next to the tea service and pulled a gold watch out of his white linen trousers. Late, of course! Was Carmen ever punctual? The Himalayan chimes on the front door tinkled. He pressed the watch back into its pocket.

Carmen, Gary, and Agnes stood outside. "I've never been to Eliot's," Gary said. His wide blue eyes blinked as he inspected the collection of jade plants in oriental jardinieres outside the flat on Union Street.

"Then you're in for a treat. Eliot's quite a collector." Carmen fluffed her auburn hair.

"Is that why he travels each summer and school break?" Gary said.

"One of the reasons." She tucked her peasant blouse in her flowered blue skirt.

The door opened. "Only five minutes late, Carmen! Did you experience an epiphany in Spain?" Eliot's eyes narrowed.

"Hardly, Eliot."

They followed him into the foyer, where he took their coats and bustled them into the living room. "Tea is waiting!"

"I see you've added to your collection of feet, Eliot." Pointing to the cherry credenza, Carmen sat down on the rose damask sofa. "From the summer's trip?"

"I picked up a few odds and ends. Lemon or sugar, Agnes?"

"Sugar, thank you."

"I'm impressed, Eliot. Living on Russian Hill with all the nobs!"

"If that were true, Gary, I'd be on Nob Hill. I'm comfortable here. It's far enough from the college, yet close to downtown, the theaters, restaurants. What do you want, Gary?"

"Cream, thanks."

He gave Agnes and Gary their tea and handed Carmen her tea with lemon. "I know what you prefer, Carmen." He passed the platter of sandwiches.

"How was your trip to North Africa, Eliot?" Agnes wiped the corner of her mouth with a napkin.

"Hot, Agnes! It's always hot there."

"Eliot and I rendezvoused in Barcelona. We had lunch at a favorite spot of mine." Carmen's leg was crossed over her knee, her foot swinging back and forth in its own rhythm.

"Summer's over," Eliot snapped. "We need to strategize for the negotiations, prioritize our demands." He opened a drawer in the table next to him and took out a tablet and a gold fountain pen.

"The admission procedure. The faculty needs more input." Gary set his teacup on the polished butler's table, lining it up with a bowl of roses.

"Do you think we'll fare better this year, Eliot?" Agnes said.

"Of course. The negotiator Dom is nothing but a thug, a second-rate Mafioso. We certainly have the brains to outwit him, and now we have a year's experience."

"Don't be overconfident, Eliot. Look what happened last year." Carmen continued swinging her leg.

"Have you seen the dean of students yet?" Gary said, changing the subject. "It will be a relief to have her return. Her absence was a disaster."

"We had lunch. I happened to run into her at Stonestown. She looks well after her sabbatical." Carmen bit into a cucumber sandwich.

"Sabbatical, or was she looking for another job?" Eliot sniffed.

"It's good she's back. The students need a dean. She's been on a city commission the past year." Carmen popped the rest of the sandwich into her mouth.

"I think she was job hunting." Eliot carried the plate of sweets over to the group.

"Where's Magdalena these days, Agnes? Did the order take any action after the opening?" Gary chose a petit four from the dish.

"Nothing. Since Vatican II, the order's focused on social justice. Of course, not everyone agrees with Magdalena." Agnes straightened her beige scarf.

"At least her actions got rid of Babcock. He was sleazy, despite his high social standing." Eliot bit into an éclair.

"That article in *Mother Jones* was rather harsh." Carmen uncrossed her leg and sat back against the settee.

"What can you expect? It's nothing but a slick *Enquirer*. I wasn't at all surprised to hear that Jack was involved in the investigation. Look at the drivel he publishes in the school newspaper."

"Not anymore. Dorothy's the editor now. He resigned last semester." Carmen folded her napkin.

"I know, Carmen! I do read it. It's one way to find out what's perceived as happening on campus. I think Dorothy will be kinder in her editorials." Eliot flattened his lips in his frog smile and put his cup on the table.

"I have good news," Agnes said. "Sarajane's been appointed a trustee."

"That is good news. Now maybe we'll have some backing on the board. We'll have to bring her here for tea." Eliot rubbed his hands together. "See when she is free."

sixty-eight | A CHANGE IN PLANS

The library floor plans were scattered across the conference table in the president's office. A carafe of coffee, two empty mugs, and a plate of doughnut crumbs bordered the blueprints. Outside, the fog lingered, a few joggers circled the lake, and a solitary sculler rowed.

"We could convert the top floor to a conference center. It's a study hall now, but the students could study somewhere else." Gudewill's face glowed; he swept his arm to encompass the campus. "Imagine, Stein, what this could do for Lakeside. A think tank for tomorrow! BJ and Harvey are behind it. Between their contacts and mine, Lakeside could be a place that the world flocks to!"

"Don't send out the invitations yet, JG. There might be space and interest, but what about the board? Now that Babcock's gone, who's on your team?"

"Sarajane."

"Sarajane?" Stein rolled his eyes. "Really! And what's the price?" He rolled his eyes again.

Gudewill eyed Stein. "It's very simple. We announce that Lakeside is returning to a single-sex college at the undergraduate level, and she'll back my proposal for an institute."

"And that's it?" Stein's eyebrows shot up.

"Nothing else. Of course, it involves meeting with her, but our relationship is strictly business."

"Have you told her that?"

"I don't need to."

"Right, and I just won the Irish Sweepstakes. Don't say I didn't warn you." He stood up and fastened the bottom button of his blue blazer. "I'll see you later. Time for the public safety meeting."

"Don't forget two o'clock. The meeting with Justine."

"How could I possibly forget my first meeting with the wandering dean?"

Gudewill moved the blueprints to the end of the table and settled in a chair to examine them more closely. He was making notes when Katherine burst in, dragging Gladys behind her.

"I told you he was in trouble. I asked you to do something. Now he's dead." She threw her arms up hysterically.

"Katherine," Gudewill soothed.

She glared at him. "You don't care! He's dead, and you don't even care."

"I'm sorry, Katherine. I know Elvis died, but it was an accident." He pulled himself up from the chair.

"It wasn't an accident. It was a conspiracy. I told you. You should have done something. I told you to!" She sobbed uncontrollably.

As Gudewill moved toward her end of the table, she pulled herself to her full height. "Don't come near me. You're part of it." She picked up the Waterford ashtray from his desk and chucked it at Gudewill. The ashtray sailed across the room and bonked Gudewill on the temple. With his eyes wide in astonishment, he fell backward. Trying to regain his balance, his head jerked forward and hit the table as he collapsed. Muttering, Katherine spun around and stormed out of the office.

In the outer office Dorothy was waiting for her interview.

"The crazy woman's finished," Lily said as Katherine brushed by them, mumbling. "Go in. He's expecting you."

Dorothy found Gudewill crumpled over the conference table. "Lily, call public safety," she yelled through the open door. "Something's happened to the president!"

Within minutes, Stein, Charlie, and Noah were in Gudewill's office.

"You think he had a stroke, boss?" Charlie asked Stein.

Noah peered at Gudewill. "I don't think so. Look at the mark on his temple. Something hit him."

"There's an ashtray on the floor. Maybe that did it," Dorothy said.

"It had to be thrown by somebody." Charlie went over and picked it up.

"For God's sake, put it down, Charlie. It's evidence." Stein knelt down and felt Gudewill's pulse. "He's alive. Call 911 and the police."

After the police finished interviewing Dorothy, she hurried to the Barn to tell Carlos what had happened. As she passed Eliot's office in the Brown House, she ducked under a cypress, jarring a branch and showering herself with tiny drops of condensed fog. She could hear someone crooning "That's All Right." It sounded like Katherine. Dorothy slowed down and looked closely at the darkened building. Sure enough, Katherine sat on the bench outside Eliot's office. How odd, Dorothy thought. Then she remembered it had been Eliot who had invited the strange woman to the revolution party. Dorothy hesitated. Should she run back and get someone? By the time she returned, Katherine might be gone.

There was no predicting what she'd do. Like hitting Gudewill with the ashtray. Dorothy felt certain that Katherine meant no harm. She was just highly excitable. Dorothy had talked to her after the mock funeral, calmed her down when she became hysterical over the burial of Lakeside's spirit. Maybe she could persuade her to go to public safety. The police were looking for her.

Dorothy called softly, "Katherine, Katherine. Is it OK if I talk to you? I can hear you singing." It dawned on her that Katherine might be upset about Elvis's death. She was his number one fan. Of course! There must be a connection between Elvis and Gudewill! "I want to talk to you about Elvis."

The singing stopped. "Who's there?"

"It's me. Dorothy. Remember? We talked about the play the students put on about Lakeside's spirit dying."

"I remember."

"Can I talk to you?"

"I guess so."

Dorothy joined her on the bench outside Eliot's office. "I'm sad about Elvis too. I can imagine how you must feel."

Katherine started to sob. When she calmed down, she said, "I knew it was going to happen. The dreams told me. That's why I told the president, only he didn't do anything to stop them."

"Stop who?"

"The conspirators, the ones who killed Elvis."

"And who are they?"

"Colonel Parker and that girlfriend of Elvis. They made it look like an accident, but I know." She sobbed, and Gladys joined her, both howling into the fog.

Dorothy fished a tissue from her purse and handed it to Katherine. "When you feel better, why don't we go back to public safety and tell them. Maybe they can help." Soon the two were walking back through the woods to the main building.

*S*tein paced up and down the corridor outside Gude-will's room at St. Francis Hospital. For all the talk about the progress of modern medicine, the cocka-mamy doctors couldn't do a thing to help JG. The small man glowered at the nurse walking by. Stein's shirt was unkempt, as if he'd slept in it, except he hadn't been to bed in two days. He hadn't left the hospital since Gudewill had been admitted to the ICU. You can't die on me now, you bastard, Stein thought. Not now. Things are starting to look up. Babcock's gone; two of the army buddies, BJ and Harvey, are interested in the institute; the students have a dean again; and the faculty's copacetic. This is a lousy time to quit.

If Stein were a man who prayed, he would have prayed. In-stead he railed against his friend.

And about the returning dean of students. Justine the Ama-zonian. You should have warned me. Our meeting was brief but not sweet. When the ambulance took you to the hospital, I saw Marian to tell her I was in charge—after all, I am your assistant and the director of institutional services. She and Justine were meeting. Justine, whom I hadn't met yet, tells me that she, as dean of students, and Marian, as dean of academics, are in command. Institutional services isn't academic, and an assistant is just an assistant. Nervy broad. It seems they'd already checked it with Sister Stack, the board chairman. So I'm supposed to keep a low profile: just tend to public safety and maintenance.

How tall is Justine anyway? Six feet? Amazing! If she weren't so bossy, I might be interested. But then my attention is focused on lascivious Lucy. Were you right when you coined that moniker! I didn't get to tell you about the bath. My God! It was better than Bathsheba's. The lady does know how to put on a show. No action yet. But she's certainly leading up to it.

If you're wondering where the boys are, I sent them out for dinner. They've been here nonstop. They're good kids, JG. You're lucky. Another reason not to check out. They need you. Yeah, and so do I. Oh, your favorite board member was here with a bunch of purple orchids, what else! Going on about "Johnny" and all the plans you two have. You'd better watch out. The trade-off for a single-sex college might be a marital bed. Here comes the doctor.

T he campus was as crowded as the day of the food-in.
Cars filled the parking lots, the driveways, and John
Muir Boulevard. The late-August sun threatened to
burn off the fog, but the mourners, who in their dark suits and
funeral attire, gathered to pay final tribute to Gudewill, barely
noticed. The memorial service had been held in the auditorium;
the chapel was deemed too small to hold the large crowd, which
included people assembled from all the pages of Gudewill's life.

Stein stood with Gudewill's sons in the gallery in front of the
lavish buffet, Lakeside's way of saying goodbye to Gudewill.
Wine, soda, salads, breads, rolls, chicken, sliced ham, turkey, roast
beef, vegetables, dips, chips, cookies, brownies, cakes, coffee, tea.
Name it, and it was on the tables set up in the gallery, library, and
even the cafeteria.

In a corner, Eliot, in white as always, was talking to Agnes
and Carmen. "It's poetic justice: the king being struck down by
one of his subjects."

"That's not a nice thing to say, Eliot." Agnes shook her head
and sipped her wine.

"The banker was not a nice man. Which brings us to the
matter of the vacancy, Agnes. You must make it clear to Sarajane

that I'm the best candidate for the interim president. It's crucial that Justine and Marian not continue." Eliot curled his lip.

"Are you sure that's what you want, Eliot? Being president is a giant headache." Carmen bent down to straighten the skirt of her black suit.

"Of course, I'm sure! Why do you think I have everyone working on a telephone campaign to the board? Obviously, I'm the most qualified. Believe me, I've learned from the union experience. And I was president of the academic senate. There's no better choice."

"I'm not questioning your qualifications, Eliot, just if you really want it." She shifted her black bag to her other shoulder. "It isn't as easy as it looks."

Across the room Sarajane stood with Margaret Phelan, who grazed from the bulging plate she held in her plump hands. Sarajane waved a purple Chinese fan in front of her; it matched the purple jacket and purple heels she wore with a black A-line dress. "I don't see how you can eat at a time like this."

"Starving yourself doesn't do any good. You need to keep your strength up, Sarajane. You'll get sick if you don't eat. Go help yourself."

"Don't you see that I'm in mourning?" Sarajane fanned herself and lowered her lavender eyelids. "Johnny and I were . . . you know . . . becoming more than associates. Now that I'm a board member . . . he looked at me quite differently. Our roles paralleled. I think further down the road, I might have been Mrs. President." She dabbed at her eyes, making sure she didn't smudge her heavy black mascara.

Noah heaped a paper plate high with samples from the buffet. Dorothy put a few pieces of turkey and some green salad on hers. "So Carlos is back in the kitchen again," Noah said, munching on a chicken leg.

"Let's go out into the hall. It's too crowded in here." Dorothy led Noah through the crowd. "Yeah, he's working in the cafeteria, to make sure that Rick sticks to the new food arrangement." They sat down on an elaborately carved bench. Dorothy crossed her knees and balanced the plate on her long black skirt. She wore a houndstooth-check jacket and a wide-brimmed felt hat that matched her black boots.

"What's with Katherine?" Noah positioned his wine glass between them. A tweed jacket and white shirt dressed up his uniform Levis.

"The police charged her with manslaughter and have her under observation. They say she's not competent to stand trial."

"They're right on that one. You could have knocked me over when she came back to the office with you."

"Everything has changed! It's hard to believe. Gudewill dead. Me editor. Carlos student body president. All in a year. What about you? I guess you're not going to Mexico."

"Not for a while, anyway. I took your advice and decided to finish the year. I'm curious to see what happens and who the new president will be. Maybe I can be on the search committee." He laughed.

"That would be a switch. It wouldn't hurt to get involved in things . . . in the right things, that is." Dorothy looked knowingly at Noah. She had never confronted Noah, but how else had the tapestries and rare books made their way to his uncle's storeroom? She and Carlos had discreetly dropped the artifacts by the public safety office while Charlie, the officer in charge, was on a break. Oddly enough, she never heard mention of the goods again.

He shrugged and chomped on another chicken leg.

ustine Tuliver and Marian Jackson sat at the conference
table in the president's office. Outside, the wind howled
and late-summer fog crouched around the building. Cross-
ing her long legs, Justine shuffled insurance papers in front of her.
Across from her, Marian rested her left foot on the edge of her
tan pump.

"Having Phelan and Phelan as the insurance brokers could
be a blessing in disguise." Justine looked through her oversize
glasses at Marian. "Now if Stein would only conduct the tour so
Barry Phelan doesn't discover the true state of the college."

As if on cue, Stein appeared at the door. "Good morning,
ladies. It's all set. Phelan arrives at ten. Maintenance and public
safety have secured the ship. Everything's in top condition." He
sat down.

"What about the theater? If the inspectors go backstage,
they'll close us down." Justine cupped a mug in her hand and
looked at Stein curiously. The board had named Marian and Justine acting co-presidents because of their roles as dean of students and academic dean. A poised woman in her thirties, Justine
projected efficiency and coolness. Her brunette hair was pulled
back off her face in a long ponytail, and her only makeup was a
splash of lipstick. She wore a simple gray dress and flats.

"We're bypassing the first floor west. Charlie's going to inter-rupt us and take us down to the public safety office to show off the new walkie-talkies." He grinned.

"Make sure nothing goes wrong. It'll help alumni relations if Phelan and Phelan decide to become our broker." Marian sat forward. "Union negotiations are going well."

"Our negotiator, Dom, is a pro." Stein reached into his pocket and pulled out a pack of cigarettes.

Justine's eyes focused on the package, then targeted Stein. "I hate smoking."

Stein looked at her. "I should go back to my office anyway." He stood up. "I'm taking the Phelans to lunch after the insurance inspection."

In Stein's office, Big Anna, a giant blond in a white uniform, sturdy nurse's shoes, and hose, fidgeted. When Stein walked in, she jumped out of her chair, almost knocking the short man over. "Sorry, Mr. Boss, sorry. I need talk to you. Can we shut the door?"

"Of course, Anna." He closed the door, strolled behind the desk, and sat down. "What's the problem?" He pulled out a ciga-rette and lit it.

"I not know how to tell you." The large woman fumbled with her feather duster. "That cuckoo guy, the gardener with the base-ball hat, the one who plays the . . . the . . . the what you call it? The thing you put in the mouth?"

"Harmonica?"

"Yes. He had meeting yesterday after work in glass house."

"Glass house?"

"The house he grow dope in."

"The greenhouse."

"Yes. He wants to get rid of Pete. Says now that big boss gone, he in charge. Mr. Boss, you know him communist?"

"I heard something. So Dooley's planning a coup. Thanks for

the information, Anna." That's all we need, Stein thought. A gardener taking over the maintenance department. This place gets screwier every day.

"That OK, Mr. Boss. We don't want work for him. He cuckoo." She twirled her finger around her temple.

Feather duster tucked under her arm, Anna left, passing Pete, the maintenance chief, on his way in. Pete took her seat.

"All set, boss."

"You hear anything about a meeting in the greenhouse?"

"No. I miss something?"

"Nothing much. I'll take care of it. When you run into Dooley, tell him I need to see him."

"Sure, boss. Everything's set for the insurance guys. The main thing we got to avoid is the wiring in the theater. You don't want them inspecting that area at all. Nothing's up to code. The drama department runs a wire here, a wire there, thinks nothing of it. The place could go up in a flash."

"Things will be fine so long as Dooley's not digging holes without roping them off. We don't need the insurance agents falling down."

Soon Stein and Pete were leading Barry Phelan and his son around campus. Pete pointed out highlights. "The elevator doesn't hold a coffin. We found that out when the first sister died in the new building. Had to carry her down the stairs." Just before they reached the theater, Charlie intercepted them, lauding public safety's new walkie-talkies. He insisted that Barry see their setup in the public safety office, diverting the tour from the theater. When the inspection of the campus was completed, the Phelans and Stein drove to Westlake Joe's for drinks and lunch. Stein made a break as soon as he could. He needed to find Dooley. The seditious gardener was about to join the unemployed.

Stein parked his car in front of the college and headed for his office. No sooner had he sat down than the phone rang. "Stein here. Christ, what is it now, Charlie? What? Where? The library? I'll be right over." Sighing, he replaced the phone and hurried out of his office, oblivious to the fog that canopied the quad and the students huddled in the corridor. Charlie had been cryptic on the phone. Just said to get over to Lucy's office right away. Stein straightened his tie as he passed the main desk.

Lucy, Noah, and Charlie stood in the center of Lucy's office. Stein could have cut the tension with a knife. A silly grin was plastered on Noah's face, and Lucy was extremely flushed. "What's up, Charlie?"

"I caught your thieves, Stein. Here they are," Charlie said.

"What?" Stein jerked, his eyes darting from Lucy to Noah and back.

"I caught them red-handed. Loading books from the Delaney collection into Lucy's car. Like they were going to drop them off at the main library. Cool as cucumbers."

"Is that true, Lucy?" He searched her face.

"Just as the man says." She looked directly at Stein.

"Should I call the cops, boss?"

"Jesus Christ, no. I'll take over, Charlie. You can go. You were right to call me."

"Sure, boss." The round man left the room.

"What do you two have to say?"

"Are you going to turn yourself in, too, Stein?" Lucy boosted herself up on the desk and crossed her legs, her short skirt hiking above her knees. She smiled smugly.

"What are you talking about?"

"You're an accomplice."

"What?"

"Remember the box of books you carried up to my apartment the night I took a bath?" She swung her leg back and forth.

Stein groaned. "They were the college's books?"

"That's right, and my staff saw you carry them out of here."

"Shit." Stein fell back into a chair. "You set me up."

"Let's say I took out insurance." She laughed. "It really isn't that bad, Stein. Lakeside never prosecutes anyone. The guilty ones just leave very suddenly. I'm sure you'll follow precedent." She recrossed her legs.

"You're right, Lucy. I'll follow precedent. You need to return all the things you have in your possession, and then you're finished. Noah, you clear out your things and leave campus. Go enroll in some other school." Stein sighed. "Tell me, did you take the tapestries, too?"

"Not all of them. We had some competition. Who, I don't know. Probably other students besides Noah." Lucy swung the other leg.

"And you two have been working together for . . . ?"

"For quite a while, Stein. Before I met you." She smiled.

"You planned all along to set me up." His face fell.

"That was a recent development. After Magdalena's opening."

Stein groaned. Insurance was right. Insurance that, now that Babcock was out of the picture, Lucy could use to avoid prosecution. Stein was her ace in the hole.

Seventy-two | BOARD BOMBSHELL

Indian summer had arrived at Lakeside. Temperatures soared and cormorants dried their wings along the shore. A black-backed phoebe darted from its perch to nab a grasshopper sunning in the dry grass. However, as far as the crowd filling Lakeside's main theater was concerned, the college could have been buried in fog. The room buzzed with speculation. What was the reason for the mandatory all-college meeting? Soon the theater overflowed with faculty, staff, students, and administrators. Seated on the stage were the board members, Marian, and Justine. Sister Stack, trustee and head of the order, stood and walked to the podium. The audience hushed and, like the phoebe outside, cocked its head in anticipation.

"Thank you all for coming. I'll make this brief." She took a sip of water from the glass on the podium. "After much consideration and many hours of discussion and trying to arrive at a solution, the board of trustees has decided to close Lakeside. The college has been operating at a deficit for a number of years; there is no other recourse. The doors will close in December. We will find placements at other schools for students in their final year and offer counseling for all students."

The audience gasped collectively.

"You don't know how sorry I am to tell you this." As the diminutive woman listed the various ailments that had contributed to the death of the college, the crowd's whisper grew to the rumble of an earthquake.

Eliot jumped up. "Why didn't you do something before? This action shows a lack of responsibility on the part of the board."

Others stood and berated the nun. She sipped water from the glass and calmly answered their questions. The tirade continued until she raised both hands. "That's all. The meeting is adjourned." She turned and left the stage, followed by the other board members, Justine, and Marian. Outside, reporters lined the lobby like turkey vultures, interviewing the angry crowd.

CHRONICLES

T he following day, the *Chronicle* devoted page three to Lakeside's demise, with a sidebar column of interviews under the heading "Why Did Lakeside Close?"

Eliot Blanc, professor of English: "I'm hardly surprised. They threw out the baby with the bathwater when they cast aside academic tradition. It was inevitable."

Sister Agnes, theology professor: "I think the problem began when they switched from a single-sex college and lost the traditional religious and philosophic values."

Carmen O'Doyle, professor of languages and drama: "The graduate programs began competing with us for students, and too many adjunct faculty were hired. How were we supposed to work with people who were there only once or twice a week?"

Gary Rubin, psychology professor: "Empire building developed. The faculty was pitted against the administration. There was divisiveness all around."

Marian Jackson, academic dean/acting co-president: "It happened when the faculty unionized. It drained us. All our resources—time, energy, money—were spent at the bargaining table."

Justine Tuliver, dean of students/acting co-president: "Leaving the students without any support didn't help. I see myself as playing a role. I thought the administration would hire someone when I was on sabbatical, but they abandoned the students. No wonder the students revolted and enrollment dropped."

Harry Stein, director of institutional services: "The college was destined to die. All smoke and mirrors. The smoke backfired and choked the college."

Sister Magdalena, art professor: "The death of Lakeside marks the end of one era and the beginning of another. We are living in a time of turmoil and change. Lakeside is part of the change. Hopefully, everyone has learned from the experience, especially the students, and they'll bring about their own changes in the new era."

Margaret Phelan, director of alumni: "It was the name change, going from Our Lady of the Lake College for Women to Lakeside. What kind of name is that? There's no association with the church. It could be a community college. The identity was gone."

Sarajane Thomas, alumni trustee: "Ultimately it was the death of the president, John Gudewill. He could have saved us all."

Dorothy Owens, student: "There were many reasons. Maybe the right hand didn't know what the left hand was doing."

Carlos Torres, student: "Vision was lacking. The administration and board won the intellectual game. The system was theirs; they called the shots and manipulated power, but it backfired on them. Magdalena was the only one with vision."

Jack Harrison, student: "Responsibility. Responsibility was what the board and the administration copped out on. We gave them four years of our lives and ten thousand dollars, and what did they do? Flushed it all down the toilet."

Keiani Jones, student: "Lack of commitment and process. I'm glad I was here. I had some great experiences and made great friends, but I think the biggest truth I learned was don't trust the system."

$\mathcal{T}$he day after the announcement of the college closing, Dorothy and Carlos sunned themselves on the front stairs leading up to the main building. Along the lake the tall fennel towered above the path, and the blue water reflected the winking orange nasturtiums.

"I still can't believe it," Dorothy said as she rubbed suntan lotion on her legs.

"Life's change, so they say. Here comes Jack. Maybe he'll have more information." Carlos waved to Jack, climbing the steps.

Jack sat down on the step below them. "You'll never guess who I saw driving his uncle's Caddy this morning . . . Noah!"

"I thought he took off for Mexico." Dorothy globbed some lotion on her arm.

"Guess not. I waved, but he didn't stop. Odd how he left without saying goodbye."

Dorothy and Carlos glanced at each other over Jack's head. "You know Noah, always doing his own thing. He said he wanted to take a semester off." Dorothy examined the lotion on her forearm.

"Maybe he knew something we didn't. Speaking of . . . what're we gonna do? We're supposed to graduate in May, but if the college closes in December . . ." Jack grimaced.

"I talked to a lawyer I know," Carlos said. "He's offered to advise us and said we should threaten the college with litigation."

"Good man, Carlos. I'm glad one of us is doing something. When should we go see the administration?"

"The sooner the better."

"I agree. I'll find Keiani, and the four of us can go." Dorothy put the lotion in her backpack and stood up. "Meet you in the quad."

Stein stood at his office window and stared into the quad. With the sun shining so brightly on the basking students, it was hard to believe that they would all be gone in a few months. He looked up to the blue sky. You really pulled a fast one on me, JG, he thought. Leaving me with your mess, yours and Babcock's. I don't even have the diversion of Lucy. What moxie she had, blackmailing me, and just for carrying a box of books. I hear she's still in the city. I told Marian Lucy had to take a leave because of personal reasons. I didn't mention the real one. She and Noah cleared out immediately. I never did trust him. Remember? And I was right. My gut's always right. And right about Katherine, too. Who'd have thought it would be the Wicked Witch who downed the great wizard? She and her cockamamy dog. And I'm stuck doing the cleanup! A lot has happened. The peanut farmer brokered a deal between Sadat and Begin. And your damn Yankees are looking good. They might even make the playoffs. Too bad you're missing them!

The ringing phone interrupted Stein's reverie.

"Yes? Speaking. Bernie? From the Way? Of course, I remember you. An appointment? What about? Luz's interested in buying Lakeside?" Stein bolted upright. "Of course, I'd like to meet her. Tomorrow at ten? See you then."

Looking up at the blue sky, Stein laughed and danced a jig around the room.

seventy-five | NEGOTIATIONS

orothy and Jack were in their usual spot on the front steps enjoying the October sun. Students clustered on the lawn; a group in shorts and T-shirts tossed a Frisbee back and forth. Jack was watching for Carlos's Chevy. "Look who's back." He pointed to a long white Rolls that climbed the driveway.

"Luz the entrepreneur." Dorothy popped her book in her backpack and stood up. "Wonder what she wants. More rentals?"

Keiani had joined them. "Maybe she wants to buy the place."

"You think so?" Jack said. "Wouldn't that be a fitting end for Lakeside?"

"Or beginning." Keiani dropped her backpack next to Dorothy's. "You know, what goes around comes around."

"Remember when Katherine's dog peed on Bernie, Luz's front man?" Jack laughed. "Look at the heavy-duty bodyguards." He pointed to the black Cadillac behind the Rolls that was spilling out four men in military gear. "Looks like guerrilla warfare time."

"They're scary." Keiani shuddered.

A red-and-white Chevy pulled up next to the Rolls, and Carlos hopped out. Immediately two guards rushed over to him. "Wait a minute, guys. I'm a student here." He pulled out his ID.

They scrutinized the picture and then Carlos and nodded.

Shaking his head, Carlos crossed the driveway to the stairs. "I see the buzzards are circling and the body isn't even cold."

"That's what I say, Carlos." Keiani nodded.

"What do you expect? Being bought by a millionaire charlatan probably fits right into the administration's plans, bigger profits for them." Dorothy folded her arms.

Carlos turned to watch the Rolls. "I talked to the lawyer again. He's going to come this afternoon. We've got a two o'clock appointment with Marian and Justine."

"How do you greet a woman who claims to have had an encounter with an angel?" Justine asked Stein and Marian. They waited for the clairvoyant in the president's office.

"Just like any other Lakeside nut. She isn't all that different." Stein grinned. There was a knock. Stein opened the door. "Good morning, Ms. Seer, Bernie. It's a pleasure to see you again. I hope our meeting will be mutually beneficial." He introduced them to Marian and Justine.

"Would you like some tea or coffee or something to eat?" Marian pointed to the lavish array of food at the end of the conference table.

"No, thank you. I only eat food prepared by my people." Luz nodded to the four bodyguards. "You may wait in the reception area." They backed out the door, closing it behind them.

Luz sat down at the end of the table. "Bernie told you I'm interested in purchasing Lakeside." She moved her arm to encompass the room and campus beyond, and her many gold bracelets tinkled like tiny bells. A petite woman, Luz carried herself as if she were ten feet tall. She wore a white chiffon dress cinched at the waist with a wide gold belt, and on each of her ten fingers was a gold ring with a different jewel. Cropped short, her silver hair accented her porcelain-fine skin.

"I like the location of Lakeside, isolated yet close to an urban center and the airport. It is the perfect place for a training center. Because the campus is a peninsula surrounded by highway on three sides, I could fence it off and security would be optimum. I'm willing to offer fifteen million dollars."

Stein's eyes popped. "Fifteen million?"

"Fifteen million. I've already had an appraisal, and my offer is well above market value. We don't intend to subdivide."

"It's certainly generous," Justine said. Luz continued to watch Stein.

"We need to talk to the trustees," he said. "This is a board matter."

"I'm aware of that, Mr. Stein." She rose from the chair. "Call Bernie when you have an answer." Luz swept out of the room, Bernie in tow.

"Wow!" Justine said. "She has some presence. I've never seen anyone like her before."

"I find her intimidating," Marian said. "And those guards! They look like they spend their days engaged in hand-to-hand combat with no survivors." She reached over and poured herself a cup of coffee.

"Remember, only a few years ago she was Betty Brown, an Oregon housewife. She's human," Stein said.

"Still, she's not the kind of person the board is going to want to sell the college to. I don't see the archdiocese letting someone like Luz take over Church property. No matter what she offered. We'll present the offer at the meeting tonight. In the meantime, Carlos is bringing a lawyer to see us. I think the students are planning to sue the college for breaking its contract in providing an education." Marian spooned some sugar into her coffee.

"Just another day at the office," Stein said, walking out and leaving the two women behind.

seventy-six | FACULTY FANTASIES

Eliot stormed into the faculty lounge and threw his white fedora on the table. Outside, the wind howled and knocked over a trash can in the middle of the quad, littering the unkempt flowerbeds. Students scurried in out of the rain.

"What's the matter?" Carmen looked up from the papers she was correcting.

"Not only has the administration sold the college to USF, they've set up a program whereby the students who have a semester left can finish their course work at USF. We are left holding the bag."

"They have a moral obligation to the students, for heaven's sake." She laid her red pen on the table.

"It's their moral obligation to us that's the problem. Of course, they should take care of the students. But they should do something about us also." He pulled out a handkerchief and wiped the sweat off his forehead.

"Calm yourself. We can apply for jobs at USF."

"The English department is full." He glared at Carmen.

"Well, you've always wanted to write." She glanced down at the papers in front of her. "I'm planning to do more directing and to run a workshop or two."

"Would you stop being so Pollyannaish! I can't bear it." He folded the handkerchief and placed it in his jacket pocket. "If they'd only sold the property to that Luz woman, we'd have received a generous settlement. She offered ten million, so I heard. We would have benefited."

"You can't fight the Catholic Church. They claimed that sale would be an alienation of Church property. So they sold the college to the Church's university. There's nothing anyone can do. They do hold the deed."

Gary and Agnes hurried in from the quad. "There's a gale outside!" Agnes unraveled the long knit scarf around her neck and removed her wool coat.

"What do you expect? It's almost December." Eliot sat down.

"Don't remind me." Gary took off his gloves and sat next to Carmen. "I need to make reservations for the holidays. It'll be strange not to return to Lakeside."

"I for one am glad that USF bought Lakeside instead of that awful woman. I can't imagine this beautiful campus becoming the training center for some cult." Agnes shuddered.

"What about Magdalena?" Gary's eyes widened.

"She's devoting herself to her art, which means we'll probably be seeing her on the front page of the paper." Eliot sniffed. "At least she has something to do."

"Quit feeling sorry for yourself, Eliot. Something will turn up."

"Thank you, Pollyanna."

They continued discussing the USF takeover.

"Two and a half million is what I heard," Agnes said.

"Your sources are as good as any, Agnes." Gary pulled his calendar out of his vest pocket. "I heard the clairvoyant offered twenty million."

"Twenty million. Think of all that money." Carmen drifted

off into a world of stacks and stacks of dollars. The others joined her, each building his or her own castle.

seventy-seven | ALL'S WELL THAT ENDS WELL

The December fog hovered around Lakeside, a blanket protecting it from more Pacific storms. Inside his office, Stein tossed papers into the large garbage can he had commandeered from Anna. Thank God, the board had come up with a small settlement for the Russian maids who had worked for the college for decades. He'd worried that they would be left out in the cold, but the nuns had taken care of them. Stein sighed as he trashed the past eighteen months of his life. Not much point in saving anything. When the new crew came in, they'd reinvent the wheel. He'd been through enough takeovers to know the routine. He surveyed the room. The filing cabinets were empty and the desk was clear. The college was deserted—only a night guard was on duty. Everyone else was home preparing for the holidays. He heard a knock at the door.

"Come in." He chucked the last ball of paper in the bin and looked up. "Lucy, what are you doing here?" He stood up.

"I came to see you, Stein." Lucy shut the door behind her and removed her Burberry raincoat. She was barelegged and wore a white silk blouse and short black skirt that hugged her body. "I hope that's all right."

Stein sighed. "What can I do for you?"

"May I sit down?"

"Be my guest."

Lucy slid into the chair across from him and crossed her legs, her skirt reaching up to where her panty line should have been. Stein took inventory and sighed again.

"I'm here to give you a going-away present, Stein. You never asked for anything, and I appreciate that. So get ready for the unexpected." She laughed.

"Here?"

"Here." She stood up and walked around the desk.

Stein was a happy man that night. He grinned from ear to ear, and the song of his grin resounded up over the quad, across Lake Merced and the city, and all the way to the Golden Gate. Even the fog lifted.

Acknowledgments

I would like to thank the following: Deirdre McDonald Greene, who did a marvelous job editing; Marilyn Cooper for the first edit; Anthony Nash, Dorene Cotter, Candyce Griswold, Jane Kimmell, and Pat Yium for their feedback; Susan Robinson Clark and Karen Giambruno for their help on research; Louis Owens and the Community of Writers at Squaw Valley for their early encouragement; She Writes Press for giving me the opportunity to publish *Slipsliding by the Bay*; and, last but not least, my family and friends who cheered me on.